I0619760

Galway Publishing

Cover art: Cedar Sanderson

ISBN: 978-1-947648-07-4

CONTENTS

A POCKETFUL OF STARS

MARGARET BALL

CHAPTER 1

I WAS MULLING over the Klein bottle problem when he interrupted me.

Coming out of a strong visualization can be tricky. Fortunately, I wasn't exactly trying for one. I was just thinking about the fourth-dimensional version of a Möbius strip and wondering exactly what would happen if I could hold an image of it in my mind and traverse the dimensions. I wasn't all that eager to find out, so the image in my head was rather fuzzy.

This meant that I was able to respond to the interruption relatively quickly. Fingers drumming on my desk, check. Do not whack fingers with a book, good for me. (No matter what Ben says, I have never chopped anyone's fingers off with a cleaver. I don't even have a cleaver in my desk.)

Fingers... attached to a man who might have been attractive if he hadn't looked so impatient. Oh hell, scratch that. Even wearing that unfriendly expression, he was hot. Being a little, dark Greek type myself, I'm a sucker for that California beach boy look. This one had the blond hair, a little too long, and a squarish Northern European face with – of course – dark blue eyes. And you could sort of tell that under his loose-fitting jacket he had a body no surfer need be ashamed of, compact and muscular. With impressively broad shoulders.

"Well?"

I blinked. "Well… what?"

"Aren't you going to offer me a chair?"

"No." I'd never seen this man before; what was he doing in the Research Division? He shouldn't even have been able to find it.

He dragged a chair from the corner, ignoring the horrible screeching sound of wooden legs on a wood floor, and plunked it beside my desk. Then he sat down, straddling the chair and resting his arms on the back. "I need to talk to you."

"How did you get here?"

"Huh? Jet Blue, rental car from the airport."

"Here. The Research Division. Topologically speaking," I hinted, although I didn't for one minute believe he would have been capable of the necessary visualizations. He'd initiated contact; his pretty blue eyes met mine whenever I glanced at his face; he was, right now, invading my personal space. Almost certainly not a mathematician.

"Walked up the stairs and through the door."

I waited.

"With Dr. Verrick."

I relaxed slightly. That's the other way to find the Research Division; get escorted by someone who already qualifies. This guy himself didn't have the talent; he had already convinced himself that there was a door in the wall that he'd been Möbiused through. But if Dr. Verrick had personally escorted him, he must want me to make the man happy… whatever that took.

Could be interesting.

I was still thinking vaguely about making him happy when he began removing all desire to do so.

"I'm from your sponsoring institution."

"The Moore Foundation?" He didn't look like a Foundation person.

"If you like."

An odd answer. I'm pretty sure that if we had any sponsors besides the Moore Foundation, I'd have noticed, if only because of the time wasted to appease them. Dr. Verrick makes all of us dress like adults and stand around at the Foundation's occasional formal parties. (If they throw any other kind, I haven't been invited.)

"We have need of some information that you people may be able to procure for us. We want you to look at the computer user behind a series of messages and find out what he's planning and who his associates are." He plopped a folder onto my desk and knocked off Darth Vader, five poker chips, *An Overview of Hyperbolic Geometry* and my notes on strongly connected graphs.

(Don't you know that a neat desk is a sign of a sick mind? Countless studies confirm the link between a messy workspace and creativity. And I happen to be very creative.)

"Aren't you even going to look at the messages?" he asked while I was still giving his folder the evil eye.

"*After* you pick up my things." I folded my hands in front of me and stared off into the distance. Well, where the distance would have been if it hadn't been blocked by a bookcase.

Grumbling audibly, he condescended to abandon his chair and collect the stuff that had fallen off my desk. When he stood up again, he placed the textbook, my notes, and Darth Vader in a neat stack, very precisely. He put the poker chips in a separate stack, perfectly aligned, beside Darth Vader. As body language went, it was an excellent projection of "I'm patiently putting up with this tiresome female."

"Now let's get down to work," he said, straddling the chair again. He wasn't that tall, but I felt like he was looming over me.

I don't take well to being loomed at.

"Not so fast! We're a research institution. We don't just take on odd jobs from every Tom, Dick or Harry who strolls in here." Not that Tom or Dick or Harry would have been able to stroll in, unless they were really good at visualizing and mentally traversing a Möbius strip - or were escorted by a staff member. Well, you couldn't get a higher-ranking escort than Dr. Verrick himself. If this fellow's story was true, Dr. Verrick presumably wanted me to cooperate with him, and I should comply.

If, on the other hand, he'd been smuggled in by Ben or Ingrid as part of an elaborate practical joke aimed at me - which I was beginning to think must be the case, as surely no one could be this irritating by accident - it was high time I stopped letting him pull my leg.

"What I don't understand," I said, tapping the folder, "is what interest the Moore Foundation has in your problem, why they should think we could solve it, and why I shouldn't be worried about the legal penalties for hacking into someone's computer." Not to mention the fact that I hadn't the faintest idea how to do that, and I didn't think my colleagues did either.

"If you'd look at the messages you might understand better."

Oh, all right. I flipped the folder open and looked at... a confusing collection of very innocent-looking emails. There was one cluster about a birthday party, another about travel plans for someone's niece and her friends, another on a hotel in Austin where they could stay.

"What are you, the Division in Charge of Investigating Birthday Parties? I do not see anything relevant to research in pure mathematics, which is the purpose of the Moore Foundation. Much less the relevance to applied topology."

"I am not... exactly... from the Moore Foundation."

Aha! I knew it! I looked around. Ben and Ingrid must be hiding somewhere, ready to leap out and yell, "Surprise! Candid Camera!"

If so, they were very well hidden indeed.

"I'm from the sponsor which actually gives the Moore Foundation the funding which they pass on to you, and I've been seconded to your group for the duration of this investigation."

"And that sponsor would be?"

"I'm sorry, but that's on a need-to-know basis. All I can tell you is that this is a matter of national security."

An ugly thought chilled me. "If it's a matter of national security... Was I cleared to read this folder?"

"You are now. The entire staff is cleared to be read in on this investigation." He looked very pleased with himself. It wasn't a good look for him. "I do still have some influence within the... agency."

"Does Dr. Verrick know?"

"Of course."

"And this silly business is important to your employers because...?"

"The messages are coded," he said impatiently. "I thought anybody working here would be bright enough to recognize that without having it spelled out. We believe these emails and transcripts are actually from a shadowy group involved in smuggling Middle Eastern terrorists over the border and transferring them to a safe house here in Austin."

I glanced at the contents of the folder again. All right, I could see that with a simple substitution code his interpretation would make sense. The "niece" could stand for a terrorist leader, the "friends" for his supporters, the "hotel" for a safe house. And I didn't even want to think - "What does the 'birthday party' stand for?"

"What do you expect?"

I *expected* it stood for something involving bombs and bloodshed. It would have been nice to be told otherwise. "We need to shut this down before the 'party,'" he went on. "Or - at a minimum - find out the time and place, so that we can increase security."

"Why would they be based in Austin, instead of closer to the border?"

"People who actually live near the border," he said, "do not feel nearly so benign about illegal aliens."

"In Austin," I corrected him, "we say 'undocumented immigrants.'" At least, if we didn't want to get a lecture from Ingrid Thorn about it.

He waved one hand. "Tomato, tomahto. In... the agency... we still speak English. Well, I do, anyway. Austin's a sanctuary city; as long as these people pretend they're just helping poor Central Americans to escape violence and find a better life, they'll get support from most of the population. And anybody raising questions will find themselves the target of a high-tech lynch mob dedicated to shutting down the opposition."

I had to think about that, but not for long. I'm as apolitical as you can be while still having a pulse, and I haven't felt the need to have an opinion on border controls and illegal immigration given that everybody else in Austin had already staked out a position. But the bit about shutting down opposition was different. Those were fighting words for Thalia Kostis, Girl Mathematician. I've been loudly and vocally opposed to all manner of things during my life, beginning with the family's plans for me. He was beginning to get my interest.

"But why us? Despite its name, the Center is a pure research facility. We don't do applications."

"You do now. As a first priority, you do whatever the sponsoring agency requests. After that, you may play with your little research papers to your heart's content."

And I'd actually contemplated trying to make Mr. Nameless happy!

"If you're representing a three-letter agency, surely you've got computer experts and other resources to throw at this problem."

Now he looked not so much irritated as like someone who'd just bitten into a green persimmon. "There are... various groups within the agency... with various goals. A lot of my colleagues built their careers during the previous administration, and they don't approve of 'persecuting undocumented immigrants.' Even suggesting that we should focus on potentially dangerous illegals made me persona non grata. Oh, I tried to start an official case. It's been tied up waiting for approval from several committees. It may never get out of committees. The funding for your group via the Moore Foundation has already been allocated, I don't have to get special approval, and it's about time you did something to justify that funding."

"Riiight. We always jump up and kiss the ring of a nameless man from a secret agency."

He looked faintly amused. "At the same time?"

"What?"

"Simultaneously jumping up and bowing down to kiss a ring would seem to be contra-indicated. Unless your meaning is that you're constantly falling over yourselves."

He stood and extracted a card from his wallet. "I do have a name, actually. Talk to your boss if you need to check my bona fides, then look at the folder and decide on a plan of action. I'll be in touch."

He dropped the card on top of the folder and walked away. I hoped

Dr. Verrick would escort him out; otherwise he'd probably return to my office, complaining that he couldn't find the door.

The card was less than informative. There were only two words on it, probably his name. No issuing agency, no email, no phone number.

Bradislav Lensky.

What an all-American name.

Just like Thalia Kostis.

On the way to his hotel, Brad Lensky kept thinking about that meeting. Whatever he'd been expecting to find at the Center for Applied Topology, it certainly hadn't been a snippy girl half his size who clearly just wanted him to go away so she could go back to staring at the wall. He chuckled, remembering her quick comebacks. It could be fun, making the sparks fly with that one.

Most of the woo-woo groups the Agency covertly funded were only too eager to convince him of their mystical powers. This little bare-bones operation - really? Three 'researchers' and a few offices in an antique building? - didn't seem to have anybody in charge of generating the smoke-and-mirrors effects he'd come to expect of this type of groups. Or maybe his unheralded arrival had taken them by surprise, and they planned to put on a better show for him tomorrow.

That didn't seem like this Kostis girl's style, though. She'd actually been more interested in getting him to go away than in persuading him that they were on the brink of performing miracles. Paradoxically, her insistence that this Center couldn't do a thing to help his investigation, no sirree, no way, had only made him believe that maybe there was some truth to the stories his boss had mentioned. Maybe these nuts really were succeeding in harnessing some of those mental powers the Agency was always wishing for.

Him? He was officially agnostic on this stuff. He'd wangled this assignment because it gave him a chance to see Linda. If the math geeks could actually flesh out the data on this suspected terrorist cell, so much the better; if not, he'd be home soon enough. It shouldn't take him more than a week to settle the matter.

At least it wouldn't be a boring week, not with the Kostis girl around. She made him think of a black kitten, all eyes and claws and sharp little teeth, but ready to curl up and purr when you stroked her the right way...eminently strokable... He killed that thought. He was *not* thinking of stroking that girl, she'd probably take his hand off if he tried, and anyway she was not his type: not restful, not agreeable, and definitely not blonde.

A challenge, though. And he would get her on his side. He just needed to stop being distracted by inappropriate thoughts and take the no-nonsense, all-business approach that she clearly wanted.

Right, buddy, I know you want to get into her business.

He shut that mocking voice down in a hurry. Thoughts like that were distracting as hell. Was he really that desperate to get laid? If a short little girl with spiky black hair and an attitude to match could get under his skin so easily, he was probably doomed to fall hopelessly in lust with some of the leggy Texas blondes he'd seen on campus. Maybe with all of them.

Close your eyes and think of Linda, the mocking voice advised him.

Yes, my name is Thalia. Rhymes, more or less, with "failure" if you leave off the final "r." And yes, I've heard all the jokes and no, I don't go by Thalia in real life. By dint of extreme stubbornness and a pretty good right hook for a girl, I had persuaded all my friends to call me Lia before I was nine years old. Well, both of my friends. I've never been all that social; blame my dear parents, who saddled me with that name. Or all the teachers who couldn't be satisfied with calling me Lia, but had to make their uninformed stabs at my first name. I've been roll-called as Thallia (a sea anemone commonly known as the glaucous pimplet), Thule (a frozen Northern land imagined by the Greeks), and Sally (I would have been happy to answer to that one, but even the teacher realized it couldn't be right.)

This is one of the many reasons why I love Dr. Verrick. He's about a hundred and ten and runs the Center on lines that would probably have been approved by Queen Victoria: never calls me anything but Miss Kostis. And I call him Dr. Verrick. For all I can tell, he isn't aware that I even have a first name. And I'm quite sure that he doesn't have one.

Dr. Verrick wasn't in the Center offices… either side. Presumably he had walked Bradislav the Spook out. Quite likely he had then hidden in his other office, in the mathematics department, to give me time to cool down after dropping this bombshell. He wasn't stupid.

The Center for Applied Topology, despite its name, isn't part of the math department and isn't housed anywhere near it. We have the top floor of an ancient Victorian gothic building called Allandale House, formerly the residence of the Chester Allandale who left the university a sizeable bequest on condition that they preserve his home in good condition and keep it in continuous use. The rest of Chester's land has gradually been covered with modern university buildings, with Allandale House in the center: an anachronism in red brick with towers, turrets, and balconies growing up and outward like an explosion of red lichen. I'm personally rather fond of it, but the roof problems and the retrofitted, inefficient air conditioning and the absence of an elevator all make it rather unpopular with most of the faculty. At present the first and second floors house the Allandale Memorial Library and, as I said, the Center has the third floor. (AKA Ground Zero for roof leaks.) The floor is divided into two sections. The larger part has the stairway access, empty offices, plumbing, and the coffee room. The smaller part consists of offices for Dr. Verrick and the three Research Fellows who constitute the entire staff of the Center.

There is no door in the wall dividing the two parts. This is actually in deference to the sensibilities of non-Fellows, who might be perturbed at seeing the results of our research activities. To reach the inner section you need to visualize yourself walking a Möbius strip at right angles to and crossing the wall, which will in due time deposit you on the other side. People who can't do that have to be escorted by one of us, and they sometimes get seasick. It makes recruiting for the Center simple: if you can't get here, you don't belong here.

Dr. Verrick managed to stay invisible until late afternoon, when there was a decent chance that all three of his research fellows would have decided to pursue our research elsewhere, for instance, evaluating the temperature gradient between air and water in Barton Springs. It was May in Austin and the air conditioning in Allandale House was not really up to the task. However, research fellows are noted for their adaptability. With both of my colleagues out – Ingrid at a seminar and Ben who knows where - I stole their desk fans and waited for the boss in reasonable comfort.

When he finally did show up, he did little but confirm Bradislav-the-Spook's story. Yes, the Center was actually funded by a government agency that preferred to remain anonymous; yes, the Spook was a representative of that agency; and yes, we really did have to cooperate with any reasonable requests that he made.

I could see some wriggle room in that word "reasonable," but Dr. Verrick left it there with a promise that there would be a meeting the next morning at which Everything would be Clarified.

"You'd have to hear this jerk to believe him, Ingrid." I lay back on the living room floor and poured some more water on my chest. As long as my T-shirt was soaking wet I could pretend that the air sighing out of our ancient window unit was actually cooling the place down.

Ingrid Thorn, my colleague and roomie, never did anything so uncouth as pouring water over her body. Mind you, it was just as well she didn't make a habit of it. With what she had under her blouse, she'd probably be responsible for a breakdown of civil order if she ever cooled herself off that way in public. I, on the other hand, could have stood under a sprinkler for half an hour and then walked through the math department without eliciting any reaction other than, "Hey, Kostis, did you know your hair is wet?"

Ingrid shrugged. "Maybe I'll get the chance tomorrow. You did say, a staff meeting?"

"Ten o'clock." Dr. Verrick, being one himself, understands that topologists are not morning people. "In the break room, like always." We didn't exactly need an auditorium for Dr. Verrick to speak with all three of us. On the other hand... "It may be a little crowded if this Bradislav Lensky shows up."

"One guy? We've got eight chairs in there. Not a problem."

"I... don't know. He has this way of taking up space. You should have seen him, Ingrid, he dragged a chair right up to my desk and straddled it and *leaned*. I felt like he was trying to dominate me."

"He should be so lucky! *I've* been trying to dominate you into not taking long showers in the small hours ever since we moved into this place."

Ingrid wasn't all that interested in my personal hygiene; it was just that the pipes in this apartment building clanked and groaned and generally carried on like the ghost of Hamlet's father whenever one of the tenants asked them to do something like, oh, providing water. "There are eight apartments in this building. Somebody's always going to be using the plumbing. You need to learn to sleep through it, Princess."

Ingrid stopped unplaiting the braids she wore wrapped around her head all day and threw a Kleenex box at me. "Remind me again why I share living space with an unsocialized infant like you."

"Because you can't afford a place this close to campus on your own, and you don't dare share with anybody else."

It was, after all, the same reason why I put up with her and her yards of blonde hair and her D-cups and her exalted status as an actual graduate student who might get a Ph.D. some day. Neither of us could risk having a normal roommate who might freak out over us making buttons dance in mid-air or scooting a couple of feet forward without visible means of propulsion.

"If this Lensky comes to the meeting tomorrow, you'll see..."

"What I don't see," said Ingrid, "is why you can't stop going on about this man you talked to for all of fifteen minutes. Is he incredibly handsome or something?"

"Or something. Not exactly pretty." I knew, because I could still see his arrogant face clearly when I thought about him. "Good body, though."

"Ha! I knew it! He's hot, isn't he? And you're crushing on him."

"Don't be silly. He's annoying, is what he is." I reflected for a moment. I had been very briefly interested in making him happy... before he started laying down the law. "To be fair... I guess he would be kind of hot - if he weren't so obnoxious. You'll see tomorrow."

CHAPTER 2

THE BREAK ROOM, like most of the Center's space, is on the public side of the top floor, so anybody at all can show up there. It's not intrinsically a bad room: a nice long solid table, a row of cute little Gothic windows high on the outside wall, a few chairs, and a cabinet where we keep the coffee mugs and other supplies. We don't get a lot of visitors, because the coffee is really bad and the doughnuts disappear quickly and let's face it, how many people are longing for a nice conversation with a math nerd?

Well, Vern Trexler, but he was an aberration. When I got in on Tuesday morning he was already in the break room, sitting tilted back in his chair with his feet on the table. "Thalia, I need to talk to you." He did the sad-puppy-eyes thing at me. The guy wasn't actually repulsive: floppy hair, big brown eyes… Full, moist, quivering lower lip. Okay, that *was* kind of repulsive.

"Maybe some other time, Vern? We're about to have a staff meeting here." The 'other time' I had in mind would involve ice-skating in Hell, but there was no need to be explicit and hurt his feelings.

"Well, that's what I want to talk about, Thalia. Staffing. Haven't you read my application?"

If you can't say anything nice, lie. "No. And it's Lia."

"You should look. I've explained time travel. See, time isn't really directional: it's, like, this fourth dimension and we can go either direction along it."

He must have been reading pulp science fiction from the '40's to come up with that staggeringly original idea. It was also staggeringly wrong, but of course I wasn't allowed to tell him how I knew that.

"Why won't you pay attention to my application? Are you afraid I'll show you up? You really need some creative people here, you know." The longer he talked, the more the underlying whiny tone of his voice came out.

The thought of sharing office space with Vern the Whiner made my skin creep. I did feel sorry for him; he was graduating this year and clearly wasn't going to go on to graduate school in math. He'd probably wind up doing some clerical job for the State of Texas. He was desperate to get back in with the cool kids. And since he was the only person in the world who thought *we* were the cool kids, I really should have liked him better than I did.

"Vern, I'm not in charge of hiring. Dr. Verrick is. You need to submit your job applications to him." There's a reason why I put that in the plural.

"I tried, but he said he isn't paid enough to read any more reasons why he ought to hire me." The whine was coming through loud and clear.

"Well, neither am I. And you need to leave before the meeting."

"Yes, but…" More whining incoming.

"Go *away*, Vern." I put enough of a snarl into my own voice to make him ooze out of the room, and busied myself re-stacking the clean coffee cups until he was gone.

"Good job, Lia." Ben Sutherland was seated at the far end of the table with a yellow legal pad in front of him. The floppy brown hair over his forehead looked more natural on him than the same style did on Vern, or maybe it was just that his was the result of not getting a haircut often enough while Vern's was the perfectly blow-dried and combed product of his barber. Vern… Wait a minute. I'd missed something, hadn't I? "When did *you* come in?"

"Part way through your attempts to evict Trexler." He looked remarkably self-satisfied. "I was testing a new algorithm. It camouflages me with open subsets of the background. I got the idea from Photoshop."

"How do you place them?" Then the penny dropped. "You rat. You were hiding and waiting for me to throw him out. Sticking me with the dirty work, as usual."

"It's just that you've got *such* a talent for alienating people," said Ingrid, coming in. "Why haven't you refilled the coffee maker?"

I sketched a bow in the general direction of her coronet of blond braids. "It's just that you've got such a talent for carrying water, Ingrid."

Fortunately for the peace of the Center, Dr. Verrick showed up just then with the spook.

"Ah, good, you're all here already." His fringe of white hair was more frazzled than usual, and Lensky looked unhappy. He cheered up, though, when he saw the sign over the cabinet. "Coffee and doughnuts?"

"The coffee maker is empty," Ingrid said.

"And the doughnuts seem to be gone." Lensky looked mournfully at the empty tray.

Dr. Verrick does frequently bring doughnuts, though he hadn't bothered today; I think he considers it a morale-raising gesture. But they never last more than five minutes, which makes the sign superfluous. Still, Ben had spent an hour with stencils to create the neat lettering that read "THESE ARE COFFEE CUPS," on one side of the sign, and "THESE ARE DOUGHNUTS," on the other. It didn't cost anything to leave it in place.

"Right, then," Dr. Verrick said. "Everybody please take a seat, then I'm turning this meeting over to Mr. Bradislav Lensky, a representative of our sponsor with a problem he wishes us to work on."

Lensky strolled back from the cabinet to stand at the head of the table. "The agency I work for has picked up chatter and email which suggests there is a group smuggling terrorists over the border and hiding them in a 'safe house' somewhere here in Austin."

"What agency would that be?" Ben interrupted. "It doesn't sound like something the Moore Foundation would be interested in."

"It's not," Lensky said, "but the Foundation actually channels funding from my agency to you people."

"And your agency is...?"

"Need-to-know, and you don't need. I'm your liaison."

"With some nameless three-letter agency," Ben muttered.

Lensky gave him a grim smile. "Exactly. Now that we've cleared up that little matter...."

"Or obfuscated it?"

"Oooh, a spook!" Ingrid cooed. "It's not Bradislav, it's...*Boris*. Where's Natasha?" She was a big fan of "Rocky and Bullwinkle." She'd even gone to see the movie as a child.

Lensky ignored her and kept going. "What I need from you is a comprehensive list of everybody in this people-smuggling operation, their contacts, and, if at all possible, the location of their 'safe house.'"

"Can't the NSA do that?"

"There are sometimes slight difficulties with inter-agency cooperation. And there is a time factor here. Recent chatter points to an upcoming 'party.' We believe that's code for a major terrorist action here in Austin. It's imperative we identify the individuals involved, and their location, before that time."

"And just why should we help you persecute immigrants, *Boris?*" Ingrid demanded. "Don't you realize that Austin is a sanctuary city?"

"Not immigrants," Lensky said. "Illegal aliens. *Terrorists.*"

Reluctantly, I gave him some points for talking to Ingrid's face instead of to her breasts.

"So you say! They're probably innocent people just trying to get away from the violence of their home countries."

"That is not your call to make."

Ingrid Thorn was the only person I knew who could flounce while seated in a straight-backed office chair. "Well, I just hope that if I'm ever forced to flee my war-torn country, I'll be greeted by people a little more open-minded than you!"

"I'm sure I can leave this in your very capable hands," said Dr. Verrick. He knew when to make himself scarce.

Ingrid, Ben and I looked at each other after the boss escaped.

"Who wants to break it to him?" Ingrid said eventually.

"You go first," I suggested to Ben. "Explain the limitations of applied topology."

Ben sighed deeply and pushed the hair off his forehead. "Look, 'Boris,' we've only just discovered this phenomenon. We're in the very, very, very earliest stages of figuring out how it works. No, scratch that. We don't have the foggiest idea how it works, but we've started figuring out what we can do with it despite our near-total ignorance."

There was a reason I had pushed Ben to do the explaining. Of the three of us, he was the one most comfortable with phrases like "our near-total ignorance." Ingrid and I preferred to describe our situation as "open research."

As in, wide open. As in, so wide open that we had no clue what we were doing.

But with the spook clearly thinking of us as some kind of action team of super-beings with super-powers, we needed Ben to disillusion him with the humiliating truth that we were more like a few lost souls groping around in an undefined non-metric space.

"But you can do *some* things that aren't... possible in the real world."

"If we do them," Ingrid snapped, "they are, by definition, possible in the real world."

"Real or not real," Ben returned to his point, "they're just not... very *impressive*... in any world. You need to understand that... *Boris.* We visualize certain topological elements and align them with real-world places and things. Ingrid can move small objects. Lia can move herself about two feet by the Brouwer Fixed-Point Theorem."

"The *what?*"

"It's a statement about a continuous function of a compact convex set onto itself."

That was nasty; he knew perfectly well that wouldn't clarify a damn thing for Lensky. And anyway, it was a lemma of that theorem that I used, identifying the point where I was with the place I wanted to be and visualizing a continuous function of reality onto itself. (Lensky tells me this isn't any clearer than what Ben said. This is the last time I let *him* read anything I've written.)

"And I've been working on a personal camouflage system."

Ben went briskly on without detailing just how his new algorithm worked. "All of us can cross barriers by mentally walking along a Möbius strip; we don't know yet whether it's easier because we're moving ourselves from one side of a space to the other, or because we're physically moving at the same time. Or for some other reason that we haven't thought of yet."

"Aren't you leaving something out?"

Ben shook his head.

"Oh, come on. When I walked in here Thalia was asking you how you had made yourself invisible."

I did rather like the way he said my name, with a broad "a": "Thah-lya." Didn't even come close to rhyming with 'failure.' *Much* better than the usual "Thay-li-uh."

"Unnoticeable, not invisible," Ben corrected him. "You should think of it as a type of camouflage. I haven't yet proved that it establishes true invisibility."

"Tomato, tomahto."

All three of us glared at him. We're *mathematicians*. We don't deal in approximations or it's-all-the-same-thing rationalizations.

I had to admire the way Lensky stood up to our combined stare. Strong men have been known to wilt and put away their calculators under the glower of all three Center Research Fellows. Lensky didn't even look away.

"You can do teleportation." His blue eyes pinned me like a bug in his collection. "Telekinesis." Ingrid got the treatment. "Invisibility." Back to Ben. "You people can be very useful to me. You're just trying to wriggle out of it."

18

"Ingrid," I said wearily, "would you bring something over from the coffee cabinet?"

She closed her eyes and moved her lips soundlessly. There was a furious jiggling in the condiments rack; then a plastic stir stick dropped on the table in front of her.

"Thank you. Now how about a sugar packet?"

This took longer. Eventually a pinch of brown sugar fell onto the table.

"Ingrid can't move an entire sugar packet," I explained to Lensky. "It's too heavy. The best she could do was to move a little sugar out of the packet."

"Without tearing it!" The man was determined to be impressed. I soldiered on.

"If you'd like, I can go to my office and get the plastic pieces I use for set selections, and you can verify that they too aren't very heavy." I wasn't eager to demonstrate the measly six to twenty-four inches that constituted my current teleportation range, so I tried to focus his attention on the accidental telekinesis that started this whole thing.

"Poker chips," Lensky said, "and Darth Vader. And other action figurines."

I was surprised. He flashed a tight smile. "What, you think I'm totally unobservant? Noticing things like that is in my job description. And even granting you have some limitations, you people can make yourselves useful. I want a look inside one of our suspects' computers. A man called Raven Crowson. I don't have enough for a warrant. But *you* should be able to get access by changing bits inside the computer. Little, light things moving very tiny distances. Piece of cake, right?"

What did he think we were, computer nerds? "Wrong! To do that, we'd have to have a detailed image of how a computer works."

"You're math majors, don't you already know all that stuff?"

"We're *pure* mathematicians," I tried to explain. Naturally, that meant nothing to him.

"So that means what? I need to find some slightly sullied math majors? Some who've already lost their virginity? Or do I need to sully you... personally?" He gave me a slow once-over, obviously trying to embarrass me. I did *not* blush. Well, not very much.

"Clean up your act!" Ingrid snapped. "She just meant, you'd have to talk to *applied* mathematicians for this."

"Actually, I don't think that's going low enough." Ben joined the argument. "He might need a computer science major."

"These days, they've gone all theoretical. He really needs an... engineer." Ingrid looked as if she wanted to wash her mouth out with bleach after using the E-word.

"And there's no way anybody in engineering could visualize abstractions well enough to do applied topology," I finished. "So you see, it's not possible to make this work."

"Sure it is. I'll get somebody who understands computer architecture and they can explain it to you, then you guys can do the voodoo part. Or are you just giving me the runaround because you actually can't do anything at all with your so-called magic?"

"We do not," Ingrid said icily, "call it magic. *Boris.*"

"And you were just arguing that we could do *more* than we were admitting! Can't you even stay on the same side of your own arguments?" I'd begun a slow burn when he tried to embarrass me, and this contradiction turned up the flame. "You ignorant, intellectually challenged imbecile, can't you even follow a simple logical argument without holding onto the rope with both hands? It's not our job to educate a dysfunctional kindergartener."

I had more to say along those lines, but "Boris" had tilted his chair back and was laughing. "Go on," he urged. "How many more polysyllabic insults can you come up with?"

"For *you*," I said, "I'd better stick with insults of one syllable. Try this: If you want a big bang, you don't need us, you need a gun!"

He pushed his coat lapels back. "That, I've got."

CHAPTER 3

AFTER THE SPOOK took himself off on some unspecified errand, Ingrid actually lowered herself to refill the coffee maker. "It's just because *I* want coffee," she said, giving me her standard unfriendly stare. "I do not consider it my *job*. We need a receptionist."

Actually, I liked the idea. "Somebody to keep spooks out of our offices."

"To take telephone messages," said Ben, who refuses to learn how to use a cell phone.

"To buy a better class of pastries," Ingrid said.

We all sighed. The Center probably did have sufficient funding to hire a general-purpose dogsbody. Finding a normal person who wouldn't be fazed by representing us was another problem entirely.

"Anyway," I told Ben, "you really want someone to *lose* telephone messages. Why do you keep giving girls the Center phone number, if you don't want them to find you?"

"I don't have another phone number."

"Lia," Ingrid said, "I have an idea. Let's buy Ben a cell phone and whenever one of his girl friends calls here, we can give them that number."

"Waste of your money," Ben said. "I'll lose it. I don't actually want any of my old girl friends to find me – not now."

Ingrid rolled her eyes. "He's in love again!"

"Just don't tell us about this one," I suggested, "and we'll... keep losing your messages."

"The real problem," Ingrid said, "is how to lose *Boris.*"

She had a definite talent for bringing us back to earth. Grudgingly, I gave up fantasies of fresh pastries and good coffee, and shoved my mug over for Ingrid to refill. "This may take a lot more caffeine. Does anybody have an idea for how to satisfy him?"

"I suggest we wrap up Lia in a pretty pink bow and deliver her to him," Ben said, then pretended to flinch away from me. "What? Didn't you notice the way he was looking at you?"

"Sex maniac," Ingrid said.

"Well, he is."

"I meant *you*," she told Ben. She looked at me. "Notice how Ben gets like this every time he falls in love?"

"Only until he gets the girl."

"Then, of course, he falls *out* of love."

"And starts losing her phone messages."

"It's not fair for you two to team up on me," Ben protested. "I call sexism, workplace harassment, um…. anti-diversity working environment… Anyway, I have an idea. What about the Königsberg Bridges problem?"

Ingrid and I both looked at him. "What *about* it?" It had, after all, been solved nearly three hundred years ago.

Ben waved his hands and talked about arcs and vertices. Or if you prefer, lines and points.

We all stared at our coffee cups for a while. Frankly, I would have preferred to be staring at a doughnut, but that was one topological identity that did not transfer to the real world.

"If we haven't seen the target computer, how do we visualize the arc?" Ingrid asked after a while.

"And isn't it likely that if it did work, it would move one or both of the computers instead of giving us access?" I added.

"I didn't say it was a fully worked out solution… Do you think he's with the CIA?"

"Well, he did imply that he wasn't NSA," I allowed.

"Can the CIA run operations inside the country? I thought not."

"I think there's some sort of loophole for counter-terrorism if it involves another country."

"I expect all those agencies do a lot of stuff they 'can't' do," said Ingrid. "Anyway, it's bound to be CIA. Weren't they the ones behind Men Who Stare At Goats?"

"What happened to the goats?"

"Nothing much, I don't think."

"But they probably lost their funding."

Ben had backed off the graph theory approach to computer hacking after I mentioned physical transportation, but neither Ingrid nor I had any better ideas. She escaped to a class (funny, I thought all her classes were in the afternoon) and Ben and I batted ideas around without much progress. Convergent nets? Ultrafilters? By mid-day, we had covered two whiteboards with diagrams but still had not managed to persuade my laptop to bypass his password protection and read data directly off his iPad. "We can visualize the *concepts* just fine," he said glumly. "We just don't know enough about the insides of computers to visualize how they could be affected."

"That's what I hate about applied math. You wind up having to think about all this messy and basically irrelevant stuff."

"Let's get out of here for a while. Lunch?"

The sandwich shop in the Student Union was loud, crowded, and stocked with cellophane-wrapped sandwiches that had probably been assembled in my freshman year. However, it was also cheap, air conditioned, and close to Allandale House, making it the Center's favorite lunch place. I shoved a bill into Ben's hand and plopped down inelegantly on two built-in plastic chairs at once. More or less. I had my butt in one, a hand and a knee on the next one, and *An Over-*

view of Hyperbolic Geometry marking our space on the white plastic table.

"Get me anything but tuna salad," I yelled over the babble. Ben nodded and threw himself into the maelstrom around the sandwich cooler. I sat back and enjoyed the air conditioning. After a morning of pretending that Allandale House was perfectly comfortable, I was in the mood to let the Student Union's much more powerful system chill me until tiny ice crystals formed in my blood.

Or at least until Ben got back with the sandwiches. It didn't take him long today; I wasn't even shivering when he dropped two cellophane-wrapped packages of white bread, brownish lettuce, and anonymous filling on either side of *Hyperbolic Geometry*. I peered at mine.

"It looks like tuna salad."

"No, it's egg salad. See the yellow bits?"

"If it's tuna salad, those yellow bits are cause for grave concern."

"Oh, unwrap it. If it's tuna salad, you can have mine instead."

"What did you get?"

"Tuna salad. Like always. Look, Lia, I need to talk to you," he yelled in my ear. "I need advice."

"Well, I think we should look at knot theory…"

"Not about that! It's about this girl."

When wasn't it? "You really want to shout your love stories out to the entire Student Union?"

"We could go to the Turtle Pond."

"Too hot!"

Ben looked to his left. "No, it isn't. Get up!" He grabbed my arm and hauled me out of the chair I'd worked so hard to defend.

Vern Trexler was between us and the exit, with a tray full of hot, non-portable food. Well, I assumed it was food. Something brown flanked with wedges of something yellow, anyway. He mouthed something inaudible at us.

"Sorry, Vern, we were just leaving!" I shouted.

Sometimes I felt like we were not just the Cool Kids, we were the Mean Kids. But Ben was willing to be ruthless in search of privacy today, and he was my best friend. He definitely outranked Trexler in my private hierarchy.

Of course, so did box turtles, water weeds and rounded rocks, all of which were in evidence at our second-favorite lunch spot.

"Doesn't that guy have any classes?" Ben griped. "How does he have the time to hang out on campus pestering us?"

"Maybe he's flunked out." Not likely, this late in the school year. Still, it wasn't a comfortable thought; Desperate Vern would be even worse than Whiny Vern.

I hadn't managed to get my blood so chilled that it was actually comfortable to sit by the Turtle Pond. But in early May it was bearable; Austin hadn't yet settled down to the daily bombardment by sun that made it questionable whether human life could be sustained without air conditioning. By mid-July, the only way I'd be willing to hang out here would be if the turtles would make room in between the water weeds.

"You're Greek," Ben said when I mentioned the heat. "You're genetically adapted to this kind of climate. It's pallid Nordic types like Ingrid and me who should be complaining."

"I may be of Greek heritage, but I'm not insane. You're mistaking me for the rest of my family. Anyway, I was born in New Jersey. I'm just as American as you two Nordic types." I ripped the cellophane off my sandwich.

"It's… Annelise," Ben said.

"It's tuna salad," I corrected him.

"Never mind that. I need some advice."

"I told you. Knot theory…"

"About Annelise!"

I took a bite of my disgusting tuna salad sandwich. Ben was still looking hopefully at me when I had swallowed it.

"Why? I don't even know your latest true love."

"Well, she's a girl. And you're a girl." He looked at me as though this biological fact was enough to give me special insight into his ladylove's mind.

"Technically."

"Huh? Don't tell me you've suddenly decided to identify as male?"

"Oh hell, no, I just mean I don't have a lot of experience with dating." I thought it over. "Or with other girls, actually. I'm not very social."

"No kidding, I'd never have guessed."

I pretended to swat him with the sandwich. "So, you want advice or don't you?"

"She – oh, never mind. You'll laugh at me."

"Promise not to. I owe you."

"You do?"

"For last year, when all this started." We'd both been graduating seniors, both in Dr. Verrick's general topology class for second-year graduate students (no, we weren't lost; the four years of Verrick's Honors Topology course covered six years of topology by ruthlessly ignoring all other types of mathematics), when it happened. My attempt to illustrate the Axiom of Choice for a kid I was tutoring, using the toys my little brother had left in the living room, went sideways and... the earth moved. Or, to be precise, Darth Vader moved out of a collection of action figures; a poker chip moved out of the chips scattered on the carpet; and one of Andros' Cracker Jack prizes had separated itself from the rest of the pile.

And I was freaked out of my ever-lovin' mind.

First I told my boyfriend. That... did not work out well.

Ben had been the only other math student I dared tell at first. He hadn't laughed at me when I tried to recreate the experiment and it didn't work. And then he hadn't run away when I tried again and it did work. He'd been the lone member of the "Lia Kostis isn't crazy" club until first he, and then Ingrid Thorn, had discovered similar capabilities.

It didn't, as far as we could tell, have anything to do – directly, anyway – with mathematical talent. It seemed to be connected with *how* we proved theorems, rather than with how many theorems we proved. Each of us was known for having a killer intuition in general topology, for *knowing* when a statement was true even if we stumbled over translating that knowledge into a formal proof. Each of us had the same, eerily similar way of getting to that knowledge: we moved into a space inside our heads that was mostly black and empty, populated by glowing points and lines and planes of light. We manipulated the images in that space and saw, without words, why certain theorems had to be true. And now, when we consciously linked those images to real-world objects... little things happened in the world that shouldn't have happened.

Dr. Verrick not only refrained from turning us over to mental health professionals; he wrote letters, pulled strings, and created an independent Center for Applied Topology out of thin air. Got us office space at the top of Allendale House, paid us miserly stipends, and completely changed our lives. This was not exactly what I had envisioned doing after I got my degree.

Not that I had any complaints. My last semester as an undergraduate had been devastating to my ambitions of getting a Ph.D. and becoming a serious topologist, and four years of studying with Dr. Verrick hadn't prepared me for anything else. I had a place to live that wasn't controlled by my family, almost enough to live on comfortably, and all the time I could ask for to explore what else a visualization of topological spaces could do by way of warping reality.

Of course, Dr. Verrick hadn't bothered to explain that we were not actually funded by the Moore Foundation, but by a secretive three-letter-agency using the Foundation as a pass-through.

"You know what?" I said when my thoughts got back to that little bombshell. "If we're actually being funded by the CIA, maybe Dr. Verrick won't make us keep going to the Moore Foundation parties."

"He already knew about the CIA or whoever it is," Ben pointed out, "when he started making us go. I think he's got a secret agenda. Forcing mathematicians to be social."

"I don't think so. He usually complains that we're all too social at those parties. Anyway, it's not like we're all total introverts. I mean, look at you, you've got a girlfriend." With great restraint, I left the word "another" out of that sentence.

"She doesn't take me seriously..." Ben complained that Annelise went out with him, sure, but she was also seeing other men.

"Well," I said, still exercising restraint, "you've seen a number of other girls."

"That was before I met Her. It's different now." Ben went on for a while about how his entire life was now dedicated to cherishing and caring for Annelise, until a turtle climbing up out of the water distracted him.

"Look!"

"Yeah? It's a turtle. In case you haven't noticed, there are a number of them around here."

"Yes, but I could swear that's *Caspica caspica* – a Caspian Box Turtle."

"So?"

"They're only found in Mesopotamia. I just need a look at its plastron." Ben grabbed for the turtle and it slid into the water with a startled *plop*.

"Oh... I forgot you had a second major in Reptiles and Amphibians."

"Marine and Freshwater Biology. Oh well, I'm probably wrong. What would *Caspica caspica* be doing in central Texas?"

"Maybe a veteran brought him back as a souvenir?"

Ben scowled. "That's terrible! This is way too far north for him to survive in the wild."

The humid May air lay heavily on my equally humid skin. "Wow, that has to be the first time anybody described Austin as 'too far north' of anywhere."

"Don't be so provincial. For all you know, millions of Mexicans may think of Austin as the frozen north."

"Frozen? That's pushing it."

"Hey. We did have some snow a few years ago, remember?"

"Vividly." And that time the snow didn't even stick to the ground, but the city practically shut down anyway.

"You and I were the only people who made it to class."

"And Dr. Verrick. Most of the other professors took off to dance in the falling snow." We enjoyed the memory in silence for a few minutes before Ben got back to the topic of Annelise, who was apparently the most wonderful girl in the world except that she didn't take him seriously.

It was an easy mistake for anyone to make. Ben wasn't exactly the most impressive person in the world – not physically, anyway. Oh, he was tall enough, and not only by my own unexacting standards; he was actually a couple of inches taller than Ingrid, who could have been cast as a Norse shield-maiden. But he didn't get his light brown hair cut nearly often enough, and when he wasn't wearing glasses his brown eyes had the vague look common to the extremely near-sighted. Because he was too impatient to try on clothes until he found some that actually fit his lanky frame, he tended to buy shirts that were way too big for his shoulders so as to get sleeves long enough for his arms. If you weren't equipped to recognize the world-class intelligence behind those unfocused eyes you might easily underrate him.

The only reason he was so successful with girls was that until he fell in love with someone else, he bent all his impressive intellect on the current girl. He would study her so intently that she thought he understood her soul... and then he'd lose interest before she had a chance to realize that he was that intense about everything in his field of view, and she wasn't so special after all.

If he'd been chasing this Annelise long enough for her to discover that he was exactly as interested in the appearance of a Mesopotamian box turtle in central Texas as he was in her soul, she was probably a lost cause for him. Ingrid and I would just have to listen until some new planet swam into his ken, or –

"*Ben.*" I jerked my chin towards the Student Union. Vern Trexler was coming this way, and we were sitting ducks unless – "Can you do your camouflage thing *right now?*"

I was unaccustomed to being within the field of someone else's visualization; generally I was the one creating the visualization, not a ride-along. From my perspective, being included under Ben's protective cover felt like being in a time-lapse video of a blue norther sweeping down on Austin. The sky darkened over us and the sounds of people outside the cover faded away. The air around us took on a strange consistency, almost like clear Jello, blurring our surroundings to my sight. On a sunny May afternoon in Texas, I felt chilled and the little hairs on my arms prickled.

By the pricking of my thumbs... But it was only Ben thinking about open subsets of our background. Wasn't it?

~

The unnatural chill invaded the water around Niiqarquusu and shocked him out of his lazy, sun-baked dreaming. Here was a working worthy of the Magi of the Medes, nothing so trivial as a hand grabbing for his shell. What had caused this? The water seemed almost solid around him, the light died. He lifted his head and searched for the source of the disturbance. Light warped and twisted in ways he had not seen in... how long had it been? He could barely count the centuries. He tried to call to this new mage and the ring binding his neck tightened, burned, absorbed his strength. The Lights were buried deep within him and the ring kept them, too, asleep. Niiqarquusu woke to a bitter awareness of his diminished powers. Bound as he was, he could not influence this strange wizardry of lines and planes in the slightest. He could only exercise the common defense of his kind. Frustrated and frightened, Niiqarquusu tucked in his head and limbs and pulled the two parts of his shell together until he resembled a rock.

~

Some distance south of the university, the man who called himself Raven felt a quivering in the air of his office. The chill that briefly surrounded the Turtle Pond had no impact on this air-conditioned building, but there was a disturbance in the air, a shaking of the light that was both familiar and strange. Familiar, because he had felt similar workings before; strange, because it seemed to be based on a cold geometry rather than on any warm, living animals.

He summoned his blue-black feathered servant, Lamashtu, and gave her instructions.

The light and heat of a normal late spring afternoon rushed back as Ben drew a long, shaky breath. Vern had walked past us; no one around the Turtle Pond seemed perturbed. I supposed they had been as blind to Ben's work as I had been that morning, when I was on the outside of Camouflage.

"You have *got* to show me how you do that!"

He started to speak, but was drowned out by harsh voices crying, "Gack! Gack!" A flurry of black feathers darted down, snatched the last of his sandwich and left a whitish splotch on the edge of the pond.

"Blast it! A cackling of grackles," he said. "I *hate* this time of year... We might as well get back to the office; I can't concentrate on anything when I'm worried about grackles shitting on my head."

CHAPTER 4

WHEN WE GOT BACK to Allandale House there was another stranger in the break room: a tall skinny redhead with nerdy glasses, whom Lensky was regarding with a self-satisfied smile. I would have been willing to Möbius right past the stranger so that Ben and I could get down to details on Camouflage, but Ben made the mistake of asking about him.

"Folks," Lensky said with a sweeping gesture, "allow me to introduce James DiGrazio –"

"Jimmy," the redhead said, "James is my-father-the-CEO."

"Jimmy DiGrazio, computer analyst extraordinaire, who has generously volunteered to educate you on the fundamentals of computer architecture."

So much for that afternoon's research. Jimmy started talking almost before Lensky stopped. After the third sentence I got a legal pad out of the cabinet and started taking notes and drawing pictures.

We had a momentary respite when Ingrid joined us; Jimmy's overlapping sentences and rush of words slowed, then stopped while he took in everything from her coronet of pale braids to the D-cups under her white shirt. The usual reaction.

"*Jimmy,*" Lensky hissed, and the lecture slowly restarted. (What, you think he couldn't hiss a word with no fricatives? Spooks get special training in this sort of thing.)

Getting Jimmy from comprehensible generalities to the kind of nuts and bolts we needed wasn't easy. As soon as he got into details he became incomprehensible, and we wasted a lot of time translating computerese into mathematics only to discover that these particular details weren't the ones we needed.

"It might help," he suggested after the fourth or fifth such detour, "if you told me exactly what you needed to know."

Lensky scoffed. "If they could do that, they wouldn't need you!"

"Well… what exactly do you want to *do*?"

Ben tried to talk around it and only shed clouds of obfuscation. Ingrid couldn't help; every time she opened her mouth the computer nerd goggled at her and quit thinking. I wound up stuck with the job, and inadvertently revealed a bit more detail than we really wanted to share with anyone outside the Center.

"So," he summed up. "You're thinking of some way to change interior states of a computer without authorization and without being physically present. What do you think, computers are magical?"

"Don't overstate the case," Ben said hastily. "There are lots of ways to change the state of a computer without being in the same room. Isn't that basically what hackers do?"

"Yes, but you're not asking me about networking and remote connections. You're not asking how to make the changes, you're asking what changes need to be made. Obviously you're not telling me everything. And I'm not going to play until you do."

"We'll have to get authorization from our boss…"

Lensky interrupted. "*I'll* authorize him. Get on with it."

I had already slipped up, and the man was incapable of keeping his brain in gear when Ingrid spoke, so it was up to Ben to explain as little as possible about our research.

He might have done that a little too well; Jimmy looked confused and dissatisfied.

"We manipulate objects in real space via mathematical visualization," I summarized.

"You do magic?" His voice went up on the last word.

"You're not freaked out?"

"No, why would I be?"

"Then you must not believe me." Another recruit for the "Thalia Kostis *is* crazy" club.

"I believe you think you're telling the truth. And I believe you're delusional."

"Good, humor me. Tell the deluded mathematicians here how to force remote access to a computer behind a firewall."

Jimmy chalked some diagrams on the whiteboard. "If you *could* directly affect internal registers, which you can't, you'd want to flip the states of this… this… and this. Probably."

"Maybe it's as simple as a Jordan Curve problem," I said. "No way to that side of the plane…"

"Let C be a simple closed curve," Ben said.

"And let AB be an arc of C," Ingrid contributed.

"Delete AB from C, and there is now only one side of the plane," I finished.

The last drawing on the whiteboard fell off, leaving its section of board pristine and gleaming. You could just make out the inked diagram, now draped over the molding at the floor. Jimmy's eyes got wide. "You set that up, didn't you?"

"Set what up? It didn't work," Ben said. He sounded frustrated.

Jimmy picked up the deleted diagram, a tenuous shape formed from tiny splodges of ink. It wrapped itself around his forearm. "This is for real, isn't it?"

"If I say yes," Ben said cautiously, "are you going to run away screaming?"

"Hell no! You couldn't beat me off with a stick! Real magic? This is *so cool*! Way better than *World of Wizardry* or *Nebulosity*."

Ingrid rolled her eyes.

～

I couldn't *think* around Jimmy DiGrazio with his ebullient enthusiasm for what he imagined our research to be. Neither could Ben. Ingrid claimed, later, not to be affected by the man's presence, but she was the first one to retreat to the privacy of our offices on the far side of the wall. We left Lensky the job of explaining how we'd turned sideways and vanished (Möbius-ing to the other side looks very strange to onlookers). It seemed only fair; after all, he'd brought the guy here in the first place.

And with all of us safely on this side of the wall, Lensky couldn't even get at us to complain about the arrangement.

"Okay, so it's not a Jordan Curve problem," Ben muttered. "I wonder..."

His eyes got even vaguer than usual and he wandered off to his own office, mumbling. Ingrid and I split up without any discussion at all. It had been exhausting, trying to get the information we needed out of Jimmy; all three of us badly needed some time in a normal environment.

(You don't think being alone in an office, drawing diagrams on a whiteboard, is normal? Look, you don't have to be introverted to the point of mania to be a mathematician, but it's a good start. Even being around Ben and Ingrid for too long was tiring, and they felt the same way about me. Being around a bouncy type like Jimmy DiGrazio was *exhausting*.)

Dr. Verrick yanked us out of our cocoons, I mean offices, before any of us were even half recovered from all that interaction. He wanted reports, and he wanted to discuss staffing. The spook was leaning on him for results and the Allandale House trustees were unhappy about the way we were using the third floor – or rather, the way we weren't using it.

"I've wasted half a day trying to persuade the trustees that we are making good and appropriate use of our space here," he announced as soon as we filed into the coffee room. From habit, I glanced at the tray under the "These Are Doughnuts" sign. Still empty. "I don't want to have another such meeting."

"What's their complaint?" Ingrid asked. "They said we could have this floor for office space. We have offices. They take up space."

"By their accounting, three and a half people don't need the entire floor." Dr. Verrick looked as if he expected us to go forth and multiply on the spot. "We have the funding to hire more people; we need to use it. If we don't put more warm bodies here, they've threatened to make us share the floor with someone else."

"That's not exactly a fate worse than death," Ben said. "As long as we don't have to share the *Research Division* space…"

Dr. Verrick looked ill. "The Office for Diversity Compliance was mentioned. As a possible co-tenant."

I *felt* ill. So, to judge from the silence, did Ingrid and Ben.

"It's not just a matter of funds," I pointed out eventually. "There just aren't that many visualizing topologists around. And even if we could find more, they might have lives." I could appreciate – as a theoretical matter – that some people might prefer real life to bouncing around the top floor of a Victorian house with misfits like us.

"Not really a problem," Ben drawled. "Anybody who can visualize well enough to join us is unlikely to have a life."

Ingrid and I objected. "Fine," he said, "come up with a counterexample. Who here has a real life?"

We thought.

"You have sequential girlfriends," I pointed out.

"They don't last. That's more of an *attempt* at a life."

We brooded a little more, under Dr. Verrick's expectant gaze.

"I had to pay a late fee on my library books last week," Ingrid said eventually.

There was a momentary silence.

"We don't have to hire more Research Fellows," Dr. Verrick said finally. "The need for support staff has been mentioned. In this very room."

"A *receptionist*…." Ingrid sighed happily.

"Someone to make the coffee."

"Bring doughnuts."

"Take messages."

"Find one who won't have a nervous breakdown within a day of starting work here, and I'll hire her," Dr. Verrick said. "Him. It. Xer. Whatever."

He did know how to squash an idea flat. "In the meantime," he went on as soon as we seemed adequately squashed, "Mr. DiGrazio will join us as a consultant. He'll have an office - *outside* the Research Division," he added before we could start complaining, "and will make himself available to answer your questions about computer architecture."

"Jimmy," Ingrid said flatly.

"Could be worse," Ben said. "He's not exactly an extrovert."

Ingrid sniffed. "You could have fooled me."

"*World of Wizardry? Nebulosity?*"

"You know what those are?"

"I looked them up," Ben said. "They're online role-playing games. That's how he spends his free time. It's not exactly social."

It was a bit more social than any of us liked to be, but I did take his point. "He's like us in that he has virtually no life."

"Or," Ingrid suggested, "you could say that he has a life… virtually."

Ben did seem to be able to deal with Jimmy better than Ingrid and I. He took his copy of the suspicious-messages folder and the name Lensky had provided and actually invited the computer nerd into his office for a bit of experimentation. "At least I don't have to conceal what I'm doing from Jimmy," he pointed out. "That makes this a *lot* better than having to be around normal people."

Ingrid and I looked at each other. "Do you think Ben might be a trifle… *extroverted?*"

"He does attract girls. That's more than you can say for either of us."

"Speak for yourself, Lia. I don't want to attract girls!"

"No more do I. I was speaking generally, and you know it. Besides," I dug in the sharp point, "now we know what you attract… computer nerds!"

"No way. Clean out your mind." She stalked out of my office.

The only noticeable result of Ben's experimentation was that his hair looked even more like a disheveled haystack than usual. I deduced that he'd been running his fingers through it for most of the two hours he'd spent with Jimmy.

"No results?"

"I wouldn't say that. I can actually mess with nearby computers to a certain extent."

"What are you using?"

"A variant on Ingrid's mapping trick. But I think I need to be physically closer to the computer Lensky wants us to target. He didn't even give us an address, but my range right now is more like ten feet and I'm pretty sure Crowson's computer isn't in this building."

"Um. How do you know that? About your range, I mean."

Ingrid stamped into my office and answered the question. Sort of. "Ben, get your tiny mind out of my laptop! Did you think I couldn't feel you messing around in my folders?"

Ben gave me a sickly grin. "That's how I know."

Lensky was lying in wait when we headed out for food. "Any success?"

Ben repeated that he needed to be closer.

"I'll have an address for you tomorrow."

Ingrid and Ben headed out, but Lensky lingered. "Did you need something?" I said. I didn't care for the idea of leaving him alone in Allandale House to do whatever spooky spy-type stuff he was used to.

"Thought I might buy you a beer," he said, following me down the stairs.

"Huh? Why?"

"Oh, I don't know… clear the air, improve diplomatic relations… apology? I did come across kind of crude this morning. That really isn't usual; I don't know what came over me."

What I mainly remembered about that morning was blowing up at him.

"Oh, well. I think we're even. I seem to recall throwing a few insults your way."

"Then *you* can buy *me* a beer."

"On a Research Fellow's stipend? Dream on!"

"I was hoping to establish friendlier terms. Is that even remotely possible?"

"I don't know. Are you going to stop being patronizing about my research?"

"I don't know," he parroted back at me. "Are you going to stop being patronizing about everybody in the world who isn't a mathematician?"

"I'm not!"

"Oh, yes you are."

"You're thinking of Ingrid, she's the snob."

We'd reached the parking lot and I was beginning to wonder what to do next. I'd automatically set out towards the west of campus because that was where my parents lived. But I didn't live there any more; Ingrid and I shared an apartment north of the university, where there were still old buildings that hadn't been replaced by luxury condominiums..

"All three of you are insufferable intellectual snobs," Lensky said. The annoying thing was, he sounded as if he thought that was funny.

"Okay, I won't prolong your suffering in my company. Good night!"

"Are you offended?"

"What do you care?"

"Well, that gets us back to me having to buy you a beer, doesn't it? Come on."

He *would* have one of the coveted and strictly limited FDP parking permits. His car was the closest air-conditioned space available.

CHAPTER 5

THE SPOOK DID DESERVE some credit for knowing where I'd want to go if I were going to have a friendly drink with him. Not much credit, though. After all, he was a professional collector, sifter, and sorter of information. And it wasn't that hard to discover the oldest business in Austin.

Yes, I'm talking about *that* beer garden; what did you think I meant? That guff about "the oldest profession," applies to less civilized places. In Texas, selling beer *is* the oldest profession. We have a long history of getting our priorities right. (So I was born in New Jersey. Doesn't count. I got here as soon as I could.)

He was also pretty good at claiming space. Within minutes of arrival, he had identified the best of the shady spots at a table under the trees, snagged two chairs, and arranged for a pitcher of cold beer and a couple of frosty mugs. (If you keep them in the freezer, it's like having ice cubes in your drink, without the melting and dilution. Did I mention that we have our priorities right?)

After inhaling the first refreshing mug of beer I did begin to wonder why he'd worked so hard to get me here. Perhaps his suspect also liked beer? Was I cover for a covert investigation? The thought made me snicker quietly into my second mug.

"What's so funny?"

"I don't see anybody who looks like a terrorist. But then, what do terrorists look like?"

"Remarkably like normal people," Lensky said grimly. "Why, are you going to tell me they spin their plots over a pitcher of beer?"

"Isn't that why we're here?"

"Actually, no. Are you laboring under the illusion that everything I do is about work?"

I gave that some thought while working on my second mug. "You do give that impression."

"Well, you're wrong. I'm human enough to enjoy having a drink under the trees with a pretty girl."

I started liking him a little better. I even regretted blowing up at him this morning.

"That's okay," he said easily, "I admire a woman who can explode with so much elegance and elan. Not to mention alliteration. I don't think I've ever been called an ignorant, intellectually challenged imbecile before. Besides," he added, "you didn't call me 'Boris,' and that was a nice change."

He wasn't glancing around; his eyes were fixed on me. Very dark, very blue. In the shade here, at the beginning of evening, the air was actually cool and pleasant, but for some reason my face was getting hot. I probably needed more beer.

"I thought that whole Boris-and-Natasha joke got old pretty fast," I said. It was only the truth. "And - I don't much care for that kind of teasing. Jokes about people's names," I amplified, so he wouldn't think I disapproved of teasing spooks. I didn't. I just thought it should be done more cleverly.

"Don't you now? I've noticed that everybody calls you Lia. What do you have against a lovely name like 'Thalia?'"

Nothing at all, the way he pronounced it, with a broad A. "Oh, people can't decide how to pronounce or spell it, that's all." Damned if I was going to tell him that everybody else rhymed it with 'failure' and thought that was just ever so funny.

"Ha! Try going through school with a name like Bradislav. And it was even worse before I talked my mom into letting me change it to that. I was christened 'Wladislaw.'" He spelled it out, and I had to admit it.

"You win. Your parents were even more vicious than mine."

He put his hand over mine, as if we were old friends. After a couple of beers, in the warm soft air under the trees, it seemed perfectly natural. "Does it have to be a contest?"

He was sitting so close now, it would have been easy to lean towards him and rest my head on his shoulder, just like any normal girl on a date with her boy friend. Why did that even occur to me? I didn't do it, of course. I was a professional, and so was Lensky, and this wasn't a date.

More like a temporary truce.

There was an ominous cackling above us; the grackles must be moving in for the night. I decided to ignore them.

That wave of blond hair rolling back from his forehead was really quite attractive. So were his hands and wrists, if you liked that kind of big, muscular look. Which, actually, I did. I took a sip of beer to cool myself off.

"Your wrists must be twice as big around as mine."

"Regular practice at the range."

"Oh, come on. Your gun can't be that heavy."

"Oh, would you like to handle my… gun?"

Just when I started thinking that I could like the man, he let off one of his crude double-entendres. Change the subject.

"You could have built those muscles doing deep-sea fishing, or wrestling, or…" Oops. Not a good choice of examples. "Do you *have* any life outside The Agency?" I asked quickly, before he could invite me to a wrestling contest. Much more of this conversation, and my mind was going to be right down in the gutter where his appeared to reside.

"I'm… working on the concept." He took a long pull on his beer. "Haven't had a lot of spare time, up to now."

I looked politely interested; he touched on some of the high – or maybe low - points of his life. A father who died young, growing up in a not-so-good neighborhood, after-school jobs to help with rent and groceries, taking eight years to work his way through a night-school degree in Criminal Justice….

"An outsize sense of responsibility." I suppressed a hiccup.

He looked unhappy. "Balancing my older brother, I guess. He had no sense of responsibility at all."

"Had," sounded very, um, past-tense-ish. Another death in the family? Or just a rift? He zipped back into the impersonal, very quickly. "Just working, instead of working and going to night school and writing term papers on the train, is still kind of a new experience for me."

Who outside of New York said train, not subway? And with that accent... Not a surfer boy, after all. More like a Jersey boy. I had a couple of cousins who sounded just like him.

"You haven't been with the agency that long, then?"

"Long enough. Finally got that degree five years ago. But... I've been busy with other stuff until recently."

Paying back student loans, probably.

"Is that where you got that outsize chip on your shoulder? Working your way through college?"

"Ha! Where did you get yours? It's so big you must get back pains from carrying it around."

"No such thing. I'm just... not good with people. A lot of us aren't."

"A lot of who? Greeks? I thought you guys were always dancing and swigging retsina."

I gave him a dirty look. "Aren't you a little young to have been influenced by *Zorba the Greek*?"

"I like old movies."

"Anyway, I didn't mean Greeks. Besides, I was born in America. I meant mathematicians."

Lensky pursed his lips and whistled. "The world-view is impressive. You really do think you're a separate, superior caste, don't you?"

"Me? No. The real mathematicians are doing actual research and discovering new mathematics. I'm just a girl with a bachelor's in math, with a really good intuition for point set theory problems and this funny trick of applying it to the real world."

"So... I understand Ingrid's going for her Ph.D. Does that make her a real mathematician?"

"She certainly thinks so!"

"I'm not interested in what she thinks." He leaned even closer. "*You*, on the other hand, do interest me. I'd like to know more about what you think."

There was nothing between us but my mug, which seemed to be empty again; how had that happened? I bought time by refilling it and chugging the contents. Understand, I was *not* flustered. I just wasn't ready to spill my personal thoughts to a near-stranger.

"Let's start with something easy. Did you always live in Texas?"

"Regrettably, no. My parents moved here when I was in middle school."

"From New Jersey?"

I was startled. "What, have you got a dossier on me?"

"Regrettably, no. Though it's a thought... I'll have my minions get right on it. You haven't quite lost the accent."

"Ugh."

"No, it's cute. A Texas-size attitude coming out of a Jersey girl's mouth. You love it here, don't you?"

"Yes."

"Why?"

"This is the only place I've ever felt like I belonged. When I started at the university and stumbled on Dr. Verrick's topology classes, I felt like I was coming home."

"Don't you think that would have happened in any university you went to? I'm sure there are mathematicians at Princeton who'd have made you feel right at home. Or MIT. Yale. Take your pick."

"Yes, well, none of those were options for some reason. Any more than they were for you."

"Family couldn't swing it? Even with - I'm sure you could have gotten scholarships."

"Family *wouldn't* swing it. According to my father, it's a waste of time for girls to go to college because they'll just get married and have children. Also, nobody will ever want to marry a freak like me who not only went to college but majored in mathematics instead of early childhood education." I tilted my beer mug.

"He doesn't have a strong need for intellectual consistency, does he?"

"Got it in one." I refilled my mug from the pitcher. Talking about the family made me thirsty.

"So… now that you've got your degree, what are you going to do next?"

"Continue to manipulate objects in real space via topological visualizations?"

"If that's what you want to talk about." Why did he look disappointed? "Or we could talk about what you were planning to do with your life before you discovered this talent, or even what you're planning to do with it now. I mean, mathematics isn't exactly a religious vocation. You can date… get married, have children…"

"Oh, sure. Just as soon as I meet somebody who isn't totally freaked out by my… abilities." I'd faced this fact last year, when my problems started.

When I broke up with Rick.

OK, to be honest, when Rick dumped me because "all this was just too weird for him."

"I can't marry a normal person," I told Lensky now. "I can't even *room* with a normal person. Ingrid and I don't share an apartment because we're such good friends, we share because neither of us has to worry about the other one freaking out when something a little bit unusual happens."

"But that's only an extension of the way you've always felt, isn't it? That your intellect cuts you off from normal life?"

"Well, it does. There aren't many men in the math department eager to date a girl who can come up with a proof faster than they can." Rick had been my one counter-example, and he hadn't actually asked me out until I was having trouble in class.

"And you couldn't, of course, consider hanging out with anybody who wasn't a mathematician."

"It makes life simpler," I said, "if you stick to people who speak the same language."

"Ah! 'Mathematicians are like Frenchmen; whatever you say, they translate into their own language, and forthwith it means something completely different.'"

"Yes, that's your typical normal attitude."

"Not necessarily mine. Goethe said it."

That raised my brows. "And studying Goethe is what part of a criminal justice degree?"

"I read a lot. You shouldn't be so quick to assume that everybody who's different from you is a moron."

And he shouldn't be telling me what I should feel. I raised my beer mug. "Why not? Statistically, it's more often true than not, and saves a lot of time."

"And cuts off a lot of possibilities."

I was about to refute that when a raucous "Gaak! Gaak!" right over my head totally startled me; I hadn't been paying attention to our surroundings.

Lensky started swearing. He'd come off worse than I had; the grackle might not have startled him, but it did poop in his beer. Fortunately it got the mug, not the pitcher.

Remarkably good aim, those birds. I toasted the responsible party with my fourth mug.

The next morning, while I was working on my third cup of coffee and regretting having had a pitcher of beer for supper, Ben came across to the Research side looking disgustingly bright and eager for action. Worse, he walked Jimmy in with him. The computer nerd didn't have as strong a stomach as Lensky; he looked like somebody staggering off a small boat after crossing the English Channel. Being led along an invisible Möbius strip tends to affect non-mathematicians that way.

"Got the target's office address from Boris," he announced.

"You guys are working already? This early?" Now *I* was beginning to feel like an unhappy sailor. Today was unnecessarily bright, the grackles outside were noisier than they really needed to be, and I did not need to be surrounded by early-morning enthusiasm. I was only here because Ingrid sings and does exercises first thing in the morning, and walking to Allandale House was better than sticking in ear plugs and cursing her.

"What's gotten under *your* skin?"

"Be nice to the lady, I expect she's hungover," said Lensky, a beat behind Ben and Jimmy. *He* didn't look even mildly greenish after being taken over the virtual Möbius strip. But then, it wasn't his first rodeo. "Last night I was impressed by the amount of beer she could handle. Possibly over-impressed."

Ben blinked. "*You* went out drinking with *Lia*? And survived?"

"I must have twice her body mass," he pointed out.

"Yeah, but she trained with ouzo-drinking Greeks from Jersey." Ben had met my parents a few times, once at a wedding where the toasts were flowing freely.

"Ah, that explains why she scoffed at retsina."

"I'm disappointed in you, Lia," Ben said. "Letting a *spook* out-drink you?"

I fished out a couple more aspirin and washed them down with my cooling coffee. "It wasn't the beer. It was forgetting to eat."

"You do that too much anyway," Ben scolded me. "It's not healthy."

"Well, if people keep trying to force stale tuna fish sandwiches on me, what do you expect?"

"What's your worry? She looks healthy enough. She's certainly not wasting away just yet," Lensky said, and his eyes conveyed an appreciative appraisal of my shape. Which really isn't all that worth appraising; I'm just a short dark girl, not very memorable. Not fat, not skinny, and definitely not striking like Ingrid. He was just taking his chance to make me uncomfortable. Why couldn't he stare at Ingrid like every other man in the known universe?

I turned to Ben. "Why don't you take Bo - Lensky to your office and see if knowing the exact address makes it easier to get into the computer?"

That got rid of him. As a side benefit, Ingrid turned up just then, and Jimmy got that stunned look again and followed her.

I closed my office door and crunched a couple more aspirin.

Much too soon, all four of them were back. "Knowing an address isn't good enough," Ben announced. "I really do need to be physically closer to the actual computer."

"Is that safe?"

Lensky shrugged. "The man calls himself a financial advisor. I doubt that he's carrying." A slight, barely perceptible movement of his hand towards his hip. Was the gun some sort of security blanket for him?

"How would just outside the building work?" Ingrid asked. "There are some nice oleander bushes where we can hide."

"How do you know?" She couldn't have zipped down to the building and back already. Ben hadn't been busy that long.

"Google Street View."

I goggled. (As opposed to Googled.) "Since when do *you* use Google Street View?"

"I downloaded it on her laptop," Jimmy volunteered, "while you two were trying to get into Crowson's computer."

"Let's see if just outside the building is close enough," Ingrid said. "I'll come with you and do Camouflage while you peep at the computer."

"I'd better come too." If Ben was teaching Camouflage, I wanted to be there.

"And me," Lensky said.

Ingrid sniffed. "There aren't that many bushes."

Riiight, that was why we were sending the blonde Valkyrie instead of the pint-sized Greek, was it? Because she was so inconspicuous?

But I wasn't actually ready for a dose of blinding mid-morning sunshine, so Ingrid got her way.

After she and Ben left, Jimmy announced that he was going to do some conventional research on this Crowson, if somebody could help him get back to his office on the public side. "It's not that hard, this way." I started him on the correct path and watched him dwindle to a line, then a blinking line, then nothing.

That left only Lensky to get rid of. "Don't you have anything to do?"

"Are you always this friendly in the morning?"

"Only after I've been plied with way too much beer. The least you could do is get me some water."

Only, of course, he couldn't, because the plumbing was all on the public side of the third floor and he wouldn't be able to get back in.

"Why," I wondered aloud, "does everybody use my office as a meeting room?"

"It's too much trouble doing your magic shuffle to pass the wall," Lensky said, "and all the extra chairs on this side are in your office."

So they were.

Finally the spook's muscle came in useful: I made him move all the extra chairs into Ben's office. This wasn't a completely trivial chore, because Ben had craftily picked a very small office. However, there was room for the chairs after I stole Ben's big box fan. After Lensky stacked the chairs to fit, he went off for lunch muttering about being exploited by unscrupulous women.

CHAPTER 6

THIS NEXT BIT is out of order, because I didn't actually know about it while I was eating lunch and going through the Student Union's supply of cold bottled water; if I had, maybe I could have done something to mitigate the fiasco. I only learned about it afterwards, from Ben. Ingrid refused to discuss the matter.

Crowson's office was in one of those elegant converted houses between the university and downtown – you know, the kind with little round windows in front and a white gingerbread frieze hanging off the porch roof. He was actually in his office when Ingrid and Ben got there, slightly unhappy – not to mention sweaty - after driving around several blocks in search of a parking space and then hiking back to the address Lensky had forked over. It was close to noon by then and the Austin sun was just hitting its stride.

Ingrid went inside to pretend she was looking for the (nonexistent) Past Life Therapy Group in the (also nonexistent) office 21F. Crowson Financial Services was in 21B, and while "looking" for 21F Ingrid verified that 21B was on the second floor, by the east wall.

"He came out of his office to ask what the hell I thought I was doing in the building," she told Ben when she got back outside, "so no,

I don't think we can lurk by the stairs while you riffle through his virtual files. It'll have to be the east wall."

That was where the oleanders were planted, so it seemed – briefly – that at least some luck was with them. It was also where the building was shaded by live oaks, which they thought – erroneously – was another piece of luck.

Ben had taught Ingrid the basis of Camouflage while they were driving to the office address. Now they both ducked behind the oleanders and she started visualizing while he concentrated on getting a remote look at the computer.

He knew when her visualization got shaky because they were, abruptly, standing in the sunlight instead of under a dark blue virtual cloud. "You dropped it," he whispered.

"It's the damned grackles. I can't *concentrate* when I'm trying to dodge grackle feces."

She *would* say 'feces.'

"Okay, trade places."

They shuffled around each other and Ingrid yelped. "You didn't mention the pyracantha!"

"I thought you were bright enough to look where you were shuffling. Now concentrate, dammit!"

"Maybe the, uh, 'lady' could concentrate better if she came out of those bushes," said a third, and distinctly unsympathetic, voice. "You too, sir."

"*Shit.*" Ben reserved 'feces' for biology classes.

"Now would you like to tell me what you were up to?"

That was when Ben had what he considered his inspiration. "Ah, isn't it obvious, officer?" He snaked an arm round Ingrid's waist. "My girl and I were just looking for a little privacy."

The cop looked less than fully convinced. "Behind two oleanders and a pyracantha? You're lucky you didn't get any farther with her, I'd have had to run you both in for public indecency."

"It was an emergency," Ben said. "Honey-babe here just agreed to marry me, and I wanted to kiss her."

"Riiight. Do you always propose to your girlfriend in a very public place? And without a ring?"

"Sorry, I don't have a settled technique for proposing. Next time I'll be sure to ask you for lessons."

The cop made it clear that he wasn't going anywhere until they did, so they retreated down the sidewalk towards Ben's car.

"*Honey-babe?*" Ingrid muttered as soon as they were out of earshot.

"Hey. I was improvising, all right?"

"You're lucky your precious Annelise wasn't there!"

"Actually I wish she had been. That girl is a genius at making up plausible stories. She'd probably have persuaded the cop to give me a boost up so I could work standing on the ledge outside Crowson's window."

"Well, next time bring your little girlfriend and let me know how that works out for you!"

"What really ticked Ingrid off," Ben insisted when he was telling me this bit, "is that one of the grackles pooped in her hair and another got her down the neck of her blouse."

That explained why she'd disappeared into the bathroom as soon as they got back to Allandale House. She didn't come out for forty-five minutes, but when she did, she was fully combed and groomed and wearing a clean, if damp, blouse. The only other sign of her unfortunate experience was that the blond braids wrapped around her head were still wet.

By that time the rest of us were gathered in the break room. Observe the benefits of forethought; Jimmy had started by trying to take over my office to announce his discovery, but the absence of chairs inspired him to move elsewhere. He didn't actually have anything worth forty-five minutes of discussion, but Ben was tired and I was on a mild aspirin high and Ingrid, of course, was de-grackling, though I didn't know the specifics until later. So we let Jimmy have all the time he wanted to talk about Zillow and AirOffice and real estate rental listings before he got to the big reveal: 21A in Crowson's building was vacant right now.

"We could rent it!"

"Takes too long," Ben said. "Boris wants results now, not two weeks and a questionnaire and a rental history from now. And *we* want to get rid of Boris. No, we'll just go in tomorrow. Jimmy, you'd better come with us in case I need to know more computer architecture."

"Speak for yourself," Ingrid said before she was quite in the room. "I've had quite enough of this clandestine business. Why don't you take the wonderful Annelise, Ben?"

Not having heard the full story by then, I was mildly curious as to why Ingrid was snubbing Ben. Not desperately curious; she was usually more likely to put me down, and I was okay with having Ben become the designated snub-ee for a change.

"Believe me," Ben said, "I would much, much rather have Annelise's company than yours. But she does have class tomorrow morning."

He'd memorized her schedule?

On second thought – why was I surprised? He was at least as interested in this girl as he was in *Caspica caspica*, and he'd already given me an earful on the box turtles of Mesopotamia.

"How do you think you're going to get in?" Jimmy wanted to know.

"Fiddle the locks. Mathematically. Now *that's* an application of topology with lots of uses. Move a small object a short distance for a big reward."

Ingrid rolled her eyes. "It's also just slightly illegal."

"How can it be?" Ben demanded. "Everybody knows it's impossible to open locks without a key or a lock picking kit. Since I won't have any tools on me, clearly the lock was carelessly left open and I was just taking a look inside to make sure nothing was damaged."

"You might have used a credit card," put in Jimmy.

Ben gave him a tired look. "That doesn't actually work nearly as well as the movies would make you think."

"When did you become an expert on picking locks?"

"When it occurred to me that moving a latch or deadbolt back was sort of the reverse of how Ingrid moves objects towards her, except I stay in metric spaces."

The guy did have a talent for coming up with slightly twisted applications of very standard topology. He'd probably be the next Director if Dr. Verrick ever stepped down.

"Might be a good idea to practice," Jimmy suggested. Ben nodded and took his arm, and the two of them turned sideways and disappeared, presumably to practice fiddling all the locks in the Research Division.

Ingrid and I sat back for a moment and just enjoyed the silence. Ben and Jimmy were presumably busy with their locks, and Lensky had gone out somewhere.

"I hope," Ingrid said eventually, "Ben never starts thinking about moving small bits of high explosives around."

"Mmm, could be useful, don't you think? If these people Lensky's after are planning a bombing?"

"I just have this feeling that if you let a guy mess with explosives, his intuition is likely to come up with ways of creating a big bang rather than ways of stopping it."

That did seem too likely to be comfortable. We'd just have to stop the terrorists before they built a bomb.

"So how was Scholz's? Last night?"

"Same as always. People. Tables. Uncomfortable chairs. Beer. Grackles."

She winced at the word "grackles."

"I really meant, what was it like going out with Boris? Is he actually human?"

"We weren't 'going out.' Just, well, just having a beer together. And yes, he's human, and he doesn't like being called Boris."

"Tough. He's not my type." She thought that over. "Actually, I don't see how he could be *anybody's* type."

"Too crude?"

"Too short."

"Isn't that a function of where you start measuring from? If H_K denotes my height and H_T denotes yours, then given that $H_K < H_T$, in the set of real numbers there exist infinitely many values of x such that $H_K < x < H_T$."

"Do you girls ever stop talking about mathematics?" Lensky walked in with a white paper bag from Upper Crust. He dropped it on the coffee cabinet and began unloading the contents onto the tray beneath THESE ARE DOUGHNUTS. I could just reach it if I leaned back carefully.

"Technically," Ingrid said, "Lia was *speaking* mathematics. We were *talking about* men." She looked at me. "And it's a weak argument, you know. I don't care how cute you think he is, he's still a spook."

"A spook bearing gifts," I pointed out, my mouth half full of chocolate croissant.

Lensky raised an eyebrow. "If I go out and pretend I didn't come in yet, can I hear the part about how cute I am?"

"Ingrid's just teasing you," I explained. "That part didn't actually happen."

"I'm crushed."

Fat chance.

In any case, he was sufficiently uncrushed to invite me out for dinner. "I have to make sure you eat something to soak up the beer. El Patio?"

One of my favorites. He must be compiling that dossier after all; I can't resist their guacamole cheese enchiladas. Also, they have the best chips in Austin, paired with an authoritative salsa.

They also have frozen margaritas.

"I've been thinking about your family issues," he said after we ordered.

"Let's not. I want to enjoy my food."

"And mine. Issues, I mean, not food."

"Probably not quite the same."

"No… You reminded me, though, that I'm not the only person in the world with family problems."

"I wasn't exactly clear what yours were. Apart from financial issues, I mean. Want to tell me more?" I'd rather talk about his stuff than my stuff, which would never have come up if he hadn't plied me with beer the previous evening. Tonight I was being prudent and sticking to frozen margaritas. They went well with chips and salsa. I loaded another chip and crunched away, waiting.

He sighed and moved the basket of tortilla chips out of my reach. "You're going to spoil your appetite, gobbling chips like that."

Bossy. Another major flaw.

"I need something to balance the margaritas."

He moved my glass out of reach as well.

Extremely bossy. But after inhaling half my drink on an empty stomach, I was feeling just a tad light-headed. Might be as well to wait until the enchiladas arrived.

"Money issues... get mixed up with other issues. My brother."

He appeared to have come to a full stop.

"Your brother?" I prodded gently.

"Ten years older. No sense of responsibility. Also, as far as anyone could tell, no ethics. He made his living playing poker. He always insisted he was just good at counting cards and reading faces, but eventually he made the mistake of winning far too much from somebody who didn't take losing well at all." He frowned and tossed back the remainder of my frozen margarita, but I didn't complain. This was my chance to get the dirt on the spook.

Or, maybe, to find out what made the man tick.

"People who upset the Latin Kings tend to disappear, or - well. Aleksi turned up floating in the Delaware."

"A family tragedy."

"For my mother, maybe. Something of a relief for the rest of us." He raised my empty glass and caught a waiter's eye. "Can we get another of these?"

"Make that two," I added.

"What? You shouldn't be drinking that much."

"I've hardly had a chance to drink at all. If you remember, that was my glass you just emptied. A relief?" While he was thinking that over, I leaned over the table and snagged the tortilla chips.

"In a number of ways. Not least to his wife. He had a kid, too... Linda was too young to remember him. And Pamela was more relieved than anything else. She felt that working would be a lot easier than trying to get Aleksi to pay child support." I noticed that he did not mention his own feelings about the loss of his brother. Clearly he found it easier to talk about his sister-in-law.

"They were divorced?"

"Oh, no. Nothing so straightforward. She would throw him out for a while, then he'd make a killing at some poker game and show up throwing money around and claiming he wanted to reconcile – get a steady job – whatever he thought she wanted to hear. And she'd take him back! I will never understand women."

"So what happened after Aleksi died?"

"Oh, Pamela went to cosmetician school or some junk like that. Cost – well, it seemed like a small fortune to me at the time. But I finally got that paid off too, and she wasn't doing badly until she took it into her head to move some place that doesn't have snow. Here, to be precise."

"And is she still doing okay?"

"That's what I'm here to find out." He moved the chips out of my reach again. That was okay; we were down to the crumbs in the bottom of the basket. "Apart from investigating terrorists, that is. She's not exactly the world's greatest communicator... or the most stable mother. I want to look at her living situation. See how my niece is doing."

Pedro brought our margaritas and a second basket of chips, which – the chips, not the drinks – Lensky waved away.

"Bossy" might have been too mild a word. I mentally substituted, "dictatorial," and wondered how his sister-in-law felt about his showing up like a representative of Child Protective Services. Not that it was any of my business.

The food came then, and we both dedicated ourselves to it: me because I wanted to think about this hitherto undisclosed side of Lensky, and him, I think, because he was wondering whether he'd said too much to someone he barely knew.

Or possibly he was thinking about getting to know me better. A lot better. I have to admit that I was more open to this possibility than I had been since he started throwing his weight around in the Center. But there was no point in thinking about that right now. Before we finished our meal he would probably find some new way to be offensive that would put me right off him again.

He actually managed to stay civilized until the very end, when I was enjoying the quarter-cup of sorbet that El Patio calls a dessert. I like to take it slowly, trying to convince my mouth that it's actually had dessert, and... well, he just had to comment on my ability to swirl sorbet around on my tongue indefinitely, didn't he? And if the words were conceivably innocent, the smoldering look that accompanied them was not.

CHAPTER 7

IT WAS STILL dark outside when I was awakened by what the Geneva Convention ought to define as torture. The aroma of actual good coffee wafted through my room. That in itself would have made for a big improvement in my dream. The way it kept insinuating itself into my nostrils and then receding: that was the torture part.

First I had to pry my eyes open, then persuade them to focus on a most improbable sight: Ingrid, fully dressed and waving what looked like a very large paper cup from Quack's.

"Gimme!"

"I *told* Ben that would get you up faster than pinching or shaking," she said smugly, "and without any danger of violence."

That was only partly correct. If she didn't hand over the coffee before I got my nervous system in gear, there was definitely going to be some violence in here. I may be small, but I was in the Jersey City Girl Scouts before we moved to Texas and I was totally eligible for a badge in Fifteen Ways to Hurt Bigger Girls Without Leaving a Mark. Too bad National never approved that one.

"Gimme. *Now.*"

It was a medium dark roast, so rich with flavor it would've been a crime to mess it over with creamer. Large size. By the time I'd worked through half the cup I was close to forgiving Ingrid. I was also able to articulate more than two syllables at a time.

"What's the idea of waking me up at this hour? Whatever that may be." The darkness outside didn't give much of a clue, except that it was a lot earlier than any normal human being would get up. "Is it just an experiment? Because..."

She interrupted me before I could get into detailed threats. "Ben's idea. We're going in *really* early, to make sure we can get into position before there's any risk of an audience. Get up and get dressed."

I did so, not because I'm in the habit of taking orders from Ingrid, but because I felt more able to deal with life after I changed from the oversize tee I sleep in to my favorite cutoffs and a well-worn vintage Clash T-shirt. "You couldn't have mentioned this last night?" I gulped down the last of my coffee and looked for my sandals. One was under the bed.

"We *could* have," Ingrid said, "if you hadn't been lollygagging around with the spook, and if we didn't want to do this without him breathing down our necks."

"He bought me food," I said. "Guacamole cheese enchiladas. At El Patio."

"Really, Lia. I never thought you'd sell yourself for guacamole on your enchiladas."

I'd done no such thing. It was dinner, not an orgy. He had even laid off the double-entendres... for a while.

The other sandal was behind my alarm clock.

"*Five o'clock?* Are you insane?"

When I dragged myself downstairs, Ben and Jimmy were waiting in his car. He had another medium roast black grande for me. The boy wasn't bad at planning. Just in case he thought I would sell a decent morning's sleep for two cups of Quack's coffee, though, I grumbled all the way to Crowson's office that five in the morning was something human beings were not meant to see, much less function in, and that if I'd wanted a life of secret missions that started at oh-dark-thirty I'd have become a Navy SEAL, not a research fellow in topology.

"Do they let women into the SEALS?" Ingrid asked.

"Irrelevant. Lia would never pass the training program."

I bared my teeth at him and he threw up a shielding hand. "Sorry, Lia, but you probably don't weigh ninety pounds dripping wet. I can't see you as a rough, tough SEAL."

"It's a *mean* ninety pounds," I told him.

"And she'll probably weigh a lot more if she keeps letting Boris ply her with beer and Mexican food," Ingrid said.

"Don't tease the animals," I warned her. "*Cette animale est tres méchante; quand on l'attaque elle se defend.*" This animal is vicious; when attacked she defends herself. That set Ingrid's lips moving as she worked it out. She might know enough to satisfy the language requirement, but mathematical French is a lot easier than bits of French doggerel.

(My Aunt Alesia's husband was French, and fifteen years after his death she still pretended to speak French as her first language and bombarded us with French phrases over the morning *koulouri* and cheese. In case you were wondering. It's not just my *parents* who are insane.)

A third cup of coffee, with maybe some pancakes, would have done a lot to improve my mood. Unfortunately, what I got was a chance to observe Ben doing Lock Picking 101.

From a distance.

One thing I had to (grudgingly) admit in favor of a pre-dawn mission: it was actually possible to park within sight of our target. Ingrid and Jimmy and I sat in the car while Ben worked on the front door. Ingrid didn't seem to be invoking Camouflage yet; presumably she was saving her best efforts until we got into the building. Finally he beckoned to us to come on in.

"About time," I said.

"You expected a high-speed result? I should maybe have just shot the lock off like your boyfriend would probably have done?"

"He's not my boyfriend, and yes, a little more speed would have been welcome. Two *large* cups of coffee, remember?"

Fortunately, there was a restroom under the stairs, and it was not locked. After taking care of that little matter I headed upstairs to join the others in 21A, but that door was still locked and I didn't see anyone but Jimmy.

"Ow! You stepped on my foot."

Ben was bent over the locking mechanism while Ingrid was standing back, frowning and staring into space.

"You're getting really good at Camouflage. Ben, are you *sure* it's not actual invisibility?" Praise where praise is due, and when *was* Ben going to share that algorithm with me?

21A turned out to be not just vacant, but completely empty. As in, no furniture. Ben and Jimmy slid down against the wall it shared with 21B; Ingrid and I took the opposite wall.

After a while I asked Ben how it was going.

"It isn't," he murmured, lips barely moving. "I can't sense anything. Either he left his computer turned off or he moved it. I'm going with turned off, because then we still have a chance."

"Can't Jimmy show you how to turn it on?"

"Told you, I can't pick up anything. Besides, what happens if he comes into the office to find it humming away, when he *knows* he turned it off last night?"

I hadn't realized that the second phase of the Oh-Dark-Thirty plan involved sitting on the floor of an empty office until normal business hours commenced... and who was to say that this Raven Crowson even kept regular hours? I was glad I'd used the facilities downstairs when I had a chance.

After a really long, boring wait we heard people coming in the front door. They sounded surprised; I concentrated, picked out words and worried. The first-floor tenants were bothered by the fact that the front door had been unlocked when they got there.

"Didn't you relock the door?" I asked Ben.

"Couldn't. Remember, my whole defense in case of capture is that everything was unlocked and we just wandered in."

Ingrid shushed us both.

Eventually the chatter downstairs died out as the people who'd come in settled into their offices. I heard a phone ringing from time to time, but not much else.

We waited some more. I started running through some minor problems in my head, until Ingrid kicked me and I realized that I'd been herding dust bunnies into a floor space bounded by a simple closed curve.

Finally there were feet on the stairs. Ben tensed. Ingrid closed her eyes and concentrated, and that eerie deep blue light surrounded us again. I hoped Ben could hear movements next door through the quivering stillness inside the visualization.

His eyes were closed too, now, and his lips were moving. Of course – he didn't need to listen for actual sounds; he knew when the computer was on. I hoped he was tiptoeing through the files more carefully than when he'd experimented with Ingrid's machine.

"Should have brought a laptop," Jimmy muttered. He sighed and fished out his phone, punched in the password and put it in Ben's open hand. The screen blinked on, very bright inside our little hidden space, and I could just see symbols zipping across it as Ben poured whatever he was reading into the smartphone.

There were more feet on the stairs: two people with heavy treads. The door to 21A swung open and a flashlight pierced the room; Ingrid's eyes opened and the deep blue faded, leaving us in a dusty room with natural light pouring in through the windows.

And there were two men in generic light blue uniforms blocking the only door.

"Want to explain what you're up to in here before we hand you over to the cops?"

Ben jammed the phone into his pocket. "Ah – well – nothing really. See, we're looking for an office to rent; we were supposed to meet a Mr. Fourier here. We found the door unlocked, and we wanted to make sure nobody had vandalized the space…."

If we hadn't all been sitting on the floor, it might have been more convincing. But it was fairly obvious Ben's story was not going over well. I took a deep breath. "Don't bother, Ben. Let's just tell them the truth."

I stood up and faced the security guards. "How did you find us?"

"We got a call about suspected intruders."

"From this building."

I filed that for later reference.

"Well, it's like this, gentlemen. We belong to an institute devoted to the study of magic. The head of the Center for Applied Technology likes to send us on field work assignments to make sure that what we do in the lab can be translated into actual real world results, and today he wanted us to try magically accessing an unfamiliar, randomly chosen computer when we weren't actually in the same room with it. We evaluated conveniently located office buildings and selected this one because of the empty office, which gave us maximum privacy for our experiments. Sadly, we were unable to fulfil the assignment. We were just sitting here because nobody wanted to be the first one reporting our failure."

One of the rent-a-cops was smiling broadly by the time I finished this farrago of half-truths; the other one was sniffing the air. "If they're stoned, they must have been smoking somewhere else," he said.

"I guess they're just insane," said Smiler, "or else there's some new kind of happy juice going around."

"It's not going to look good for us if we left this room unlocked," brooded Sniffer. He looked at me. "Are you *sure* it was unlocked when you got here? And the front door too?"

"It was *your* turn to lock up," Smiler said to Sniffer. "Not going to look great on your record."

"Do we look like expert lock pickers?" I countered.

Smiler and Sniffer eventually decided that if we would just go away and never come back, the whole incident could be forgotten.

Nobody spoke until we were safely back in Ben's car.

"You nearly gave me a heart attack, Lia," were the first words out of Ben's mouth. "Standing up and announcing you were going to *tell them the truth* – what were you thinking?"

"That it wouldn't be nearly as effective if I announced that I was going to lie to them. And anyway," I said, thinking back, "I actually did tell them the truth. Well, some of the truth. It would have passed the Verrick Test. Parts of it." Dr. Verrick believed that if you told people the literal truth and they misinterpreted it, you hadn't lied. I shared his opinion – sometimes – as in, when it was convenient.

"I couldn't make up a whole convincing story out of scratch."

"Yeah," Ben acknowledged. "Too bad we didn't have Annelise along."

"I am getting tired of hearing how your little girlfriend could have solved every problem we encounter," Ingrid said.

"She's got a real talent for it," Ben protested. "You should see her in action."

"Anyway, I did tell one huge lie," I said. "I hope… What were you doing with Jimmy's phone? Downloading Raven Crowson's computer files, I hope?"

"Oh!" Ben contorted himself, trying to drag the phone out of his pocket, and nearly hit a couple of students who leaped for the side of the road and yelled at us.

"Better wait till we get back," Jimmy said.

"Oh well, they looked like engineering students," said Ingrid. "It wouldn't have been a great loss if Ben had hit them."

"Bad for my paint job," Ben said, "and think of the paperwork. It could ruin my whole day." But he stopped twisting and turning and trying to get at Jimmy's phone. "We didn't even access all of the data. I did find Crowson's Contacts list. And then I found some concealed folders." He looked sick.

"Let me guess," Ingrid said. "You got complete plans for this 'birthday party,' plus a list of known terrorists, and you can pass all that on to Lensky and he'll go away?"

"I never knew you to engage in such unbridled flights of optimism, Ingrid," said Ben. "Are your hopes and dreams the same, Lia?"

"Not hardly." For one thing, I didn't want Lensky to go away thinking he'd gotten away with all his double-entendres. I wanted to deliver a crushing blow to his ego, and then…. Well… I still couldn't work up much enthusiasm for his disappearance. Probably I needed more than one ego-crushing line to even the balance between us.

CHAPTER 8

THE SPOOK WAS in the break room when we got back to Allandale House. He exploded out of there like a man looking for a fight. *"Where have you been?"* He was looking at me, but I assumed the question was meant for all of us.

His dark blue eyes were giving off sparks and there was a tiny vein fluttering in and out on his temple. Left side. It didn't seem like the best time to tease him. So I did anyway.

"Where did we go? Out," I said. "And what did we do? Nothing."

He said something in Polish that hardly needed translation; his eyes said it all.

"We've been getting the information you wanted," Ben said, dragging Jimmy's phone out of his pocket with a flourish. "Some of it, anyway. Yesterday you were complaining because we hadn't got it, now do you want to complain because we have it? *Boris?*"

Lensky closed his eyes. "Just tell me this excursion didn't involve cops or, worse, Crowson spotting you."

"Couple of rent-a-cops," Ingrid said, "and Lia persuaded them we were insane or drugged."

"That shouldn't have been hard," Lensky snarled.

"And," I said reluctantly, "somebody called them from inside the building. That could have been Crowson."

"You were in Crowson's building?"

"What's biting you, *Boris*? You gave us his office address yesterday. What did you think, we could mess with his computer by sitting in a circle and staring at the words?" Actually, Ben had tried just that, but there was no need to remind Lensky.

"You should have waited for me."

"Parking's a *lot* easier before dawn," I pointed out. I hadn't been a big fan of that starting hour, but it was done now and we needed to put up a united front before the spook.

"You." This snarl was directed at me. Lensky grabbed my wrist and spun me around him, towards the door. "In the break room. Now."

He followed me in, slammed the door and turned the thumb latch. Well, Ben knew how to fix *that*.

I didn't hear the door being remotely unlocked, though. Nor did I hear anything at all from my three co-conspirators.

So much for the united front. The cowards were leaving me to calm down Lensky all by myself.

"No more funny stuff. Get this: You. Do. Not. Go. Out. Without. Me!" He actually had the nerve to shake a finger in my face.

"Oh, sure, Mother," I said. "I'll never go down to the end of the town if I don't go down with you. Count on it."

"I *warned* you about being funny," he said, grabbing my shoulders. I think his intention was to shake me, but it didn't work out quite that way. There was a hot and breathless interlude and then he let me go. And it was a good thing I wasn't wearing lipstick, because it would have been thoroughly smeared by now.

"Is that how you convey the seriousness of your orders?" I asked, only gasping for breath a little bit, and very quietly. I backed away from him and sat down with the table between us. It wasn't that I didn't want him to touch me again. The trouble was that I *did* want him to.

A man who was only temporarily in town.

And who had no tact.

In the office, no less.

This was a three-star Bad Idea. I was counting on the table to give me time to get over the feeling.

"It's how I convey the seriousness of protecting *you*," he growled. "I wanted you and your buddies to do some nice quiet voodoo, not to risk tangling with a man like Crowson who deals with terrorists."

"You mean, you *suspect* him of dealing with terrorists. And *don't* say 'Tomato, tomahto.' I'm tired of that line."

"I should have been with you. I want you to promise that you won't go on any more field trips without me."

Like *that* was going to happen.

"For heaven's sake, I wasn't exactly playing the sacrificial virgin! There were *four* of us. Two of whom were young, healthy men."

"Neither of whom was carrying," Lensky said.

"No. Believe it or not, even in Texas we usually manage to go about our daily business without taking our six-shooters along."

Now Ben banged on the door. "If you two are quite through," he shouted, "I would like to discuss our data with Boris."

So much for Ben's protection. Interrupt a furious spook intent on doing violence to my person? Naah, leave the man alone. But showing off *data*? Definitely worth some banging and yelling. I began to warm – ever so slightly – to Lensky. He might be a rude, crude s.o.b., but he did have this streak of protectiveness toward me. Most men were pretty clear that I could take care of myself; for some reason I found Lensky's foggy vision touching.

I understood Ben's priorities better once we were all seated around the table and he put Jimmy's phone in front of him. "First thing I got was Crowson's contact list," he repeated. "But that's not important."

"I decide what's important," Lensky said immediately.

"I'm the one with the data," Ben countered.

Am I the only person in the world who thinks that life could run perfectly well without men doing their King-of-the-Mountain thing all the time? Anyway, Ben wasn't as bright as I'd thought he was if he wanted to start that kind of competition with Lensky. The spook had plenty of faults – now I could add a couple more to my growing list – but he was always going to dominate any room he was in.

"Take a look at the pictures I downloaded off of his hidden files and say that again." Ben swiped at the screen with one finger.

Then he tried two fingers.

Then he poked at it.

Talk about not being willing to ask for directions!

"Let me." Jimmy retrieved his phone and did some series of swipes and pokes that must have been different from the ones Ben had tried. "See, here are the pictures…"

His voice trailed off and he looked as if he was about to puke. I glanced around the room, just in case I needed to find the wastebasket in a hurry.

Jimmy swallowed – hard – and found his voice again. "Ben's right. We need to deal with this first."

I happened to be sitting between him and Lensky. The jerk reached out *behind* me to pass Lensky the phone, which the spook held at an angle that concealed the screen from me. One eyebrow shot up as he looked at – I guessed – the first of these mysterious pictures Ben had been talking about.

"Not within my remit," he said, sounding just slightly sorry about it. "My agency has no jurisdiction over domestic crimes. I would like you to continue working the angle we'd been discussing."

"It's got to be illegal to have that stuff on your computer," Ben insisted.

"*What stuff?*" I was tired of being excluded, and Ingrid looked as if she felt the same way. Actually, she looked as if she was ready to pull a Viking axe out of her elaborate coronet of braids.

"Believe me, Lia, you don't *want* to see those pictures. I wish *I* hadn't seen them." Ben too looked slightly greenish. Maybe I should put the wastebasket between him and Jimmy? "I want to bleach my brain."

"*I* want to bleach my *eyeballs*," Jimmy said.

Lensky started to speak, then cleared his throat and started again. "It's kiddie porn, Thalia," he said. "Of a *particularly* revolting sort."

It was news to me that one kind of child porn was more revolting than another, but Jimmy and Ben were both nodding.

"And rather amateurish photography," Jimmy said.

"Which suggests that Crowson, or somebody close to him, may be producing this stuff personally."

"As a labor of love, you might say?" Ingrid asked. She was sitting on the far side of Lensky; he turned the phone screen towards her and I could see the desire to tease the spook fade from her face. Now we had *three* people turning green. Lensky and I appeared to be the only good sailors – so to speak – in the room. And I hadn't actually been exposed to the pictures.

"We need to tell the police," Ben insisted.

"Not yet."

"But…"

"Not. Yet." Words of one syllable. "We need to finish this investigation first. I don't want Crowson alarmed over an ancillary matter."

"But whoever took those photos could be torturing more children *right now*."

Oh. *That* was the translation of "particularly revolting." I lost all interest in seeing the evidence for myself.

"I am aware of that," Lensky said tightly, "but even more people may die if the primary plot is not stopped. I assure you that as soon as we have the information we need on the terrorists, we will turn over these files to the FBI, who actually have authority to pursue this matter."

That clearly wasn't good enough for Ben. "Okay, we don't need you to take care of this. I wonder what would happen if somebody told the APD that Crowson has kiddie porn on his computer?"

"Gee, I don't know," said Lensky sarcastically. "You think maybe they'd barge in, alert the whole porn ring, and abort my investigation? Leave. It. You don't want to make a permanent enemy of me over a delay of two or three days, you really don't."

"Ben has a kid sister," Ingrid mentioned.

"I," said Lensky, "have a niece. Here in Austin, as a matter of fact. You think *I* don't want this bastard stopped? It will be a pleasure to

70

see him go down. I'm just not willing to compromise the investigation at this point. And my agency can't take him down over this."

~

When Ben and I headed for the sandwich bar, there were actual clouds covering the sky. That probably meant a torrential downpour later, most likely at the most inconvenient possible time; right now it meant that the outdoors was almost pleasant.

"Turtle pond?" Ben asked.

I nodded. "You save us a bench; I'll get the sandwiches." That way I could make sure mine wasn't tuna fish.

Being smaller than a football player could be a disadvantage when trying to get to the cooler of wrapped sandwiches. On the other hand, being vicious and *really* small was an advantage. I could wriggle into any opening, and because I was little and sort of cute nobody associated me with stamped-on toes and elbows into their sides.

"Tuna salad for you, mystery meat for me, *and* I got us each a package of Fritos," I announced upon emerging, somewhat breathless, from the swarm.

Ben looked at the labels. "Yours claims to be ham."

"Yeah, well, don't believe everything you read. All that matters is, I know that slice of pink mystery meat is *not* tuna salad."

A grackle overhead interjected a loud "Gack." See, even *grackles* feel that way about tuna salad.

"Lensky." Ben said as though the name in itself were a meaningful statement.

"It's not a slice of Lensky either," I pointed out. "He's still walking around."

"Being a *problem*," Ben griped.

"I hate to be fair to the man, but if he hadn't pointed us at Crowson we wouldn't know anything about an illegal porn collection."

"I still think I should tell the police."

I put down my sandwich and looked over Ben carefully. He looked the same as always: uncombed light brown hair, unfocused brown eyes, too-big brown shirt flopping around his shoulders. He looked like the dictionary definition of a math geek.

What he did *not* look like was somebody who ought to get into a physical altercation with a brawny spook.

"That wouldn't be fair," I said, deciding to skip the more serious problem that Lensky could probably tear him to shreds. "By ending the meeting when we did, we implicitly agreed not to call in the police until Lensky said."

Ben hunched unhappily over his sandwich. "We have to do *something....* Well," he amended, "*I* have to do something. You can stay out of this, Lia. It's not your fight and you don't want to alienate Boris."

"Oh, to hell with that, Ben. I have a feeling it *would* be my fight if I'd seen those pictures. In fact, never mind the pictures. *Su batalla es mi batalla,*" I said in possibly inaccurate Spanish. "As for Lensky, remember what Ingrid said: I have a talent for alienating people. Trust me, that is never going to be a beautiful friendship." I'd had time to think about it while I was fetching sandwiches, and had regretfully decided I was right the first time. Me and Lensky? Three-star bad idea.

The Tower chimes sounded and a number of the people around us shouldered backpacks and headed off, presumably to attend classes.

Ben tore a bit of crust off his sandwich and lobbed it at a turtle that was wandering around, looking hopefully at pebbles.

"Right. It's you and me, then. Um... what exactly *are* we going to do?"

"I'm not sure yet, but I think sneaking around Lensky might work better than going through him. He's bound to want more detail on that list of contacts you got, even if only to eliminate the obviously innocent ones."

Ben snorted. "Yep. There are going to be a *lot* of those. Fifty years ago, Crowson would have been one of those guys with three Rolodexes on his desk. He's got everybody from the mayor to the public relations office of Dell in his email. Even the head of the Moore Foundation!"

"Okay, so first we cross off the obvious business contacts, then look at the ones that are left. Anybody who looks the slightest bit interesting, we'll sneak over and you can take a look at their hidden files, see if they have any of Crowson's pictures. I understand perverts like this are into sharing."

"Ugh."

"I know, but you've become our Touch-Free Hacking expert. Anyway, you only need to take a brief look around, you don't have to *stare* at the stuff. We'll keep a list of the guilty parties and hand it over to Lensky when we've solved the terrorist problem. Then he – or the FBI or the city cops or whoever has jurisdiction – can arrest a whole set of creeps instead of just one."

"Huh. That does sound pretty okay. You're making me feel a tiny little bit better about waiting."

"That's me, a ministering angel and all that. Why don't you eat your sandwich and think about something else for a while?" Um, preferably *not* Annelise; Ingrid and I had both reached Peak Annelise. Our location gave me an idea. "Why don't you watch for capsicum?"

"For what?"

"You know, that turtle you were all excited about the other day."

"*Caspica caspica,*" Ben corrected me. "Capsicum is a hot pepper. I think. And for your information, *I* can do two things at once. Why do you think I've been donating bits of my sandwich to that guy?" He jerked his head at the box turtle that was crawling sort-of towards us.

"Gee, Ben, I don't know. Because you've finally realized that the tuna salad is disgusting?"

"Shh! Don't spook him."

It looked like just another box turtle to me, but then I didn't do a second major in Reptiles and Amphibians. Shell: high, rounded, and covered with some kind of tan-on-brown pattern. Clawed flippers, wedge-shaped head. Yep, a box turtle. As I watched, it extended its neck to get a fragment of tuna fish that had landed off to its left, and I grabbed Ben's arm. "Did you see that?" I whispered.

"Yes. It's awful. I could *kill* whoever did that to it."

A shiny metal ring was half buried in the flesh of the poor turtle's neck.

"Think we could catch it and get that off?"

"Wait. Let it get farther from the water."

The turtle halted on a patch of bare earth halfway between the pond and our bench, turned around, and started clawing at the ground with its front flippers.

"I never saw one do *that* before. What does ripping claws through the dirt mean in Turtle, Ben?"

"Nothing. That I know, anyway."

I could have sworn the turtle looked over its shoulder and gave us a dirty look before resuming its clawing action, somewhat more slowly. It didn't seem to be random; deep gouges appeared in the dirt, looking almost like some kind of pattern. The first set consisted of a vertical line with two lines at an angle meeting at the center; if you were imaginative enough, it could have been a capital letter K. The next was a single deep angle, vertex downward. Like a V. Which showed the craziness of this interpretation; I've played enough Scrabble to be pretty sure there's no English word starting with KV. Oh, sure, kvetch, kvell and so forth, but those are Yiddish really.

Another vertical line, this time topped with a perpendicular across the top.

Like a T.

"KVT?"

"It *could*," Ben said in a low voice, "be KUT."

"What, he's invoking the university radio station?" If the next two random scribbles looked like FM I would eat – the rest of Ben's tuna salad sandwich.

They didn't. The next one did look like an M, though.

The turtle moved sideways, which by the way looks *really* odd when one of them does it slowly enough for you to watch, and started a new group of scribbles.

A vertical line.

Two vertical lines joined by a perpendicular bar.

One vertical with three perpendiculars hanging off it.

A triangle with the long side vertical.

"K-U-T-M," Ben read. "I-H-E-D."

This was definitely getting too weird to put down to chance. And it was happening to two of the very few people on this campus who might be able to accept it. I mean, normal people would have flipped out last year, when a poker chip and Darth Vader moved out of my little brother's toy collections.

So I was *not* going to freak out over a turtle writing English letters.

Anyway, it was all capital letters. Printed. Way easier than cursive, right?

The third grouping was only two symbols long; a diamond followed by a verticals sprouting two perpendicular lines from the top half.

O-F?

Hey, at least it spelled an actual word.

The turtle stopped scratching. Twisted its poor tortured neck around and looked at us. Raised and lowered its top shell like a person shrugging, and added a new symbol to the last group: a dot under half a vertical.

"OF!" I said. Quietly.

It came to me then. As well as Scrabble, I used to play a particularly vicious form of Anagrams with Andros. He'd think of several words, scramble them, and write them down in groups of five letters. It was surprising how much harder they were to decipher that way.

These weren't even scrambled.

"The groupings are wrong," I said. "It's KUT MI HED OFF."

"Oh. He can't spell. He's trying to say C-U-T M-Y H-E-A-D O-F-F." Ben did have his obsessive-compulsive moments. *I* had figured that out without fixing the spelling.

It did seem more real after Ben's fixes. "We can't do that to him... can we?"

"It's probably illegal. And anyway, we can do better." Ben leaned forward and addressed the turtle. "That seems like kind of a drastic solution. Would you really rather die than endure the pain until we figure out some way to get that ring off you? Because I think I know where I can find some bolt cutters."

"IHUR TNOW"

"Fine, stick around and chat with Lia while I get the cutters."

As Ben left, a grackle dive-bombed us and shat on the remains of his sandwich. Then all the grackles overhead took off with their usual chorus of "Gack, Gack, Gackle." Only a few blue-black feathers drifted down to mark their passing. The turtle pulled in its extremities and slammed its shells together.

"It's lucky you picked us for your cry for help, Mr. Mesopotamia," I told the turtle. "Most people around here wouldn't take you seriously."

The shells opened and a long neck swiveled around, fixing me with a distinctly sardonic look.

"Look, I don't know how it works in Iraq, but around here we don't see a lot of talking – well, writing – animals."

"UDUN TLUK," the turtle scratched out. After a quick blink I deciphered the message. "Ok, maybe you're right. We *don't* look – not for that, anyway. But with everybody except Ben using a smartphone, you'd think there'd be some Youtube videos of writing turtles and composing crocodiles by now."

"KROK SSTO OPID," the turtle laboriously scratched while Ben was off getting bolt cutters.

After resting up from that communication, the turtle added, "OOT? OOB?"

"Ah. One of the twenty-first century's less attractive aspects."

It took the little guy a long time to scratch out his messages; I was spared explaining Youtube by Ben's return. He positioned himself behind the half-wall that discouraged drunk students from walking into the pond. "Can you bring him here? People might get upset if they saw me apparently attacking him with bolt cutters."

They might get upset if I picked him up, too. Wasn't handling the animals strictly verboten? Oh, hell, it wasn't nearly as verboten as the rest of our plan. But I didn't want to startle Mr. Mesopotamia into splashing back under water.

"Can I pick you up, Mr. M?" I murmured in a low voice, not to attract attention from the people remaining around the pond. True, most of them had their faces in their smartphones, but it would be nice if they stayed that way.

Scratch, scratch.

KUTM IHED OFF

"No, I'm *not* going to cut your head off. We can remove the ring without killing you."

IDON TDI

"Right, that's the idea. But we have to do it over there." I pointed, and after a moment Mr. Mesopotamia pulled in his extremities and closed his shells. I took that as permission to pick him up.

Ben's bolt cutters were huge. And ugly. Serious cutters on one end were attached to three-foot handles that gave me an idea how much force the things were expected to exert. I set Mr. Mesopotamia down facing away from the things. He might get cold flippers if he saw the size of the tool we wanted to use on him.

"Mr. M? Could you stick your neck out, please?"

After a moment, the top shell raised and the head, neck and flippers came out. Ben frowned as he studied the target.

"I don't know if I can cut the ring off without hurting him. Look how deeply embedded it is."

The flesh of Mr. Mesopotamia's neck rose up in a kind of puffy billow on either side of the metal ring. He must have been much smaller when it was put on. I mentally absolved the hypothetical veteran; Mr. M. must have been wearing this long before we sent Americans into that hellhole.

"You'll have to hold his neck while I position the cutters," Ben said, sounding less than confident.

Scratch scrabble scratch scratch...

DONT HOLD MIIM REDY

"I know you're brave, Mr. M. But Ben doesn't want to risk hurting you if you flinch or if his hand slips."

WATS SOHA RDWO NKUT

"Yeah, well, we're all hoping it works out that way." I rested one hand behind his head, then took a grip on his neck with fingers and thumb. Keeping the rest of my hand well out of range of the business end of the bolt cutters.

Ben opened the shears and tried to rest the tip of one pointed blade between the ring and the puffy flesh on Mr. M.'s neck. It didn't go down very far. The same thing happened, or didn't happen, on the other side. He slid his hands up the handles, got a good grip, and squeezed.

The cutters slid right over the ring and met in the middle.

GETO NWIT HIT

"I may have to hurt you just a little bit."

This time Ben waggled the pointy end of one blade until it was out of sight between the puffy flesh and the ring. A drop of blood oozed up. Resting the other end where it had been before, he squeezed again.

This time the bolt cutters left a very, very shallow nick in the ring.

"Successive approximations!"

I couldn't tell whether he was cursing or declaring a plan of action.

Whichever it was, Mr. M. wasn't having any. He twisted his neck to make it clear that my grip was unacceptable, then scrabbled furiously.

WATS RONG YUST UPID

KANT EEVN KUTM IHED OF

"Look, Mr. M.," I said, exasperated, "That's just what we're trying to *avoid*. We don't want to cut your head off; there has to be a better way to get the damn ring off."

Nobody ever said that a paranormal phenomenon couldn't also be intensely irritating.

STOO PIDI DONT DI

"Yes, that's our plan."

By way of punctuation, Mr. M. retracted his appendages and drew his shells together with a distinct click.

"I guess we need help," Ben said. "I'm not exactly the most mechanically gifted person. I know somebody who works in an engineering lab…"

"Just be sure and wash your hands after you talk to him."

"Her."

Why was I not surprised? Of course it would be a girl.

"Just tell me she's not still mad at you."

"Why would she be mad at me?" He blinked his myopic brown eyes. "We agreed *months* ago to be just good friends."

I scooped up Mr. M. and paused. "Wait a minute."

"What?"

"If I put him back with all the other turtles, how are we going to find him again?"

"Easy," Ben said. "He's the only Caspian box turtle."

Which was *not* going to help me identify him. I'm just not that sensitive to the variations of squarish tan-on-brown patterns as opposed to brown-on-brown, very-dark-orange-on-brown, black-on-brown... well, you get the idea. If Ben's confidence was misplaced, I could see some long hours of checking turtle necks for jewelry in my future.

CHAPTER 9

VERN TREXLER STARED in impotent disbelief as the turtle Thalia had called "Mr. M." slithered back under the water. Who knew those things could move so fast? All he knew about turtles was Zeno's Paradox – wait, that was about a *tortoise*. Oh well, same difference. For the first time it occurred to him that maybe Zeno hadn't been strictly theoretical when he "proved" that the tortoise could outrun Achilles.

For all he knew, the thing might have climbed back out of the water already and be sunning itself on one of the rocks in the middle of the pond. All the ugly things looked alike to him. And if he waded into the pool and started grabbing all the turtles to check for rings around their necks, two things would happen. All the box shells would snap shut. And somebody would call the campus police.

Scowling, Vern pulled out his phone and searched for a picture of *Caspica caspica*.

"You know that guy who's always hanging around here?" Jimmy DiGrazio had brought a large pizza to his new desk in Allandale House, and for some reason we were all drifting towards him.

"Lensky?" Ben groaned.

"Nah, he went off somewhere. This guy is younger."

I did not exactly feel disappointed that Lensky was gone. After all, we'd have a lot more freedom to act without him watching us; we could get straight to work on Ben's project without even pretending it had anything to do with terrorists.

It was more a feeling of...oh, unfinished business.

Business I had consciously decided *not* to finish, because getting involved with the man would be a very bad idea.

Apparently my subconscious hadn't gotten the message.

"Younger than Lensky," Ben said to Jimmy, "is hardly a definitive description. *Everyone* is younger than the spook."

"That's a bit of an exaggeration," I interrupted him.

"Tomato, tomahto." I might never forgive Lensky for introducing that meme into our conversation. "This is a college campus, Lia. Everybody's younger than us, too. Except for the grad students and faculty."

"You know the guy I mean," Jimmy amplified. "Looks kind of like a blurred copy of Ben, except for the big wet mouth, usually has a bunch of papers in his hand..."

"Vern Trexler?" I suggested.

Jimmy's eyes widened. *"That's* what he looks like? I always pictured something more like the Hunchback of Notre Dame in his mommy's basement."

"The Hunchback of Notre Dame was abandoned as a baby," Ingrid said.

"And even if he lived with his mother, she wouldn't have had a basement, because the Paris sewers are disgusting." Ben contributed.

Not for the first time, I wondered if the intense concentration needed for our work led to a lack of concentration outside of work. Mathematicians seem to have a unique talent for being sidetracked by irrelevant details.

"Fiction aside," I said, "how do you know Vern, and how on earth do you know him without knowing what he looks like?"

"Gaming," said Jimmy. "He's Morph the Maganimous on *World of*

Wizardry. I tracked down his real ID once because I was beginning to suspect he was a bot; I couldn't believe any actual human being could be as *whiny* as Morph, always coming up with reasons why whatever just happened to him shouldn't count. But I just glanced at the resumé, I didn't look for a picture. Why would I? I didn't expect to be running into him outside virtual reality."

"Well, now you have," Ben said, "That guy is the most persistently pestiferous pest in the known universe."

"He has this insane desire to become an underpaid Research Fellow here," I explained.

"Insanity is not necessarily a problem," said Ingrid, "but lack of talent is."

Jimmy looked skeptical. "Well, I think he might have become too insane even for this crowd. When I walked past the Turtle Pond just now, he was stuffing a box turtle into a backpack."

Ben and I looked at each other.

"Mr. M.," he said.

"Vern probably *would* cut off his head."

"To be fair, that is what Mr. M. asked us to do."

"I don't care, there has to be some other way to get that ring off him. We've got to get him back before Vern kills him."

"Jimmy, did your research on Trexler include a recent address? No? Get one. Now! It's an emergency!" Ben turned to me. "I'll get my car, pick you up out front."

Jimmy grumbled a bit about his pizza getting cold, but settled down to his research with reasonably good grace. It probably helped that he could type pretty well with the first two fingers of his left hand, leaving the right hand free to convey triangles of pepperoni and red glop to his mouth. Texting has created some very odd typing styles.

I was downstairs with the address just as Ben screeched to a dramatic halt in front of Allandale House. "Do try not to attract the attention of the campus cops, ok? We don't have time for that."

"Where am I going?"

It wasn't far; the address was just off Speedway, in an area north of campus full of old houses and garage apartments and a few small, shabby apartment buildings dating from the early sixties. The relatively cheap housing attracted a lot of students. In fact, the apartment Ingrid and I shared wasn't far away.

Unfortunately, all the students except me had cars, and they were all home this afternoon and using up the parking spaces along the street. Didn't anybody go to class any more?

"Drop me here," I said when Ben pulled up outside a shabby house with a privacy fence. "It's either this house or the garage apartment behind it. Come back as soon as you ditch the car, ok?"

"And you don't go running in there until I'm back," he ordered.

Ben and Lensky – two peas in the same pod? Or had Lensky infected Ben with the idea that I not only needed protection, but would wait like a helpless maiden until a protector showed up?

Vern was getting frustrated. This *had* to be the magic turtle that Ben and Lia had been talking to. The ring was easy enough to see, a gleam of gold digging into the soft flesh of the turtle's neck.

His first try had involved dousing the animal's head and neck with olive oil. That had been a pure waste of time. The ring was stuck so tight that not a drop of oil got under it, and now both the turtle and Vern's hands were all slippery. He would have to go to Plan B. The problem was, how could he make sure the turtle wouldn't pull its neck into the shell as soon as he let go?

He couldn't. But at least he could flip the turtle upside down so the beast wouldn't go anywhere while he hunted for his landlord's hatchet. And a good thing too, because it took him quite a while to figure out that the hatchet was hanging on two nails on the garage wall rather than buried in the kindling chopping block, where he would have left it.

Caspica caspica was still where he'd left it, waving its stupid little flippers as though it had a hope of touching the ground and flipping right side up. Good, it could stay like that for... a few...

Whap!

Vern jumped back and nearly chopped his own toes. The first hatchet blow had been a spectacular miss, coming down right in the center of the undershell and spattering turtle parts and liquids everywhere. Good thing he was wearing glasses; he wouldn't have liked to get something like that in his *eyes*.

He aimed more carefully the second time. And the third. God, who knew it was so difficult to control a hatchet? Oh well, at least now the shell was so thoroughly destroyed that the turtle's neck lay flat on the ground, barely twitching. Vern brought the hatchet down one more time and severed the neck, grabbed the twitching head and yanked off the ring. It had to be some kind of ring of power. Dropping the disgusting severed head, he slipped the ring over his thumb and frowned. Nothing felt all that different.

In fact, the "difference" was just that some parts of the universe which Vern did not believe in anyway were now invisible and inaudible to him. He did not hear the cries coming from the turtle's severed head, nor did he see the stream of bright points of light that poured from the neck. All he saw was the mess of hacked-up body parts on the ground before him. He should clean up…

Vern vomited on the pieces of turtle and backed away. *Later.* He'd get rid of the… stuff… later. He backed up the stairs to his apartment over the garage, watching the turtle parts with a superstitious fear that they were going to move and reassemble themselves, and let himself into the apartment before he realized that he was still clutching the landlord's hatchet. That, too, could be taken care of later. Right now he needed to figure out how to unlock the power of the ring.

∾

Ben pulled away and I turned towards the house. A long driveway ran beside the house and back under some ancient live oaks. A garage in this part of town virtually implied a garage apartment. Which to attempt first?

The question was answered for me. A cloud of fireflies poured out of the back yard and down the driveway – no, a firefly's blink is yellow. These were flickering points of blue-white light, like miniature stars, except their brightness wasn't dimmed by the daylight. I put up one hand to catch one as they passed by, and the whole cloud slowed, contracted, became a twister-shaped funnel pouring stars into my right hand. The first touch felt a little like a very minor electric shock; then there was just a slight prickling and a sense of absorbing something vital that I hadn't even know was missing. The edges of things around me were somehow sharper, and the minor background noise of cars and bicycles and people talking became a collection of discrete, clear sounds. And I could feel space stretching out all around me. Solar system – distant galaxies – for a moment the structure of the universe was part of me, and I was part of it, and I heard the music of the spheres.

Then I was back on the sidewalk, on a hot May afternoon in Texas, and the points of light were no longer flowing through the air.

I turned my hand over and looked. My cupped palm seemed to be holding a miniature cloud of sparkling little blue-white stars, all dashing around as if they were playing tag with each other. One zipped all the way to the edge of the cloud, caromed off the base of my thumb, and bounced back into the game.

It seemed possible that these guys were all going to bounce themselves out of my hand, given a chance. I folded my palm and fingers around them and shoved my whole hand into the front pocket of my jeans before opening it again.

They seemed to find this an acceptable playground; when I slowly withdrew my hand, there were only two little stars – sorry, I know stars are way bigger, I just don't know what else to call the guys – clinging to the tip of my index finger. I tapped it twice against the inside of the pocket and they broke loose to join the rest of the gang.

Now I could work on the incomprehensible noises coming from the yard behind the house. I'd been sort of aware of them while preoccupied with the stars, but since they weren't in any language I was familiar with I'd been able to ignore them. It sounded like a foreign student from some place very far away was excited about something, and I really didn't have time to deal with him. I needed to rescue Mr. M. The thing with the stars took longer to describe than it did to happen, but now I needed to *move.*

While I was running around the house the voice kept on, and I rather thought it was trying out several different languages now. "Abatu! Anaku qatu! Zu Hilfe, zu Hilfe, sonst bin ich verloren! Areeksis! Suppetiam implore! Au secours!"

French. *Thank* you, Aunt Alesia. Okay, somebody wanted help, but where were they? There was nothing here but a stack of kindling and a disgusting... mess... which was *not* the result of somebody dropping a loaded dinner plate, as I'd first thought. There were unmistakeable pieces of turtle shell poking out among the other... stuff.

I wasn't the first person to throw up on it, either.

"Vite, vite," the voice urged me, "Espèce d'imbecile, je suis *ici!* Sur terre, vois-tu? On the *ground*, idiot!"

I looked down at the ground as ordered, carefully *not* focusing on the place where I'd just tossed my cookies, and saw Mr. M.'s poor little severed head only a few inches from there.

His beak was moving; he was cursing my slowness and stupidity. I think. Aunt Alesia's French vocabulary – and hence, mine – does not include most of the words Mr. M. was deploying now.

I dropped to one knee – being, yes, very careful where I put that knee. "Mr. M? We came to save you. I'm so, so sorry we were too late. Is there anything I can do for you before you, um...."

"Finish your sentences," Mr. M. snapped, reverting to English. And when a box turtle is feeling snappish, it can be quite impressive. "*I am, quite obviously, going to do nothing until I am reunited with the rest of my body.*"

That was going to be a lengthy assembly job, and I wasn't at all sure that something held together with Zap-a-Gap and duct tape would function enough like a body to keep him alive. "How long can you go on like this?"

"Like what?"

"Bodiless."

"Oh, indefinitely," he said. "But it is a grave humiliation for a person of my wisdom and gravitas to have to ask you mortal types to *carry* me everywhere. Had you only paid attention, instead of whining like little girls when I told you to cut my head off, I could have explained that after removing that thrice-accursed demonic ring you could simply hold my severed neck against the matching wound on my body. I am quite capable of doing the necessary repair work. The problem is the *body*. The longer you wait, the harder it is to remind it that it has to function as part of a living being. Still, you are here now. Pick me up and hold me while I reattach to my body."

I couldn't refrain from a quick glance at the hodgepodge of turtle shell bits and other turtle parts. "I'm afraid that's not possible."

"Why not?" Another snap of the beak.

"Well..." I really didn't want to show him the damage; next thing you knew, I'd be trying to find therapy for a talking turtle. Head. "The guy who took the ring did a *lot* of damage to your body. It's all in little pieces. Trust me, you're not going to be able to reanimate *that*!"

"You have no idea of the full extent of my powers. Show me!"

"All right," I sighed. "It's your funeral."

As far as the body was concerned, that was literally true. I lifted his head up and held it where first one eye, and then the other, could get a good view of the damage.

"*Isten basz!*" Before I could ask, Mr. M. informed me, "That's Hungarian, and you don't need to know what it means. I... I think I'll take a little nap while you find a new body for me."

I slipped him into my other front pocket – the one without the stars – and, being a kind and thoughtful person, removed my wallet and keys so he'd have a nice roomy space in which to nap. It wasn't easy to get them into the back pockets, either; I like my jeans to *fit*.

Ben came pounding into the yard between house and garage just as I finished rearranging everything. "Lia, are you all right? It took me forever to find a parking place, the Unitarians are hosting a debate about open carry on campus and the Baptists are having a yard sale to raise funds for lawyers to defend undocumented immigrants." He thought that over. "Or maybe the other way around. Anyway, here you are – but where's Mr. M. – and where's Vern?"

I pointed down at the ground and up at the apartment over the garage. Ben looked at the ground first and groaned. "Too late!"

"Maybe, maybe not," I said. "Some interesting stuff has happened since you dropped me off. We need to talk, but maybe not here?"

It was quite a hike to Ben's car. Mentally, I gave him points if he'd actually run all the way from his car to the apartment. I actually felt touched by the thought that he would do that just for me. Maybe Lensky was starting a new trend: Take Care of Thalia.

Fortunately, I didn't say anything before it dawned on me that I was merely a side-issue; he'd made that mad dash through the streets to save Mr. M.

CHAPTER 10

BEN'S PLAN, if you can call it that, was to drop me off at my apartment while he mooched off to his tiny place south of the river to brood on failure. However, we had things to talk about that were better discussed in the private side of the Center. I certainly wasn't going to tell him about Mr. M. or the mini-stars while he was driving.

He wasn't exactly positive about the idea.

"I won't be able to park anywhere close, and I'm tired already."

"We need to talk," I repeated. "On the private side."

"What's so urgent about analyzing our failure?"

I didn't want to talk about it out here on the sidewalk, especially while we were being dive-bombed and persecuted by grackles. I was beginning to have a funny feeling about the way the blue-black devils showed up *en masse* whenever we had something important to talk about. Probably that was unjustified; it *was* May, and *en masse* was a pretty good description of the general grackle presence in Austin at this time of year. Still, I decided to appeal to his lower instincts.

"We haven't had dinner yet."

"Of course not, it's too early."

"After we talk, I'll order a large pepperoni pizza."

"With anchovies? And pineapple?"

Ben's instincts were even lower than I'd guessed. *"Half* with anchovies and pineapple. Some of it has to be left for normal people to eat."

"Oh, are there going to be any of those around?"

We didn't talk much more in the car.

In the event, Mr. M took a *very* long nap, so we had an early dinner. (I kept trekking over to the secret side of the office and fishing him out of my pocket to make sure he wasn't squashed or dead.) Ben was polishing off the last piece of anchovy-pineapple pizza and Ingrid was working on everybody's pizza bones when I felt Mr. M moving around in my pocket.

"Okay, guys, over to the Research Division," I announced. "Ben, you walk Jimmy over; he's entitled to be in on this."

Jimmy muttered that it was a good thing he'd had *his* pizza a couple of hours ago. I didn't have much sympathy for how crossing the wall would upset his delicate stomach; he should have seen what I'd had to look at in front of Vern Trexler's apartment.

There were, of course, no extra chairs in my office or Ingrid's, and it was impossible to get into Ben's tiny office where Lensky had stacked all the chairs. Ben took the three on top of the nearest stack and set them in my office.

Maybe I could shift them over to Ingrid's office after this meeting.

"We have *not* failed," I announced to start things off. I reached into my right-hand pocket: oops. Little tickling things that bounced off and into my palm. Possibly giggling. Possibly not.

Ok, left-hand pocket. I caught his neck right behind the jaws and pulled him out. "Allow me to present Mr. M. himself."

"Ugh," Ingrid said. "Lia, I've given up expecting any feminine sensitivity from you, but do you *have* to bring pieces of dead animals into the office? That's really not funny!"

"WHO ARE YOU CALLING DEAD, ESPÉCE D'IMBECILE?"

Mr. M. didn't really shout as loud as those capital letters imply, but he had the same effect. I found out what Ingrid and Jimmy looked like when all the blood left their faces. Ingrid reminded me of the Snow

Queen in my old edition of Hans Andersen. The look wasn't quite that good on Jimmy.

"Mr. M. is separated from his body, but he is definitely not dead," I explained. "And he's feeling a lot better now that ring is off his neck. For one thing, he can talk now."

"Ring?"

"Turtles wear jewelry?"

Of course. Ingrid and Jimmy didn't know the whole story. It took Ben and me quite a while to tell them, mainly because they kept inter-rupting. You'd think someone who floats Lego bricks around her office on a regular basis would have more of an open mind about English-speaking turtles.

Er, make that *multi-lingual* turtles. During the whole story Mr. M. was muttering in languages unknown to me. I suspected he was feeling neglected now that all the humans were talking to each other instead of listening to him.

What I didn't realize at the time was that this was a recurring condition. It recurred any time he wasn't the center of attention.

Finally Ingrid and Jimmy were in possession of most of the details about Mr. M. and his ring.

"Too bad you didn't get the ring too," Jimmy said. "It's got to be a magic ring of great power."

"Stupid human!" Mr. M. was going to have his say at last. "Not a magic ring. *Anti*-magic ring. It was put upon me by treachery of the high priest of Marutuk at the orders of Nabû-kudurrī-usur."

"Who?"

Mr. M.'s eyes closed and he appeared to be searching his memory. "I believe that in this degenerate time you would refer to Marduk and Nebuchadnezzar."

"I've heard of Nebuchadnezzar," said Jimmy. "Didn't he go crazy and start eating grass?"

"My enemy is cast down!" chortled Mr. M.

"He probably went on a vegan diet," murmured Ben.

"Gluten-free," Ingrid suggested.

"I think some other bad stuff happened to him, but I'd have to look it up."

Mr. M. ignored them. "O wise young sage!" he addressed Jimmy. "How is it that thou hast this knowledge which the other humans lack?"

"Parochial school. But I don't know anything about this other guy, Marduk."

"Thou knowest not the Great God of Babylon?"

All four of us shook our heads.

"Then is my triumph complete at last, and those who ringed me and crippled my powers are lost. Nabû-kudurrī-usur eats grass like a beast of the field; Marutuk is utterly forgotten; and my bonds are broken. Get me a new body! I wish to go now and slay Nabû-kudurrī-usur!"

"He's probably dead by now," Jimmy said. "I don't remember where he comes into the Bible, but I'm pretty sure everybody in the Old Testament has been dead for a long, long time."

Mr. M sniffed. "I take it, then, that this testament of which you speak does not mention *me*?"

"I'm not sure. What's your name?"

"Niiqarquusu Adrahasis Galammta-uddua."

"Nope. A name like that, I'd have remembered. Nikerku..." Jimmy gave up. "What would it be in English?"

Mr. M closed his eyes again. After a long pause he opened them slowly. "It would appear that I have outlived my fame; there is no modern version of my name. I can, however, translate the latter part. You may call me Niiqarquusu Great-Wisdom Goes-Forth-in-Strength."

"How about Niko for short?"

"What I just said *is* the short form of my name. My full name is..."

"Never mind, never mind," Jimmy said hastily. "Trust me, if we try to call you Nikerku-whatsit, we'll just keep getting it wrong and mispronouncing it, and that will be very irritating for you."

Niiqarquusu Adrahasis Galammta-uddua thought it over for a moment.

"This small dark person has been calling me Mr. M. That is accept-able – for the moment." His tone suggested that he expected to teach us Babylonian. Well, good luck with that. Americans are really bad with foreign languages, even living languages that we might conceiv-ably need to use some day to order a beer.

Ben had somehow managed to keep track of the thread during this extended divagation. "You were going to tell us about the ring."

"That object of ill omen was made in response to a prophecy that One would destroy Babylon with unheard-of magics. Unluckily for me, I was known to be a powerful magician – I had actually helped Nabû-kudurrī-usur with the conquest of Elam. Thus came about my downfall. At a feast to celebrate our victory I was plied with unwa-tered wine. When I awoke the ring was upon my neck, and I could make only the slightest of workings – not enough to free myself. Long centuries I slumbered, retreating into my turtle mind, until Dzaqar the messenger of the gods brought me the key to freedom in a dream, promising that I should not die. Even then..."

"You decided that it wouldn't kill you to cut off your head based on a *dream?*"

"As I was saying before I was *so rudely interrupted*," Niiqarquusu went on, "it was necessary to wait until I found an audience capable of understanding at least the rudimentary basis of magic before revealing myself; otherwise, Dzaqar warned me, the humans would ignore my demands and use me either as an experimental animal or a curiosity in a freak show. When I felt the invisibility working of this tall human I knew I was in the presence of one who was potentially as great as the Magi of the Medes, one who would understand and serve me. Or so I thought!

"I had just enough power to ensure that I was psychically attuned to the mage. On his next visit to my domicile I exited the water and attempted to communicate with him using the crude means then at my disposal. Disappointingly, I exhausted myself without persuading him to meet my demands. I had not previously realized that a master mage could be *stupid.* Not only did he refuse me, he left me to the mercy of some butcher who destroyed my body, left me lying in the shambles, and did not even catch my stars. Without them I doubt very much that I shall be able to attach to a new body, even if you provide one."

Right-hand pocket. The little things were still there. I closed my hand very gently over what felt like a small subset of them, held it out over the table and opened it. Tiny sparks of twinkling, blue-white light came spiraling out of a miniature cloud on the palm of my hand. There were an awful lot of them – I must have grabbed more than I thought. I closed my hand quickly before any more escaped.

"Are those your stars, Mr. M?"

"How did you capture them? Were you lurking unseen in the butcher's yard? No, I would probably have sensed your presence even before I was free of the ring, certainly afterwards. You did not turn up until long after I started calling for help."

Well, for certain values of "long after," that was more or less true. Mr. M. didn't have a lot of tolerance for waiting.

"I saw them when they were just past the driveway. I wasn't trying to catch them, I just wanted to know what the swarm felt like. I raised my hand and some of them bumped into it, then they all headed for me and made this, like, really condensed cluster. So I put it in my pocket."

"The Endless Lights of the Medes, carried around in a cloth bag by a small woman! And yet you too must be a sort of magus, if they really came to your hand."

I've already admitted that I'm not very tall. He didn't need to harp on it.

"Will these, ah, lights help you to reassemble yourself? If we can get a new body for you?"

"Indubitably. You may call them back now. They have danced long enough."

I had no idea how to collect the dancing lights. Visions of a butterfly net lined with Saran wrap came to me. Lacking that, I just raised my hands and hoped I'd be able to catch a few.

And they came to me as before. The palm of my right hand

prickled as what seemed like a million sparkling points of light funneled down into a glittering cloud which I put back in my pocket.

Ingrid sighed. "I want to learn how to do that!"

"Later," Mr. M. said. "Your task now is to go out and get me a replacement body."

"How are we supposed to do that?"

"Elementary. I have had ample time to observe my environment. In the place where I found you there are many, many turtles. Just pick out a nice, healthy one, bring it here and chop off its head. With the added power of a few Lights, I can easily merge with the new body."

We exchanged looks.

"We... can't do that," Ben said.

"Why not? One more or less will hardly be noticed. Even *my* departure has caused no disturbance. And if I can disappear, so can a common box turtle."

"That's not what I meant."

"Those bolt cutters of yours should work well enough."

"N-no, I mean – look, we wouldn't kill you. And we're not going to kill another living being just to give you a means of transportation."

Mr. M sniffed. "Then what is your plan? To sit by the pond and wait until a turtle expires of natural causes? We are a very long-lived people. I cannot wait that long."

"Does it have to be a *turtle* body?" Ingrid asked.

"It is not absolutely required, but that is what I should find easiest to work with. The last time I changed bodies, the Priest of Enki sacrificed two hundred turtles upon the altar and invited me to choose the most acceptable body."

"Must have been one hell of a big altar," Ben muttered in my ear.

"I was thinking, maybe a rat? From the biology labs," she expanded. "One that was going to die anyway."

Mr. M made it blisteringly clear that he would not accept the humiliation of a rat body. It was remarkable how he was picking up colloquial English; star power must be giving him enhanced access to our minds.

It was also remarkable that one of us knew *that* many of *those* kind of words.

"I have an idea," Jimmy announced. "I know this girl who's working on a robotics project..."

Ingrid made a face. I had the distinct impression she wished she were wearing a ballgown, instead of a short tight dress, so that she could draw aside the hem of her garment.

"We don't need a robot," she objected.

"No, but she's got some spare bodies. More like snakes than turtles."

"*You* know Meadow?" Ben interrupted.

"Everybody knows Meadow. It's not like she's inconspicuous."

I didn't know Meadow, and Ingrid said she didn't either. But I had a feeling that Jimmy's "everybody" was a certain subset of the human race that Ingrid and I, by definition, did not belong to.

Calling Meadow just got us bumped to her voice mail, and we felt it might not be a good idea to leave a message. She might write us off as insane. Ben and Jimmy promised to get on it first thing in the morning, which at least put off the time when she would write *them* off as insane.

When Ingrid and I got home, Mr. M was in the full tide of a complaint about having no home but my pocket. Good thing Ingrid had given me a ride; if I'd walked home, the other pedestrians might have been slightly bothered about the fact that my jeans appeared to be talking. Loudly. In multiple languages. Thankfully, he relaxed after Ingrid improvised a temporary home for him using an empty cardboard box and a red silk scarf that I had been rather fond of. I put the box on the top of my bureau and he settled in for another long nap. I hoped.

CHAPTER 11

INGRID HAD GONE out to some sort of graduate student party when Brad Lensky turned up at our front door.

"Your doormat's wrong," he said by way of greeting.

I glanced down to see if the wording on it had changed. No, it was the same as always: YOU'VE READ MY DOORMAT. THAT'S ENOUGH INTERACTION FOR TODAY.

"We haven't had nearly enough interaction today," he amplified.

"Speak for yourself, spook." But I let him in anyway, and even offered him a beer.

"I think I'm making progress," he said, shrugging out of his sport coat and leaving it dangling on the back of his chair.

"On the terrorist ring?"

"With *you*. I didn't have to bribe you with beer or guacamole this time."

I sank down on the couch, trying to look pale and wan, and heaved a dramatic sigh. "A girl can always hope."

"If we go out for anything tonight," Lensky said, "it had better be a salad bar. You eat too much junk food."

Definitely beyond bossy and into dictatorial. Good thing I'd already had some pizza.

"But first, we have some unfinished business. Don't we?"

Funny coincidence. I'd just been thinking about that earlier. And I'd decided not to finish it. Hadn't I?

By the time I'd thought that far, he had somehow moved from his chair to the couch, and had one arm around my shoulders. "I don't like leaving a project incomplete," he murmured.

This time neither of us was spitting mad at the other, and I have to admit that being on semi-friendly terms greatly improved the quality of his kisses. I really hated to remove his hand from under my shirt, but one has to maintain some standards.

"I believe this is yours," I said, dropping the wandering hand on his knee.

"I'm willing to share."

"I have a roommate. And I hardly know you."

"The order in which you stated your objections gives me hope." And he moved in again.

This time he made sure that I wasn't in a good tactical position for removing hands or anything else. In fact, there wasn't a whole lot I could do with him leaning me backwards on the couch like that. And to tell the truth, my interest in holding him off or even removing his wandering hands was fading. In fact, I was more interested in running my hands along his back - until a sharp jab in my own back sent me rocketing upwards.

"Ow!" Lensky had one hand over his face. "I thik you broke by dose."

"Oh, don't be a crybaby." I moved his hand, pinched his nose and wriggled it back and forth. "Nothing's broken. I think you'll live."

"No thanks to *you*," he said. "What did you do that for? Next time use your words. 'No' works a lot better than butting me in the head."

I stood up and pointed to the spike sticking out of the place where I'd been reclining on the couch. "Broken spring attack."

"Oh, then you *weren't* saying no." His eyes brightened and he seemed to have forgotten all about the nose.

If we kept this up, I knew where it would end. In my bedroom. The thought of Mr. M. as an observer and commenter was an instant turn-off. And just as well, because apart from that and the inevitable teasing from Ingrid, I wasn't ready to get that intimate with somebody I'd only met three days earlier, and who couldn't lay off the double-entendres. It was easier to remember this when he wasn't kissing me, so I stayed vertical when he patted the couch cushions. "I'm hungry. You want to go get that salad?"

"Salad," he said, "is vastly overrated. "I'd rather..."

"Whatever you're going to say you want," I interrupted, "it isn't on the menu." To be precise, *I* wasn't on the menu.

"Barbecue?"

We wound up at the Iron Works, where he inhaled the vast quantity of protein needed to keep a body like that and all its muscles happy, and I nibbled on a brisket sandwich and a Big Red soda because after claiming hunger I couldn't exactly admit to having filled up on pizza earlier. And when he took me home, Ingrid's little Honda was parked out front, and he didn't even ask if he could come upstairs.

We did spend some time in the car, though.

After meeting Meadow Melendez, I understood why the guys had said that everybody knew her. I'd noticed her myself, walking through a mob of other students rather as a small tank might progress through a crowd of unarmed protestors. A busty girl with a Hispanic Afro of reddish-black curls and the personality of a bulldozer does get noticed.

Confine her to a cluttered robotics lab, and the personality was overwhelming.

And – at the moment – decidedly negative.

Ben had been trying to lead up to the fact that we had a severed, talking turtle head in the box under his arm; it's not the kind of thing you want to spring on somebody without warning. Before he got properly started Meadow brushed him off.

"You know I don't hang out with people who do drugs, and I have real work to do. Go away!"

Given time – which, sadly, did not seem probable – I could begin to like this woman.

Ingrid tried a different tack. "The project we have in mind is totally unlike any robotics project ever done before. It'll make you famous." That was, assuming any editor actually believed her paper. I decided not to bring up that irrelevant little detail.

"You can't possibly need *all* those discards," said Jimmy.

Meadow had been working on developing a snake robot that could go up and down stairs, swim, climb trees, and take itty-bitty cameras into places where you needed to see what was happening. Like around the corner of a stairway where there might be armed terrorists waiting. She'd gotten the idea from Israeli war robots and was trying to take it a step farther.

Meadow glowered at him. "Why not? They're perfectly functional snake bodies. My problem is the control system. It's nowhere near sophisticated enough to use all the functionality I've built into the body."

"We might have a solution to that."

Meadow sneered. "Mathematicians? You people think that if you prove something must exist, that's the same as holding it in your hot little hand. I don't need any theoretical proofs that a multi-functional controller is possible, thank you."

"Well, actually," Ben said in a soft, apologetic voice, "I *am* holding a multi-functional controller in my hand – well, in this box." He set it on the lab bench in front of Meadow. "Our only concern is that your snake bodies may not be sophisticated enough to make the best use of the controller."

"And what would *you* know about it? Show me." Meadow pulled the tabs holding the box closed.

Looked inside.

Screamed and threw the box away from her.

Ben dived to catch it and tripped over a metal snake body. The box hit the floor, turned over once, and spilled Mr. M. onto the tiles.

100

Mr. M. began telling us what he thought of this careless treatment. At least, that's what I thought he was telling us. He seemed to have reverted to ancient Babylonian.

"I *tried* to warn you," Ben told Meadow. He uncurled his body, separated himself from what was now an oddly shaped piece of scrap metal, and stood up rubbing what was probably going to be a goose egg on his forehead.

"That. Was. Not. Funny!" Meadow announced. "What the *hell* do you think you're playing at, bringing a [fornicating] piece of road kill into *my [incestuous fornicating] lab*, all wrapped up like a pretty little [blasphemous fornicating] present? You and your friends can all go and [perform anatomically impossible acts]."

It's not wise to piss off somebody with the personality of a bulldozer.

Fortunately, Mr. M. decided to stop expressing himself in dead languages and save the day.

"Dama más elegante y hermosa, por favor perdónanos para este choque."

Meadow stared at all of us. Nobody's lips were moving.

"Okay, who's the Spanish-language ventriloquist?"

Ingrid picked up the box, patted the red silk scarf down, and gently replaced Mr. M. Then she held him out to Meadow – at a safe distance, this time, but close enough that she could see his beak moving.

"No tenia intención de mis amigos de sorprenderle."

"Oh. Oh, wow." Meadow sat down at the lab bench. "It looks so *real*. And how did you program it to do that?"

"Young person, I *am* real," said Mr. M., reverting to English and to his usual state of high dudgeon. "And if "program" has a meaning similar to "command," allow me to inform you that *no one* commands *me*. In the terms of your theology, you might say that I have free will and agency."

"And it talks as fancy as Father Hernandez on a tear," Meadow marveled. "Where did you get it?"

"Ummm… long story," I said. Most of it not exactly calculated to add verisimilitude to an otherwise bald and unconvincing narrative. "The thing is, his body has been destroyed, and it's kind of our fault, so we promised to fix him up with a new one."

"Why come to me? Plenty of turtles in the pond."

"Decapitating another turtle to save this one," Ben said, "would only perpetuate the cycle of abuse. Now, about those snakebots…"

"I've never even thought about the problem of connecting living neural tissue with the 'bot controls. The technical problems alone…"

Good, she was starting to think like an engineer again. Mr. M.'s head had been upgraded from "icky body part" to "engineering challenge."

"You do not have to solve this problem alone," Mr. M. said. "Some of your problems, I surmise, stem from the difficulty of connecting two non-sentient systems with no warning if you make a mistake. *I*, being not only sentient but highly sapient, will be in a position to provide information – I believe you call it 'feedback' – on each step in the process. You will, of course, first set up a system of mirrors so that I can see the parts you are joining."

"That's going to be a PITA," Meadow said.

"It will not be trivially easy. But since you, unlike most mortals, are capable of calculating angles of refraction in your head, that part of the problem should not be overly difficult."

Good old Mr. M! He knew how to flatter her.

Meadow sent us out to buy some nice plain rectangular mirrors and some museum tacky goop to attach them with. "*Yes*, all of you. Except for Mr. M. here. He and I need to work through some technical details." Her eyes got that unfocused look. "Did I just say I wanted to have a technical discussion with a *dead turtle*? Am I going crazy or what?"

"You do not appear to be insane, but I fear that your memory is failing," Mr. M. informed her. "I have already told you that I am not dead."

"Talking to a severed head in whatever condition is proof of insanity," Meadow said.

We skedaddled and left Mr. M. to soothe her.

Ingrid and Jimmy opted not to return, pointing out that Ms. Melendez appeared to get more irritable the more people she had to deal with, and furthermore Ben and I had started this whole thing and we were the ones who ought to see it through.

I had queasy visions of being handed a hemostat with a nerve or a blood vessel or something clamped in it, and being told to attach it to exactly the right one of a bunch of thin metal wires that all looked alike.

I never found out if that was how the operation actually went, and that was perfectly all right with me. Meadow used us to hold mirrors until she got the angles right, and then she fixed them in place and ordered us out again.

"Wait," Mr. M. said. "Thalia, we will require some of the Lights."

I really needed to figure out a better way to carry those things. I pulled a handful out of my pocket and released them into the room. Mr. M. said a few words in, I guess, Babylonian, and the little dancing lights divided into two clusters, one at the back of his neck and one at the place where a controller and camera should have been attached to the snake body.

Meadow took a deep, shaky breath. "Riiiight. We have talking animal parts and a performing firefly circus. Is there anything else you want to tell me?"

"That's about it," Ben said. Well, it was true enough; we *didn't* want to tell her about telekinesis, teleportation, and invisibility.

"*Good.* Now go away. I'll tell you when I'm through."

Our only part in the procedure was sitting on the floor on either side of the lab door and persuading various disgruntled engineering students to come back later. We heard innumerable variations on "My project's due tomorrow," "I have to have my lab notes," and "She has no right to take over the lab like this!"

By the end of a very long morning, I had come up with answers to all these complaints.

"The semester isn't over for three and a half weeks. Nobody's term projects are due tomorrow, which by the way is a Saturday."

"She told us that if anyone forces their way in, she'll burn their lab notes. And yes, she's got matches."

"You're welcome to tell her she has no right to take over the lab. In person. As soon as this is finished. Want to wait for her?"

As a graduating senior, Meadow had had four years to impress her personality on the other engineering students. Nobody took me up on that last offer.

"That woman is a real lesson in the power of stubbornness and crankiness," I said after one of the robotics students, offered a chance to wait, had paled and left quickly.

"Mmm. Remind me to keep you two apart," Ben said. "I fear that she would encourage your worst qualities."

"I think of them as valuable traits for a researcher in a field that doesn't actually exist. Anyway, we won't be seeing much more of her if this works. Or if it doesn't," I added after thinking over the possibilities. I was all for Meadow's success; the alternative appeared to be for Ben and me to become the Burke and Hare of the turtle world. But I still found it hard to believe this could work. Jimmy might be more optimistic because he was used to telling computers what to do and they obeyed him. My experience with machines of any sort – starting with the coffee maker in the break room and working upward – was more about making tentative suggestions and being sneered at by the machine.

It was after two when Meadow staggered out the lab door, leaned against the wall, and slid down to our level. "I. Do not. *Believe*. What I just did. I'm not a neurosurgeon! It couldn't have worked! And now I want to forget all about it."

Ben removed a pair of ultra-fine-tip needle-nose pliers from her hand. "It didn't work, then?"

Meadow pushed her reddish-black curls off her face with both hands. "I didn't say that. It *shouldn't* have worked, though. I thought…"

A long silvery blur zipped through the lab door and wound itself around Meadow's legs. "You have done well," the turtle head at one end of the silver thing said to Meadow. "You have earned favor in my eyes. You may call upon Niiqarquusu Adrahasis Galammta-uddua in your time of need."

"Mr. M! You're all right?"

The turtle head turned towards me. A moment later the silvery scales were coiled around one of my legs, and Mr. M.'s head was resting on my belt buckle. "You too, Daughter of Stars, have earned the favor of Niiqarquusu Adrahasis Galammta-uddua." He unwound himself from my leg and slithered down the hall in a very fast undulating motion. I could have sworn I heard a "Whee!" before he turned around and sped back to us.

There was no way we were going to get a three-foot metal snake, no matter how flexible, in the little box we'd been using to transport Mr. M. He announced loftily that he no longer needed our services, but after about ten yards of undulating along a sidewalk that had been soaking up heat all day he condescended to let me pick him up and drape him over my shoulders.

"What's my story if anybody asks what that thing around my neck is?" I whispered to Ben.

"Uh… it's a necklace?"

Mr. M. promptly coiled one loop around my neck and wrapped the rest of his body around that loop, finishing in an ornate design around his own head.

CHAPTER 12

BACK AT ALLANDALE HOUSE, Mr. M. zipped around the public side of the third floor, commenting on everything he saw. Coming from someone whose last experience of interior design was during the Nebuchadnezzar administration, there were a lot of comments and he required a lot of explanations, most of which he did not receive. Finally he consented to join us on the private side. He brushed me off when I tried to explain how to get to the other side of the wall.

"This thing you call a Möbius strip was old when the stars were new. Did you children think you had invented it?"

Actually, mathematicians – I mean the serious ones who are actually doing new work – debate about whether they are *creating* or just *discovering* the objects and spaces they define. I lean towards the "discovery" side of the debate, so I wasn't worried by Mr. M.'s comment. It seemed quite probable to me. After all, if anyone in ancient Babylon had been thinking about a Möbius strip, it would have been him. I made a mental note to ask if he'd ever seen the Hanging Gardens.

I didn't see quite how he did it, but he was on the private side after I'd walked the Möbius strip.

On my desk.

Tapping his tail.

And demanding a private office of his own.

I could see that our new colleague was not going to be any less high-maintenance now that he had a body again.

The private office demand generated a confused and acrimonious debate. We could partition off a space for him – we weren't anywhere near filling up even this side of the third floor – but he wanted a door that he could close and open.

How does a snake turn a doorknob?

Even a *very intelligent* snake?

"Could you do it by magic?" Ben suggested.

"Waste my powers on such a mundane matter?"

That was either a *no, I won't* or a *no, I can't*, and I didn't think Mr. M. was open to debate on the subject.

Fortunately, the mention of power brought something else to his mind.

"Daughter of Stars, you should share your power."

"Say what?"

"The Lights of the Medes," Mr. M. said impatiently, as if that had been totally obvious. "Each magic user should hold some. They enhance your puny little workings."

I reached into my pocket and brought out the sparkling cloud. Now that it had been suggested, I found I was very reluctant to part with my little dancing friends. "Um, I already gave some to help Meadow with the surgery. How many..."

"There is no end to the Lights."

"So...."

The tail began tapping. "I thought you were a mathematician. What is half of an infinite set?"

Okay, that was obvious. I'd have got it the first time if he'd spoken mathematics instead of mage. I dropped a handful into Ben's palm, then into Ingrid's. I took half of what I had left and held it in front of Mr. M., who opened his beak while the stars funneled down into God-knows-where. Now each of us had an infinite set of stars.

"This dress doesn't have pockets," Ingrid said. "Is it okay if I put them in my purse?"

Ingrid *would* be the last female student walking around campus in a dress and carrying a purse.

"Only if you do not wish your powers augmented," Mr. M. said, sounding testy. "They should be on your person at all times."

"Okay, I'll get something to keep them in as soon as I can." Ingrid stuffed her handful of sparkles into an interior pocket of her purse and zipped it shut. Ben was still holding a sparkling cloud in the palm of his hand and looking into it with that vague unfocused stare that usually meant his mind was a million miles away.

Then he was.

Oh, not quite a million miles away.

But definitely not *here*.

As it turned out, he was in Annelise Wilson's room in Littlefield Dorm, which happens to be a women-only residence hall.

And so was she.

This is what happened, as Ben explained it later:

He had been thinking two things at once as he gazed at the star cloud.

Part of his mind had been wondering whether the stars would improve his teleportation range.

A somewhat larger part of his mind was visualizing a scantily clad Annelise.

It remains unclear whether Ben would have found himself in Annelise's dorm room if she had not been there, or if she had not so closely resembled the image in his head. In the light of subsequent experience, I'm inclined to think he would have turned up wherever Annelise was. But at that time we hadn't even begun to experiment.

In any case – there he was. Holding something that looked like a spherical sparkler.

And there she was, in black lace underwear and not very much of it at that.

According to Ben, she didn't scream or even squeak. She grabbed an extra-large T-shirt, pulled it over her head, and demanded, "What are you doing? And how did you get in here?"

"I know you're not going to believe this," he said, "but I was just thinking about you. Just. Thinking. And suddenly here I was. I didn't *mean* to burst in on you like this."

Annelise picked a pair of shorts off the floor and stepped into them. "You're right, I don't believe you."

"Annelise, are you talking on the phone *again?*" a girl called from the hall. "Just turn the poor goof down already, and come on. We're going to be la…"

The door swung open and a strange girl – strange to Ben, anyway – stared at him.

"What's *he* doing here? The Barker is going to *kill* you if she finds out you've smuggled a *man* onto the *floor.*"

"Janice, I didn't!" Annelise said.

"Man on the floor?" squealed someone down the hall, and moments later three girls in babydoll pj's were looking over Janice's shoulder.

"Well, how *did* he get here?"

Both of them looked at Ben.

"Why didn't you reverse the mapping and put yourself back here?" I asked at this point in the tale.

"Or use Camouflage?" Ingrid asked.

"I was *rattled*," Ben told us. "I couldn't concentrate. You'd have trouble concentrating too if you suddenly found yourself in a strange place surrounded by scantily clad girls."

"Not as much trouble as you seem to have had," Ingrid sniffed. "You really need to develop better concentration, Ben."

"Like you had day before yesterday when you walked into that pyracantha?" he inquired snidely.

I didn't want to listen to more bickering. "So what happened next?"

What happened next was that a solidly built – and fully dressed - young woman shooed the onlookers away and started giving Annelise hell for having a man in her room. Expulsion was mentioned. So was the Dean's office. And there was some talk about 'the last straw.'

"I can explain everything, Ms. Barker," Annelise said as soon as the woman paused to breathe. "It's… about Daddy's new girl friend. Did you know she was Miss Ukraine two years ago, before she came to the US? Well, she... told Daddy... that the Ukranian Mob was trying to get her to spy on his business transactions with the Russians."

"And what transactions would those be?"

"I have no idea. He told me that he's not doing any business with the Russians, but the newspapers have been publishing terrible smears against him accusing him of selling our country out for profits from Russia based on the fact that he met Vladimir Putin at a State Department party five years ago, and apparently the Ukranians fell for it and threatened Anna, and she was terrified."

"And what has this international espionage got to do with your hiding a man in your room?"

"Well, I'm trying to explain, but you keep interrupting. You see, they told Anna they knew all about it because they'd been listening in when I Skype with Daddy."

"Ha! A likely story!"

"That's what I thought. They couldn't have learned anything important from my Skype chats with Daddy, do you think he tells me about his business? He thinks I'm still about six years old with pigtails and pink ribbon bows. But it's about the bows, you see."

"Pink. Ribbon. Bows."

"Yes, well, the Ukranians are why he sent one of his computer experts to upgrade the security on my laptop. And because he still thinks I'm a little girl, it didn't occur to him to tell Mr. Sutherland that my dorm has positively medieval rules and he'd have to check in at the front desk, and there wasn't anybody at the desk when he came in so he just came on up to look at the computer, and I didn't know he hadn't checked in because he didn't tell me because he didn't know he was supposed to, but it's all right because he's done all the security checks now and Daddy's private jet is waiting for him at the airport and he needs to leave right now to avoid the traffic."

Ben took his cue and hot-footed it out of the dorm as soon as the forbidding Ms. Barker accepted that story. He walked back to Allandale House, very carefully not thinking about anything except his immediate surroundings.

Then he bounded up the stairs and told us that we needed to hire Annelise immediately.

He got a wounded look when we responded by asking how he'd vanished and where he'd been. Finally he interrupted his own praise of Annelise long enough to give us the account above.

Then he borrowed Ingrid's phone and called Annelise. Could she come over to Allandale House right now? "Please... It's important... You were telling me you want a part time job to show your father that you're independent but you're not qualified to do anything, right? Well, I've thought of something you're super qualified for!"

He handed Ingrid's phone back and thanked her.

"Since when do *you* make hiring decisions around here, Ben?"

He looked wounded. "But isn't it obvious? I've seen her in action before, but this time it all came together for me. Annelise can talk her way out of anything, any time. I *told* you we should have had her along on those spying excursions. Now I'm going to wait for her on the public side."

"I shall take a nap," Mr. M announced, coiling himself up on my desk. "This has been a very tiring day."

Ben turned sideways and vanished.

Ingrid and I followed, because we weren't through with this argument yet.

All moving the site of the argument accomplished was to add Lensky to the firestorm. He must have come in while we were talking on the private side. Thank goodness Mr. M had decided to nap on my desk; introducing him to Lensky was going to be a whole new can of worms.

"She's not even a mathematician!" Ingrid complained.

"*I* decide who can be read into the program," Lensky announced.

"Well, I think Ben's got a good point," I said, mainly because I hate it when everybody in the room piles onto one person and won't stop hitting them. "To get the information you need, Lensky, we're probably going to have to go to a lot more places where we're not supposed to be. Wouldn't it be useful to have somebody who can talk her way out of anything?"

Of course, Lensky hadn't heard that part, so Ben had to tell his story all over again. He was almost through when a tanned, honey-blonde girl in shorts that displayed a couple of miles of tanned leg showed up at the top of the stairs. Lensky got *that look* on his face – you know, the one where the man looks as though he's just been hit on the head with a two-by-four but hasn't yet realized he ought to fall down – and I surmised that it wasn't going to be at all difficult to get him to clear Annelise and read her in on the project.

It was actually more difficult to persuade Annelise to join us.

No, she didn't freak out at the part about real-world effects created by visualizing mathematical spaces. Of course, she'd just had a demonstration. Even so, a lot of people would think we were insane. Annelise just said, "I saw the *Lord of the Rings* movies three times. And after that I read the books twice."

Possibly she was the insane one. The first movie in the trilogy had been more than enough for me. Although Legolas *was* pretty hot.

The hard part was persuading her that we really needed her help and that this wasn't a make-work job dreamed up by Ben to get points with her. I have to admit it sounded kind of fluffy: follow us around and be ready to talk us out of any complications? Finally I got Ben and Ingrid to shut up long enough for me to tell her about us getting caught sitting on the floor of a vacant office.

"How did you get out of that?"

"I told the truth," I confessed. Well, some of the truth, anyway.

"What? That's *never* a good idea!"

"You see? We really do need you."

Since Annelise was a graduating senior, she didn't want to sign up for a full-time job that would conflict with her classes. "Not that I have a lot in the way of classes this semester," she admitted. "I put off the most boring General Requirements classes until the last year. This semester all I've got besides English Comp. and Biology 101 is "Sex and Power in the Black Diaspora" and "Queer Identity Formation." Those satisfy the Diversity and Anti-Bigotry requirement and all you have to do to pass is show up at every class and record what the professor says so you can repeat it on the tests. But I *do* have to go to class. I heard that last year some students pooled their resources so only one guy with a smartphone had to actually show up at "Sex and Power" and record the lecture for everybody. So now the department's cracking down on attendance."

She gave us her class schedule and we agreed that we'd try to work around it.

Ingrid noticed that she didn't have anything before 10 AM. "The other part of the job is very simple," she said, and stepped on Ben's foot. "You need to come in between 9 and 10 every morning, make coffee, and set out the pastries you bought."

"Where do I get the money?"

"Petty cash," Ingrid, Ben and I said in unison. Great minds really do think alike. When Dr. Verrick had been the only supplier of doughnuts, this topic had never come up. By Monday, though, there would be a desk facing the stairs, a cash box on the desk, and generous donations for a pastry fund in the box. Jimmy and Lensky could donate too; they certainly ate enough when they got a chance.

CHAPTER 13

Dr. Verrick chose this time to call a staff meeting.

"I have a seminar," Annelise claimed, and fled the building.

Sensible girl. She had the right attitude towards meetings.

Ben thought the purpose of the meeting was for Dr. Verrick to retroactively okay Annelise's hiring and possibly thank him for having done something productive about our staffing crisis.

I don't think Ben and Annelise have a future; she's a realist and he, as you can tell from the foregoing paragraph, is an incurable optimist.

It turned out that the purpose of the meeting was to lacerate our sensibilities, offend our finest feelings, and remind us that we had all the status and freedom of slaves. In chains.

Or, as Dr. Verrick put it, to remind us that the Moore Foundation's annual May Fiesta was tomorrow night, and for us to brush up on the finer points of formal attire and behavior.

"Mr. Sutherland, despite the fact that the Foundation calls this a fiesta, a sombrero is not appropriate evening dress."

"Miss Thorn, you are not and never will be a Viking Shield-Maiden. You are particularly warned to lose the authentic sword."

"Miss Kostis, ladies do not wear cut-offs. You will dress like a lady tomorrow night. That means wearing something with a skirt, if you follow me. Preferably one long enough to cover the tattoo on your… upper leg."

I poked Ben. We'd both predicted that the outline of the State of Texas on the outside of my left thigh was going to be mentioned; Dr. Verrick really didn't like my favorite pair of cutoffs, which were frayed up to the point where you could see all the way to the Panhandle. But I'd bet Ben five bucks that Dr. Verrick wouldn't be able to bring himself to use the word "thigh" in public. It's a sin to pass up easy beer money.

He probably wouldn't use the word in private either, but there was no way we were ever going to be able to test that theory.

Lensky, the rat, was leaning back in a chair at the far end of the table, tilted so far back he could rest his feet on the table, and grinning as he heard our sartorial deficiencies listed.

"Now, as to conduct appropriate to a formal party. You will all, of course, make eye contact with the other guests, smile, and reply courteously when spoken to.

"Miss Thorn, 'Hojotoho!' is not an acceptable greeting or response to a greeting; nor is 'Heiaha!' With all due respect for Wagner, you will please confine yourself to English tomorrow night.

"Mr. Sutherland, not only is your Mexican hat inappropriate, but so is any attempt to perform the Mexican hat dance. Particularly as badly as you do it."

"Miss Kostis, 'There are a lot of numbers larger than four' is not an excuse for being found on a balcony with no fewer than four inebriated trustees, one of whom is attempting to drink champagne out of your sandal and flooding the balcony. Please wear shoes that do not leak this time."

"Mr. Lensky…."

Lensky's feet swung off the table and his chair crashed forward. "Wait a minute! I don't have to go to this thing! I'm not your employee!"

"Ms. Harris has already mentioned to me how much she is looking forward to greeting a representative of the agency which has been so supportive of the Moore Foundation."

I don't know anybody else who could have gotten so many multi-syllable words out of what was basically, "You have to go."

And what was that about Lensky's agency being so supportive? What else were they secretly funding? I hadn't actually seen any men staring at goats on campus, but maybe the remake was, "Men Who Stare at Grackles." I narrowed my eyes at Lensky, but he gave me a slight shake of his head, implying that he didn't know what Dr. Verrick was talking about either.

After Dr. Verrick had finished crushing our egos, he went off to home, or his other office in the math building, or some other place where he would be safe from muttering, resentful peasants.

To my surprise, Lensky sympathized with us.

"I would have brought doughnuts if I'd known about this."

"You should always bring doughnuts," I said, "somebody's always having a crisis. Oh, I forgot, we outsourced that to Annelise. Dough-nuts, not crises."

"I need beer. Now," Ingrid announced.

"Let's drown our sorrows together," Ben said, taking her arm.

"Don't forget to eat something!" I called after them.

The break room was remarkably quiet now that Dr. Verrick and two of the muttering peasants had left us.

"So," Lensky said, moving briskly past the pastry shortage, "you've all been pulling my leg about being introverted scholars, and the truth is that you're wild party animals."

"I think it's the open bar," I said. "It's a natural chain of events. When forced to make conversation with Deans and Regents we drink too much, and when we drink too much our... imperfect socializa-tion... manifests itself in sometimes overly dramatic ways. Also, there's the hope that we won't be invited back. They have three or four of these parties a year, you know. And Dr. Verrick makes us go to all of them."

"Party animals," he said.

"And then there's Ingrid's Viking hat. She has some sort of person-ality change when she puts on her horned helmet."

"Has anybody told her that Vikings didn't actually wear helmets with horns?"

"They do in Wagner, and that's good enough for Ingrid."

"But those aren't Vikings! They're Germans! And they didn't wear horned helmets either, nobody would, it's dumb to put *handles* on your head when you're fighting!"

"Look," I said, "you can either argue historical and military accuracy with Ingrid, or you can wait until tomorrow night and see what happens when she wears the hat."

"Didn't Dr. Verrick tell her not to?"

I thought back over his exact words. "No. He told her that she wasn't a shield-maiden, and he told her not to bring the sword. I don't think he said anything specific about headgear. Bet you five bucks she wears it tomorrow night."

"Done," he said.

Beer money was coming in easy today. But I felt a little bit guilty about winning it *this* easily. "Aren't you awfully ready to bet on somebody you really don't know all that well?"

"The way I see it," he said, "if I win, I'm five bucks ahead, and if I lose, it'll be worth it to watch Ingrid swinging from the chandeliers and yodeling. Besides, I'm already betting more than I'd like to lose on somebody I don't yet know all that well."

He looked at me as if he was mentally removing my Ramones T-shirt. Ok, it was a little small even on me, and the much-washed cotton clung to my body. My face grew hot. "If you're betting on a one-night stand before you go back to DC, you've already lost."

"I was hoping for more of a multi-night stand," he said softly, "with lots of reruns."

"I don't do long-distance relationships."

"Is that really the problem? Or is it that you're too much of an intellectual snob to dally with a commoner who got a lousy degree in Criminal Justice from a lousy state college?"

"That chip on your shoulder really shuts down intelligent conversation, you know."

"That would explain why I haven't heard any from *you* yet."

At this point, a proper couple would either fall into a long, passionate clinch or exit angrily in different directions, slamming any available doors. Another sign that Lensky and I weren't meant to be together: instead of stomping off he lingered to clear up, he said, some minor logistical points.

"I won't be in tomorrow," he said.

"What, spooks take weekends off?"

I think the funny noise I heard was his teeth grinding. Or it might have been another comment in Polish. Hard to tell.

"Not until this investigation is concluded... But tomorrow's different. I'm going to take my niece out. I haven't even seen her since I got to Austin."

That might have had some connection with the fact that he'd spent the last three evenings with me. I refused to feel guilty; he was a grown man. He had to figure out his own priorities.

"What do you do when you take her out? Go to the shooting range?"

"If that's what she wants," he said, "that's what we'll do. I don't have any firm plans made. She's eleven years old and sharp as a tack; I expect she'll have her own plans for tomorrow."

"And her parents are okay with her going around with a guy who carries a gun?"

He had a strange expression. "Remember, my brother died when she was a baby. As for Pamela – her mother – well, I don't think Pam would notice if *Linda* started carrying. You've heard of helicopter mothers? Well, Pam's like the inverse of that. She believes in giving Linda her own space. Lots and lots of her own space. So much space that for all practical purposes, Pam might as well be in the next county."

He sounded disapproving, and I felt a little bit sorry for Linda's mother. It couldn't be easy having your child-rearing critiqued by a spook.

"But I'll pick you up tomorrow night. Say, seven?"

"We don't have to be at the party until nine. And you don't have to pick me up; there's no rule that we all show up together in one tight, unhappy, anti-social clump. Though," I admitted, "that seems to be the way it always happens."

"Well, maybe it's time for a change. I thought we could have dinner first. And then I'll escort you to the Foundation Fiesta."

"You don't have to do that."

"I insist on it," he said. "From the sound of it, I'll need somebody to watch my back."

CHAPTER 14

LENSKY HADN'T SAID what he was doing Friday night, but evidently it didn't involve me. Which was really just as well; after Ben's experience, Ingrid and I were dying to see what we could do with the stars augmenting our visualizations. I got a ride home with her because the clouds rolling overhead looked like the prelude to a May downpour. There's nothing tentative about rain in Texas. We don't get a light drizzle or a 'gentle rain from heaven.' Texas can go from drought conditions to flash flood warning on a moment's notice.

We didn't experiment jointly, of course. Without any need for consultation, she headed to her bedroom and I to mine. She had a head start on me; she didn't have to scoop books, magazines, and laundry off the floor to give herself a place to work. I needed to get the room semi-organized so that I would be able to tell if anything changed.

After Ben's experience I was shy of teleportation. I decided to do set selections instead. This meant that I was sitting quietly on the floor, thinking beautiful thoughts about the Axiom of Choice, when Ingrid's mind was already careening around in non-metric spaces.

And the earth moved.

Okay, not literally. When I picked myself up after the crash, the floor was still level and none of my books had slid out of place. So it probably hadn't been the long-anticipated shift of the Balcones Fault. It hadn't been the thunder now rolling across the sky, either; that was still going on.

The sound of cursing in the next room guided me to the epicenter of the non-quake. Ingrid was sitting in a corner, and there were books, cinderblocks and boards strewn all over the room.

"*One book*," she said. "Yesterday I couldn't lift a sugar packet. Today I thought that using the stars to augment my work, I'd be able to bring something as heavy as a book to me. I was trying for *Counterexamples in Analysis*. What I got was the bookshelf and all its contents."

"We need to calibrate the effects, don't we?"

I got back to my own visualization before she could draft me to help rebuild her cinderblocks-and-boards bookcase.

There were trees around the apartment building. I didn't know what kind of trees and I thought they were probably not all the same kind. Deciduous, not conifers, and that was about as far as my nature study went. It would be interesting to collect a selection of their leaves and get Ben or somebody to identify them. The rain was already pounding them; it should be easy to detach a wet leaf from each tree.

Slow, counted breaths to calm my mind. Clusters of bright points in the darkness; sets. Let the leaves of each tree denote a set... I reached out with imaginary hands and touched a rain-wet leaf, felt the connection going one way down into the earth and the other way into a mapping onto the bright points of an imaginary set. This was easy! I could sense the other trees around the building and map each tree's leaves onto another set. I could sense some of the space around the trees, too; the rain-slick shingles of the roof below the leaves, birds huddled under branches. But that wasn't relevant. I thought about the Axiom of Choice, let a single point move out of each set, leaving a glowing line behind to denote its path...

For a moment I thought it was raining in my room, as wet leaves pattered down around me.

Success!

The leaves were followed by harder, heavier objects. I put a book over my head for protection and recognized... shingles.

And now it *was* raining in my room.

~

Saturday morning.

A *reasonable* part of the morning: around ten. No pre-dawn shenanigans today. At least, not jointly.

Lensky was off, it was the weekend anyway, what were we doing in Allandale House?

Comparing notes, obviously. We'd all given in to the temptation to experiment with our augmented abilities. Well, Ingrid and I had, anyway. And Ben looked as if he hadn't gotten any more sleep than we had.

Ingrid and I had wondered how to get in touch with The Man Without a Cell Phone. It was probable that we could now do it without using the phone system, but communication had not been a research focus for any of us. Of course it hadn't. Look, one of Ingrid's contributions to our apartment furnishings had been the "Enough Interaction" doormat that Lensky had objected to.

It was possibly a little bit weird given that our apartment was on the second floor of the building, but we loved it so much that we put it out in the hall anyway.

So it was fortunate that we found Ben in the break room, bleary-eyed and poking ineffectually at the coffee maker. "It's about time you got here," he said by way of greeting. "Can either of you make this thing work?"

"How did you know we were coming in this morning?" It was going to be beyond creepy if his augmentation included the ability to read our minds without us even noticing. Ingrid took the carafe to the bathroom to fill it with water, and I broke open one of the packets of super-cheap coffee that Dr. Verrick provided. We thought he got them from a discount sales warehouse in California that had to ship them around the Horn to reach Texas.

"Don't worry, I didn't read your minds," Ben said. Which was not the most reassuring thing he could have said under the circumstances. "It just seemed obvious. Some of these effects are... really powerful. I think we should do our experimenting in the private side of the Center until we have a little more control."

"I hate to admit it, but you're probably right," Ingrid said. Her hands weren't as beautifully smooth and white as usual. Heaving cinderblocks around tends to mess up your manicure.

"I do see your point," I said reluctantly. The roof shingles which I'd unintentionally selected the previous night were now hidden under my bed, just in case the landlord started looking for someone to blame for the leaky roof.

"And what minor disaster did *you* get into last night?" Ingrid asked Ben.

"Uh... I'll tell you... *after* you two tell me exactly why you agreed with me so quickly." Damn! We should have bickered for a while. It was out of character for all three of us to agree on something without arguing, and Ben had picked up on that. We condensed our confessions into one sentence apiece.

When Ben headed for the pot, Ingrid blocked him. "No coffee until you tell us what happened to *you*."

Ben took off his glasses and slipped them into his shirt pocket. His brown eyes looked even vaguer than usual. "Littlefield Dorm again."

"Well, that's not so bad. You were doing that even before... oh. No. The first time it happened was right after Lia gave us the stars. Still... you didn't get caught this time, did you?"

"Not the first time."

"You went *twice?*"

"The second time was all right too."

"When *did* you get caught?"

"The seventh time, and I got away. I don't think Ms. Barker got a good look at my face."

Ingrid sank into a chair, incidentally clearing the way to the coffee maker. I let Ben have the first cup; he looked seriously under-caffeinated. "Merciful heavens, Ben, what were you playing at? Didn't it occur to you that if you kept revisiting the scene of the crime you were bound to get caught eventually?"

"I didn't do it on purpose!" Ben shouted. "It just *happened* every time I thought about... well, you know."

"And you called Lensky a sex maniac!"

"That's different. He makes crude jokes at you of his own free will."

"And you, apparently, think about *you know* every thirty seconds. How did you manage to stay out of Annelise's dorm after the seventh visit?"

"Remember what Mr. M said about us needing to be in actual contact with the stars to augment our powers? I put them in an empty jar and left it in the kitchen nook. *Then* I finally got some sleep."

Ingrid reached for the tea ball she had hung around her neck rather than sewing a bag for the stars, and took it off. Very carefully. By the chain.

I didn't have such a convenient solution. I couldn't exactly take off my cutoffs. I'd just have to remember not to stick my hands in my pockets.

"Did you punch air holes in the lid?"

"They're perfectly all right," Ben said defensively. "Look, here they are all dancing around in their jar."

The jar did seem to make a good container for his stars; even in daylight, they formed a blue-white cylinder of dancing light contained by the glass.

"That was a good idea," I allowed grudgingly. "But we're going to have to learn to work with them. We can't go around grabbing our Tea Balls of Power every time we want to augment our work and dropping them when the augmentation is too strong."

"Yes, but let's work on the private side." Ben grabbed his jar, turned sideways, took three steps and disappeared.

I poured a second cup of coffee into one of the spare mugs and took both cups over to the private side.

"Why two?" Ingrid asked when she popped into the hall a moment later.

"I want to try something."

Mr. M. had slept through our experiments last night and had been too dozy to play necklace this morning. Which was sort of ok; he was really too big to make a convincing necklace. Now I drew him out of my belt loops, making sure not to catch his metal scales, and set him down on my desk with a cup of coffee in front of his pointy little head.

He started sniffing almost immediately. Then his beak began opening and shutting, and finally he raised up his front six inches, made an arch, and dipped down into the coffee.

"What is this potion?" he demanded when he came up for air.

"It's called coffee. I don't think they had it when you were last... active."

"It must be the drink of the gods, which in my time they reserved for themselves. I feel younger and shinier already." He dipped his head back into the coffee. I chugged my own cup. I was already beginning to feel that I might need extra caffeine to deal with Mr. Younger and Shinier.

"I wonder where it goes," Ingrid whispered. "Seeing that most of him is... no longer organic."

I wondered too, but felt it might be too personal a question to ask a newly awakened Babylonian mage.

Wherever he was putting the coffee, he certainly put it away in a hurry; his cup was empty almost as soon as mine was. "Ahhhh!" he announced. "I feel young again – not a day over two hundred." He slithered from my desk to the chair and then to the floor, and began racing from office to office in a series of shimmering figure-eights. This time I definitely heard, "Whee!"

"We'd better ration the caffeine in future," Ben murmured. "About a third of a cup, you think?"

"Just wait until he discovers sugar," Ingrid said.

The first experiments were tricky, and Mr. M. was too jazzed up on coffee to be any help; he just raced around the offices getting underfoot.

We wanted to keep whatever we did behind the wall that closed off the private side. That meant *really* strict control whenever we thought about teleportation. Given Ben's recent history, we forbade him to do any personal experimenting on the first tests; he could take notes while Ingrid and I worked on office-hopping for a while. We focused on just moving between offices, and found that as long as we carefully avoided thinking about anything beyond the private side, we could make the desired move instantaneously. For me the experience was like a split second in darkness, a flash of two curved surfaces that barely touched, and then I was in the target office. Conveniently, we materialized in spaces that weren't shared by furniture. I guess that part of the laws of physics must be compatible with Brouwer's theorem.

After we felt confident that we wouldn't overshoot, we tried holding hands with Ben (whose stars were still on his desk) and jumped from one office to another without telling Ben where we were going.

One of us could move him, but it felt like wading through knee-high water. When we tried a joint effort, there were some problems with coordination. "You know what?" Ingrid said after the second time our attempt at a joint jump turned into an inconclusive tug-of-war. "We need to *name* the things that work and practice until the name triggers the image in our minds."

"Huh. I've been calling it 'Mapping' and I don't want to get triggered to jump every time some bozo mentions looking at a map."

"How about "Brouwer" for the Brouwer Fixed-Point Theorem, since that's what we're using?" Ben suggested.

"Um. I don't know. Didn't he prove a number of other theorems?"

"None as well-known, and none that we're using right now. And nobody's likely to casually mention Brouwer." He thought for a moment and appended, "As long as we stay out of the math building."

Ingrid and I practiced jumping together while he gave us the cue. He was right; after a few practice sessions, the image of two surfaces connected at a single point flashed into my mind the moment he said the word, and our combined jumps from one office to another became a thing of beauty. Adding Ben didn't help much, since we were still keeping him away from the stars, but it was a lot easier than it had been with only one of us trying to move him.

Worked like a charm. There was really only one tiny little glitch. By way of winding down Ingrid and I did a couple more solo jumps and... Well, I was hungry, and since it was Saturday nobody had brought in any pastries, and at the conclusion of one jump I found myself in the doughnut shop at 28th and Guadalupe.

So it shouldn't be a total waste, I bought a selection of doughnuts before picturing my own office and thinking the magic word.

"What took you so long?" Ingrid demanded.

"I got a teensy bit distracted." I proffered the box of doughnuts as a peace offering. Ben and Ingrid carefully set their collections of stars aside and we transferred to the break room. For some reason Ingrid and I were ravenous. We blew through three plain glazed doughnuts each while Ben was working on the one with chocolate icing.

"Workings require power," Mr. M. informed us while undulating up and down the table.

"Isn't that what the stars do? Give us more power?"

"There are different kinds of power. You will find that you need to replenish your bodies more frequently as you move to greater workings. What are those round pink things?"

Ingrid quickly closed the lid of the box on the remaining two doughnuts (pink icing with chocolate sprinkles). "Coffee cups... topologically speaking," she added, making her statement kinda-sorta true.

("I just wasn't ready for Mr. M. on a sugar high," she told me later.)

"But without coffee in them? Ah, well..." From somewhere, Mr. M. drew a great heaving sigh of disappointment and looked pointedly at the empty coffee carafe.

By unspoken agreement, we all ignored the hint.

"You seem to have made significant progress with Travel," Mr. M commented.

Ingrid frowned. "I don't know. Lia screwed up this last time."

Nice way to put it. She'd been happy enough to eat the doughnuts, hadn't she?

"More important," said Mr. M, "despite surprise and the distraction of a strange environment, she was able to invoke Travel well enough to get herself back here immediately. I believe you young mages are ready to expand your horizons."

Ben frowned. "We sort of decided that we'd keep it all inside the Research Division until we had complete control."

Mr. M. made some remarks about slackers and cowards which I prefer not to repeat.

"Tell the truth, Mr. M. You're all jazzed up from that coffee and you want to go places and do things."

Mr. M. curved his neck around and studied his reflection in his own shining scales.

Having said that, I realized that I felt that way too. Across the table from me, Ingrid's eyes were sparkling.

It was, of course, possible that we were just on a sugar high. That, or we'd been possessed by the Monumentally Bad Idea Fairy, because Ben wiped the chocolate icing off his mouth and said, "Why don't we get Crowson's computer?" and both of us agreed. It was Saturday; chances were the office would be empty. But just to be on the safe side, we agreed to focus on the vacant office next to Crowson's – a place all three of us had clear memories of.

To lean even more on the side of safety, Ben said, "We should really take Annelise with us. In case, you know, some little thing goes wrong."

If anybody ever tells you that he's taking extra precautions just in case some little thing goes wrong, *run*.

But we didn't know that at the time, and when Ben borrowed my phone to call Annelise and invite her along, we felt that we'd covered all the bases and were practically going on a picnic. And Mr. M. egged us on. As he pointedly mentioned about half a dozen times, it had been a long time since he'd seen anything but the Turtle Pond and the inside of Allandale House. Of course he *could* go exploring by himself...

A vision of coeds shrieking and athletes pouncing on the silvery streak that was Mr. M. chilled my blood, followed by the even more chilling thought of what he might say if interrogated. He didn't really understand how our world worked, he was completely devoid of tact, and I could all too easily envision him being stomped to death by someone who was freaked out by a talking snakebot with a turtle head.

The suggestion that maybe he should stay in the office did not go over at all well. And there wasn't really any way I knew to imprison a slithery, untrustworthy mage whose powers were far beyond ours – look at the languages, for instance, how did he do that? I'd sweated blood just to make it through French II. I probably wouldn't have passed if it hadn't been for Aunt Alesia, whose breakfast-table habits had given me an accent that made whatever I said sound good no matter how ungrammatical and unidiomatic it was.

Anyway, we cooperated with Mr. M. – not having much of a choice – and by the time Annelise got there, he had squirmed though the belt loops on my cutoffs and had coiled his extra length of tail around his head until he looked like an exceptionally ornate belt buckle.

Annelise listened to Ben's brief explanation, but I wasn't sure she'd really taken it in. She seemed to be more concerned with the doughnut box on the table. "I'm sorry, I didn't realize I was supposed to do coffee and pastries this morning."

"You weren't," Ingrid reassured her. "Only during the week – and even then, only after we get the petty cash box set up. The way Dr. Verrick pays, you could wind up spending your whole after-tax salary on snacks for us."

But Annelise kept apologizing, and so we may possibly have failed to brief her quite as thoroughly as would have been desirable.

"Will you take Annelise and I take Ben," Ingrid asked, "or the other way round, or should all four of us hold hands?"

Mr. M uncoiled the extra length of tail long enough to say, "Circles move and amplify power." Then he rewrapped his delicate silvery coils and, to all appearances, fell asleep. Possibly he was tired after that caffeine-fueled race up and down and around our offices.

"You know, it might be safe to let Ben use the stars," I said slowly.

"Under the circumstances..." I cut my eyes to where Ben, grinning, had already captured one of Annelise's hands.

"He's not likely to go off-target," Ingrid agreed. "And we won't get drained so fast; it's got to be easier for three to carry one than for two to carry two."

I dug into my pocket and offered Ben a handful of stars.

"Keep yours, I can use my own," Ben said.

Great. Holding Annelise's hand was already reducing his IQ. "Half of an infinite set, remember?" I held out the little sparkling cloud and Ben took it.

"Office 21A," I said, and waited a moment to be sure everybody had the dusty office in their minds. *"Brouwer!"*

CHAPTER 15

THIS WAS the farthest we'd gone yet. The inter-office jumps had seemed instantaneous; even the accidental jump to 28th and Guadalupe didn't feel as if it had taken any time. I didn't know if it was the longer distance, or the fact that we were essentially carrying Annelise as dead weight, but I had just a bare second or two to experience the in-between space we traveled through. I was a glowing point of light, sliding along an arc from one vertex to another...

My feet came down on the bare, dusty boards of Office 21A and I felt a sharp pang of loss. I looked at Ingrid's and Ben's faces and saw the same sentiment there.

"We really must try some long-distance jumps," Ingrid said.

"Soon," Ben added, and then, *sotto voce*, "Whee."

"That was, you know, really strange," said Annelise. "And uncomfortable. And I didn't like not being able to see anything."

Ben looked at his new love and disappointment was written all over his face. Here he'd just had this incredible, life-altering, beautiful experience, and Annelise couldn't share it.

It was a reminder that this talent of ours would always set us apart from the rest of humanity, and it was sobering.

"I don't hear anything from next door," Ingrid said, a little too briskly. "Do we think it's empty?"

Keep listening while I do the locks," said Ben. "Or – no. Lia, you and Annelise listen, and Ingrid, shield me once I get this door open and have to work in the hall." He gave me an apologetic look. "I really am going to show you Camouflage as soon as we have a moment to breathe."

I accepted the implied apology with a nod and ambled over to stand by the wall with Annelise.

Ben knelt and muttered to himself. A moment later the deadbolt zipped back as if it had been shot from a gun, and clanged against the metal shield in the wall. Ooookay. If nobody came out of Crowson's office to investigate that peculiar and very loud noise, I thought we could probably assume it was empty too.

We *definitely* needed to learn how to calibrate these effects.

Annelise and I stayed at our listening posts while Ben and Ingrid moved out into the hall. I felt the sense of a blue-black lowering sky replacing the ceiling, and the air quivered like Jello. I took Annelise's hand. "Don't get scared," I whispered to her. "It's just Ingrid working Camouflage."

She gave me a blank look. "I'm *not* scared. Nothing's happening."

Just then someone outside the building screamed.

I sidled up to the window and peered out. There was a woman in the yard next door, screaming again and pointing at the top of our building. "It's gone! It just disappeared!"

Oh, shit. *Calibration!* I scooted to the door of 21B as quietly as I could and shook Ingrid's shoulder. The air around us cleared and the light went back to normal. Ingrid gave me an annoyed look.

"What did you do that for? I can't hold the visualization with you grabbing me like that."

"That's why," I said in an undertone. "You disappeared the entire building."

She gaped at me. "I *did*?"

"Maybe just the second floor. This woman outside suddenly started screaming, "It's gone!" and pointing at us."

"But..." Then Ingrid repeated my thoughts. "Oh, shit. Calibration! I *knew* we needed to do more research before going out in the field."

Oh, yeah? She had been just as enthusiastic as the rest of us about this little excursion. If we'd had time and privacy, I might have pointed that out. As it was, I merely hoped – desperately – that we'd turned off the invisibility before anybody else noticed. I didn't think even Annelise would be able to talk us out of this one.

I slithered back into 21A while Ben was still working on the locks of 21B and took another peek out the window. Two men – one young enough to be her son, one middle-aged – had joined the screaming woman. Who had stopped screaming. There appeared to be a vigorous argument in progress. I didn't dare open the window to listen, but if I understood the body language at all, it went something like this:

Screamer: *It disappeared, I tell you! I was looking right at it and it just-just winked out!"*

Older man: *Sure looks to me like it's still there, honey.*

Screamer: *Yes, yes, it's back* now, *but it went away for a minute!"*

Younger man: *Mom, I ran outside the second I heard you scream, and there wasn't a thing wrong with that building.*

Older man: *Have you had your eyes checked lately, honey?*

Both guys were shaking their heads and shrugging now. Probably telling each other that women were too imaginative. Great, no corroborating witnesses. I thought we were home free. It did seem kind of rough on Screamer; I hoped she wouldn't end up in Shoal Creek Mental Hospital.

From the sounds next door, we were into 21B now. I went to congratulate Ben and to share the good news that the cops were prob-ably not going to be too interested in the Case of the (Briefly) Disap-pearing Building. Coming into the office with a grin on my face, I was startled to see Ingrid and Ben looking as if they'd flunked qualifiers.

"What's the matter, you guys?" This was a *much* classier looking room than poor old empty, dusty 21A. Built-in office furniture lined two walls, with a glass desk in the corner. Very clean, Swedish-type style. Very...hard to hide anything in here.

"We're idiots," Ben said.

"It's not here," Ingrid contributed.

"I should have realized. It's a laptop. Of course he takes it home with him."

"Are you sure about that?" If it was a desktop machine, might it be concealed behind one of those gleaming wooden doors?

"Of course I'm sure," Ben said. "I spent some of the worst minutes of my life inside that computer. Do you think I wouldn't remember the make and model? It's a MacBook Pro, same model Ingrid has."

Both of us had spent some time quietly envying Ingrid's sleek, lightweight, up-to-the minute machine. I believed Ben when he said that he'd recognized Crowson's as being the same model.

Annelise had followed me and heard the bad news. "Well, if he takes it home with him, why don't we just go there?"

"Don't know where he lives."

"There's bound to be something in here with his address…" Her voice trailed off as she surveyed the sleek perfection of the room. It did look as if Crowson had actually achieved the paperless office that "experts" have been predicting since I was in second grade. Or maybe kindergarten.

Ben straightened. He'd thought of something; I recognized the just-proved-a-theorem look on his face. "And you know what, we're still being stupid. We don't have to go to his home address, and anyway we'd have to go by conventional means since none of us have seen it. What we need to do is go where his *computer* is."

"We haven't seen that either."

"Sure we have! We've all seen Ingrid's MacBook, haven't we? Well, just visualize that… with a kind of slime oozing out of it. That's what Crowson's computer feels like to me."

At this point you might have thought at least one of us would have realized that we didn't need Crowson's computer right away, today, and that it was silly to break – excuse me, *teleport* – into a possibly occupied house or apartment on the off chance that there was nobody in the same room as the laptop just now. What if Crowson was using the thing, what were we going to do then? Wrest it from his hands?

I can only say that we were slightly over-exhilarated by the stars, the sugar, and the glory of sliding through 3-space as a point of light. Annelise had taken Ben's hand and was gazing at him in a kind of hero-worshipping way, so her intelligence was also off-line at the moment. As for Mr. M., he still claims that he thought of all these problems and a few more, and whenever he says that I ask him why he didn't speak up at the time.

In any case, we joined hands again and the three of us visualized a MacBook oozing slime. Ingrid was first to nod that she had the picture firmly in her mind, then Ben and I nodded simultaneously and I said, "Brouwer."

There was no chance to enjoy the journey this time; as soon as I said the word we were in a room furnished much like Crowson's office, all sleek wood and gleaming glass. With an elegant little MacBook Pro sitting on a table, hooked up to its charger.

We have vowed never to reveal who whooped, "Got it!" at sight of the laptop. It could have been any of the three of us, and whoever made the mistake doesn't deserve to live in infamy. In any case, just as Ben scooped up the laptop, while he paused to unplug the charger, a flurry of grackles screeched at the window and a sleek, dark-haired man entered the room. His hands flickered towards us and then stopped, frozen.

"Make haste," Mr. M. said. "This working will not bind a mage for long." He had uncoiled himself and was staring at the frozen man, his head swaying back and forth as if he were a cobra.

Even before he finished the sentence, I saw the man's lips moving. But we had all joined hands again and I said *"Brouwer,"* just as his hands began to move again.

"Next time," Ingrid said as she slumped against the wall of the break room, "we need to agree on an escape destination before we start. It's just dumb luck that we were all thinking about Allandale House."

She took a deep breath. "Ben, let's get that thing behind the wall."

A whirlwind of grackles swept through the open window and clustered in one part of the room. Ingrid's hands automatically went to her head. The grackles swooped out again, leaving two splotches of bird poop and the black-haired man.

Ingrid and Ben turned sideways and vanished.

He was closer to Annelise than to anybody else.

Annelise was the only one of us who couldn't Möbius through the dividing wall.

Crowson had already had a gun in his hand when he appeared. A split second later, he had Annelise's arm in his other hand. He yanked her around in front of him and put his gun to the side of her head. "Give it back now, and nobody gets hurt."

I turned sideways and vanished.

CHAPTER 16

PAMELA HAD GIVEN Lensky an address about ten miles north of the university. He looked around the street after parking. Not wonderful, but not too bad either: a street of aging duplexes with live oaks overhead. Probably more renters than owners, but most of the residents kept their lawns and houses in good shape. There weren't any dead cars parked on lawns or in the street.

Pam had told him that he would recognize her place by the prisms on the porch. As a rule Lensky preferred street numbers clearly painted on the curb, but fair enough; there was only one porch with so many hanging crystals that they'd probably blind a man when the sun fell on them.

Just as there was, thank God, only one Pamela Lensky.

Pam was, of course, not ready for him. Equally of course, she was full of apologies. "I *meant* to have her all ready for you, Brad, but she insisted on going over to her friend's house first thing this morning."

"No problem," Lensky said, "just phone and ask her to come home now."

"Well, I don't exactly... I *think* she was going to Angelina's... but it might have been LaTonya's, and... Jerry, what's LaTonya's last name?" she called back into the bedroom.

"No idea." A balding man in a T-shirt and jeans appeared at the bedroom door. "Don't you have the number? Christ, it's not like the kid has that many friends!"

Pam then thought that maybe she *had* written LaTonya's number on the back of an envelope, or maybe it had been the grocery list that she always kept stuck to the refrigerator, but she'd gone grocery shopping yesterday and maybe the list was still in her purse. She handed the purse to "Jerry" and asked him to look through it for her because her nails were still drying. He rolled his eyes and dumped the entire contents of the purse onto the kitchen table.

There wasn't a grocery list, although there seemed to be most of the other things you'd want to sustain civilized life in the event you were stranded on a desert island: two lipsticks, emery boards, loose cough drops, a pack of nicotine gum, a handful of bobby pins, an empty packet of tissues, a smartphone..."

"I know, it's in my phone!" Pam picked up the phone gingerly and tapped at it with the tip of one fingernail. "Just let me get to Contacts..."

"Hi, Uncle Brad," Linda said. "You're early." She tapped the oversized sports watch on one thin wrist. "You said ten-thirty, and it's only ten-twenty-five." She gave her mother a tolerant glance. "You didn't seriously expect *Mom* to keep track of the time, did you? I set my alarm so I'd be sure to be back in time."

When asked what she would like to do, Linda said firmly, "Go to the park."

"Oh, hon, you go there all the time. Why don't you ask your uncle..."

"I like the park. And I want to show Uncle Brad all my favorite places."

"Oh, all right, but do try not to get all muddy, and for Heaven's sake stay out of the creek, and don't go making poor Brad climb trees or..."

"Right, Mom," Linda interrupted. She took Lensky's hand and dragged him out of the house. "If we wait for Mom to finish the list of things not to do, we'll never get there," she explained once they were outside.

Lensky inspected his niece. She reminded him of the street where she lived: a little shabby, but basically healthy and clean, he thought. She was a delicate-looking little creature, fine-boned and slim: not much Lensky there, she was all Pam on the outside, down to the wispy white-blond hair that was at present her best asset. Someone – probably Linda herself – had pulled the long hair back and braided it. With those outsize spectacles on her face, she was no beauty, but on the whole he approved. Pamela, in the unlikely event she consented to go to a park, would have gone in high-heeled sandals and a fluttery dress. Linda's sneakers and shorts were much more appropriate. Some Lensky common sense inside, then.

"So, things going all right, Lins?" he asked, using her baby nickname.

"Just fine, Lens."

Lins and Lens; it had been hysterically funny to her at five, and the nicknames had stuck.

"Who's Jerry?"

"Mom's new friend. He's all right," Linda volunteered.

"This latest move okay with you, then? You aren't missing your friends back in Trenton?"

Now he got the I'm-going-to-tolerate-this-stupid-adult look. "I didn't *have* friends in Trenton, Uncle Brad."

"So, it's better here? Pamela mentioned a girl called Angelina and a LaTonya?" Was anything harder than getting information out of an eleven-year-old? His interrogation skills deserted him with Linda.

"Oh, well, *Angelina's* real..." The pause for thought was longer than it should have been. "Real friendly," Linda finished. "But she doesn't understand important things. Like the park."

The much-mentioned park was only a few blocks from Linda's house, a longish strip of green with a creek running through it, a jogging path beside the creek, benches between the street and the jogging path. "To get to the best part you have to..." Linda paused, looking doubtfully at a tangle of shrubbery with an approximately

Linda-sized opening in it. "Mom told me not to drag you around, but you *do* want to see the good part, don't you, Uncle Brad?"

Lensky assured her that his life would not be complete without a tour that included the good part of the park, and that he was accustomed to getting through obstacles much more formidable than a tangle of leaves and branches.

He was rewarded for scrunching down and contorting himself to get through the shrubbery by a bouncing, much happier Linda. She took his hand again and drew him along to see the layers of rock and earth exposed where the creek had cut through, the "witch rocks" that had been worn down until there were holes right through them, and – the grand finale – the Glass City. This was a collection of miniature cairns and towers built entirely from the bits of broken glass that the creek had tumbled among pebbles until all their sharp edges were smooth.

Lensky whistled at the sight of the Glass City. "That's a very impressive construction."

Linda smiled. "I built the bridge just this morning. To celebrate you coming to town."

The "bridge" was constructed of the longest scraps of glass held up by cairns of smaller pieces. But...

"I thought you were at LaTonya's this morning?"

He waited for Linda to tell him that the two girls had come and worked on the Glass City together. Instead she looked down, turned pink, and scuffed one sneaker over a tree root. "Well, LaTonya isn't exactly... well..."

"Interested in this stuff? Did you quarrel? How old is LaTonya, anyway?" Lensky thought his niece was past the age of angrily taking her toys and going home.

There was a panicked look on Linda's face. "Um, I'm not exactly... She's fifteen," she said quickly. "Almost sixteen."

Lensky wasn't sure he believed in a teenage girl content to pair off with his eleven-year-old niece. "And where does she live?"

"Um, close to here?"

"Can you show me?"

"No! Leave me alone!"

A new interpretation of Linda's story occurred to Lensky. "Would LaTonya by any chance be a... an imaginary friend?"

"Uncle Brad! I'm <u>much</u> too old for imaginary friends! LaTonya is... um... well, sometimes Mom can be..."

"Ah. LaTonya's a convenient excuse for getting out of the house alone?"

Linda nodded. "I knew you'd understand."

Lensky understood all right; he wasn't entirely sure he approved. Pam was already casual enough in her care of Linda; look at the way she hadn't made sure, this morning, that she knew whom Linda was visiting and had a phone number. He might need to have a little talk alone with Pam – perhaps Monday, while Linda was in school? Or would Pam be working?

Linda would feel that he'd betrayed her.

Could he talk Pam into being a little more vigilant without giving away the secret of LaTonya?

"Anyway," Linda said, with the air of one who'd faced down and conquered a difficult question, "I don't think I'm going to work on the Glass City much more. It's pretty, but kind of... *childish*, don't you think?"

"I think I'd like to get some pictures of it," Lensky said.

"Yeah, but..." Linda stated the real reason. "There isn't a lot more I can do with it. So... I'd like to become a geologist and analyse the rock strata here and at roadside cuts, but..." She heaved a sigh. "That's the trouble with Austin. Look at the creek here. What do you see?"

"Well, that looks like a layer of limestone," Lensky guessed.

"Right. And that's another layer of limestone, and below that is *another* layer of limestone. It's sedimentary all the way down!"

What a kid, thought Lensky. Imagine knowing words like 'sedimentary' at her age! No wonder she had trouble making friends.

"So I think I'm going to be a bird whisperer. Come on!" She tugged him back towards the shrubbery.

"A what?"

"Haven't you ever heard of horse whisperers? Like that, except with birds."

"Can you do that?"

"Sure. In *Freckles* there's this great scene where all the birds come and take food from his hands."

And the woman who wrote that book had been some kind of nature freak, hadn't she? So who knew, maybe it was possible.

"The good thing about being a bird whisperer," Linda explained, "is that I'll have plenty of material to work with."

Lensky managed the contortions necessary to get through the shrubbery again and stood up with a sense of relief. He didn't really fit into an eleven-year-old's play space.

"See?" Linda waved her arms and a dozen black birds headed for the trees, cackling their grievance. "Birds all over the place!"

Lensky looked at the birds. To him they were identical bundles of blue-black feathers. "Uh, Linda, I'm pretty sure all of them are grackles."

"Oh, I know *that*. There are *lots* of grackles in Austin around this time of year. Well, actually I think there are always grackles, but Angelina says there are more of them in spring. And people come and sit on those benches and throw them bits of bread, so they're used to coming here. See, I'm going to start small and just concentrate on calling *one* kind of bird. Then after I do the grackles I can move on to whatever birds are around here in the summer. Don't you think that's sensible, Uncle Brad?"

"Very mature," he assured her.

"And then when I can call half a dozen - *who's she?*" Linda's sentence switched directions entirely and ended on an aggrieved note.

Spiky black hair framing eyes too big for her face, oversized T shirt advertising some rock group he'd never heard of, cutoffs and sandals. She hadn't been behind them a moment ago, had she?

"Ah – Linda, this is Thalia Kostis, one of the researchers I work with. Thalia…"

"We don't have time for introductions," Thalia interrupted. "There's a problem. Need you back at Allandale House."

She sounded breathless. "Thalia, can't it wait? I've got my niece here…"

"Okay, give me your gun and I'll take care of it."

"*No!*"

Linda tugged at his sleeve. "Uncle Brad, I can go home by myself. I do it all the time." She sounded firm and sure of herself, and older than she'd been a few minutes earlier. He looked at her face and saw – yes, disappointment, but also a maturity he hadn't seen before. Blast Pam, Linda probably had to be the adult in that relationship more often than was healthy. And now he was going to do exactly the same thing to her.

"Are you *sure*, Linda?"

"It's three blocks! I was walking farther than that to get home from school in fourth grade!"

"Okay. Tell Pam I was called away by an emergency, and I'll be back as soon as I can, all right?"

CHAPTER 17

I WAS proud of the speed with which Lensky oriented himself. His gun was in his hand and pointed at Raven Crowson as soon as the room solidified around us. "Drop your weapon!"

Crowson smiled and pocketed his gun. "Certainly, now that I have what I came for." He released Annelise and picked up the MacBook that Ben had apparently just set down beside him. A flurry of black birds swooped through an open window, cawing and shrieking and surrounding him. When they scattered, he wasn't there any longer, and Ben was giving me a dirty look.

"You didn't need to bring *Boris* into this. We had everything under control!"

"I'm happy to hear that," Lensky said. His own weapon had disappeared back under his sport coat. "Perhaps you'd like to tell me what "everything" consists of? And don't leave out the part where you brought an armed enemy into the office on the one day you knew I'd be out."

He sounded relaxed and friendly, but that little vein was jumping at his temple again.

"Um – I'm sorry for interrupting your time with Linda. Wouldn't you like to go back to her now?"

"Not using the same transportation system, whatever that was," Lensky said firmly, "and my car's still parked in front of Pam's house. I'll call Uber when I'm ready to go back. But I have *plenty* of time to hear your stories." He pulled up a chair and straddled it. "Who wants to go first?"

"I have a seminar," Annelise said, and bailed on us before anybody could ask what kind of seminar met at mid-day on Saturdays.

"We might not have that much time," Ben said. "As soon as Crowson opens that laptop he'll – he'll probably be back."

"If you'd gotten here sixty seconds earlier," Ingrid said bitterly, "I'd still have my MacBook."

"Oh!" Now I got it. "You pulled a switch. That was *brilliant.*"

"It bought us time. But not much..."

Lensky interrupted. "Start at the end. How did Crowson get in here? Did he just walk up the stairs, or what?"

Ingrid shook her head. "He just... appeared. I think. There were all these grackles screeching and zipping in and out the window, and then he was in the middle of them. Same way he disappeared just now."

"Well then," Lensky said very calmly, "perhaps the first thing we should do is *close the goddamn window.*" He dragged his chair over to the outside wall, stood on it and turned the crank that opened and closed the louvered windows above his head.

"Can you magicians do anything else to close off the building?"

Ben shook his head. "Like a shield or something?"

"Like a shield or something," Lensky agreed, tight-lipped.

"We haven't actually worked on anything like that yet. Mr. M?"

"I can keep the Master of Ravens from this part of the building," Mr. M. said from where my belt buckle would have been, "but I shall require more of the magic brew."

"Coffee coming right up," I promised him, and escaped into the break room to make it. I was feeling strange: shakier than that quick teleport out and back should have made me. "Sugar," I muttered, and more or less inhaled the two doughnuts with pink icing while the coffee dripped. The sugar helped, but not quite as much as it had before; I still felt dizzy, and my pulse seemed to be racing.

When I brought out coffee for Mr. M. and me, I noticed that Lensky was also looking kind of shaky, and he seemed fixated on my waist – oh! "You hadn't met Mr. M. before, had you?"

"Is it *alive?*"

Mr. M. launched into a stream of multilingual invective that I could only admire. The general burden of his remarks seemed to be that not only was he alive, he had been alive for nearly three millennia and had forgotten more about being alive than Lensky had ever known. Furthermore, the solecism of calling him an *it*.... Well, you get the idea. I wish I'd pulled out my phone and recorded the whole thing for future reference; I could have been rude to people for a year on the basis of that tirade alone.

Even Lensky's eyes were wide with admiration – or something – by the time Mr. M. ran down, slithered out of my belt loops and deigned to accept a cup of coffee.

"Sir, I apologize for failing to use your preferred pronouns," he said very calmly – maybe too calmly. "Thalia, where did..."

Ingrid's aggrieved screech from the break room interrupted him. "Lia, did you eat *all* the doughnuts?"

"There were only two left," I said. "And I needed sugar after that transport job."

"Ben and I did rather a lot of teleporting too, you know."

"I know, sorry, how about if I go downstairs to the vending machine and buy Cokes for everybody?" That would get me out of the room while they told Lensky the story of our morning's adventures.

I came back with two Cokes for Ingrid and me and a root beer for Ben, who has peculiar tastes. They'd drifted into the break room, all but Mr. M., who was doing his cobra sway again and looking fixedly at the spot where Crowson had appeared and disappeared.

The atmosphere in the room seemed extremely tense. Lensky, Ingrid and Ben were all seated on one side of the table, looking at me. "Everybody caught up on recent events, then?" I said chirpily while handing out the soft drinks.

"We decided to wait for you," Ben said.

"Since most of it was your idea," Ingrid added.

That was not exactly how I remembered it. But since I still felt funny, even after inhaling two doughnuts, I didn't argue with them. I just thought back over the morning and tried to explain to Lensky how we got *here* from *there*.

He didn't interrupt, but I could feel a deep blue-black cloud sort of forming around him as I took him through the morning. It got darker and thicker with each turn in the story. When I finished, he took a deep breath and just stared at us for a long, long time.

"So," he said finally. "You decided to go adventuring with abilities that you admit you had not fully explored. You frightened the neighbors by accidentally rendering half of a house invisible."

"*Briefly*," I reminded him.

"You then invaded a private home without even finding out first whether it was occupied..." I couldn't quite tell what annoyed him more, the illegality or our incompetence.

"We couldn't check," Ben tried to explain, "the way we were jumping, we focused on the computer, not the place."

"And for a grand finale, you 'jumped' back to Allandale House, apparently leaving enough of a trail through the universal ether that the owner of the computer was able to follow you. The *armed* and *criminal* owner."

"And we kept the computer," Ingrid pointed out, "and could have got rid of him with no trouble. We didn't need you to show up with *another* gun. You should stop treating us like some zany undergraduates who've been pulled into the Dean's office for a stupid prank."

"Ingrid's right," I said. "Why don't you go take your niece out to lunch and leave the *professionals* here to examine Crowson's computer?"

"Do I dare?"

"If you want to sit in an empty break room all afternoon," Ben said, "we have no problem with that. *We* will be on the Research Side, doing the work you've been so desperately eager for us to do."

A sour look crossed Lensky's face. I think he really hated it that we could move into a space he couldn't reach without our help. "All right. If you need me to rescue you again, try my cell; you don't have to display your special talents all over town. God knows how I'm going to explain this to Linda."

At the door he paused and looked back at me. "Seven. And for God's sake wear something that won't get you arrested for public indecency."

～

Linda watched her uncle and the strange girl turn sideways and get... narrow. They became a blinking image that narrowed to a line and then disappeared altogether.

"I always *knew* the Narnia books were non-fiction," she said to an outsize grackle at her feet.

The bird responded with a friendly "Gack, gack, gack," flapped its wings, and went spiraling up into the sky with a very un-gracklish smoothness. Linda watched until it disappeared and then turned her attention to the nearest bench, where several more grackles were waddling about in the hope of discovering some neglected particles of birdseed from the lady who sometimes sat there, or maybe some nice juicy bugs.

"Gack?" she said questioningly as she walked toward them. "Gaaaack?"

They let her get within ten feet of the bench and then flew upwards all at once to perch over her head on a live oak tree, where they gackled and gacked loudly. Linda had a feeling they were laughing at her.

"I guess I don't speak their language – yet."

But how was she to learn it if they wouldn't stick around and chat? Linda sat on the bench and practiced being still, being inanimate, being just another bit of the park furniture. Time crawled by. The shadows of the trees shortened slightly. Grackles sailed past from tree to tree. Two joggers came around the curve to her right, inspiring a fresh burst of gackling overhead, and disappeared down the long straight path to the left. A couple of large grackles ventured down to peck around the ground ten feet from Linda's bench. "Gack?" she said softly.

The birds didn't even look up. Linda tried to tighten her throat and make the word sound more like a caw. "Gack."

One of the grackles looked up and fixed her with a bright black eye. It looked as though it was about to speak, Linda thought.

Then the Lady With Three Dogs came around the bend and both birds fled with a derisive "Gack, gack, gack!"

Linda liked dogs and was used to seeing these three in the park on weekends, but she did wish the lady had chosen to walk them earlier or later. Still, it wasn't the dogs' fault, and they were used to being petted by Linda. The lady paused as she always did, and Linda fondled Buster's floppy brown ears, scratched under Bozo's black chin, and rubbed Mutt's head. She remembered that she really did like Buster, Bozo and Mutt, and gave them as much attention as she could before the lady moved on with a friendly nod.

Now there was somebody sitting on the next bench over. Linda glowered at him. Dogs were one thing, extraneous adults quite another. How was she to achieve her destiny as a Bird Whisperer if people kept interfering like this?

While she was giving the unwanted man her best death stare, the two grackles that had been at her feet earlier fluttered out of the live oak. At least, she thought they must be the same two; both were considerably larger than the other grackles. They circled the stranger's head. Then they settled on the bench, one on each side of him. He talked softly for a few minutes – so softly that Linda couldn't catch a word – and then the grackles flew up, circled him several times, and returned to their live oak.

Linda had stood up and come closer without really thinking about it. Now she burst out, "How do you *do* that?"

"Oh, I don't do anything," the dark-haired man said. "The grackles do it all. It's just a matter of speaking their language."

Mom periodically warned Linda against speaking to strangers, but a fellow Bird Whisperer hardly counted as a stranger. She came right up to the bench. "Will you teach me?"

"Can you learn?"

～

Ben may be the only truly intelligent person in the Center. He called in Jimmy, who brought over some equipment and copied the entire contents of Crowson's laptop to a little box he called an external hard drive. "Now," he told us, "you can swap the laptops back. All of his information is in here."

Ingrid eyed the box suspiciously. "It is?"

"*Look* at it," Ben said. "The way we looked for Crowson's laptop."

Ingrid touched her tea ball and I put a hand in my pocket. The palm of my hand prickled ever so slightly, as if I'd put it down on a bowl of very fizzy soda. And now I could see that Jimmy's box seethed and simmered with the same sickly miasma that covered the laptop.

"Double, double toil and trouble," Ingrid murmured, dropping her hand. "Lia, how are we able to see this? *I* wasn't visualizing, were you?"

I shook my head. "I think Mr. M and his stars have their own magic, and it's got nothing to do with mathematics."

"I don't *like* this. How do we know what we're doing if it's not based on proven mathematics?"

It didn't seem to me that we'd known a whole lot about what we were doing before Mr. M entered our lives. The real difference was that now we were able to do a whole lot more of what we didn't understand.

And boy, was *that* ever a reassuring thought.

"There is something distinctly eye-of-bat and toe-of-frog about it," Ben agreed.

"Isn't it supposed to be bad luck to quote *that* play? Will you two please knock it off? We need to figure out how we're going to switch the laptops back."

Ingrid shivered. "I do *not* want to jump blind into That House again. Not unless we get the spook back. With his gun."

"Break room," I said. "Pizza. We're going to need fuel."

We discussed the problem until the pizza guy arrived. Ben was in favor of simply dropping Crowson's laptop off with the police. Ingrid and I explained, separately and then in chorus, that this was an excruciatingly bad idea. Not only was it unlikely that the cops would bother to examine a laptop that had been dropped off at their equivalent of a Lost and Found box, but when Crowson discovered he'd been cheated we'd have nothing to trade him for our lives.

"*And* my MacBook," Ingrid finished. "I want that back."

Paying for the pizza was a slightly fraught experience. I pointed out that I had already sprung for soft drinks and doughnuts that day; Ingrid and Ben pointed out that these cost considerably less than a large pepperoni half-pineapple pizza. In the end it was less a question of fairness than of what we could find in our pockets, which left all of us feeling equally broke.

"Wouldn't it be nice if Dr. Verrick authorized a credit card for the Center?" I said after the delivery guy left with most of our liquid holdings.

Ben looked thoughtful. "This *is* a work-related expense, isn't it?"

"And Annelise could use it to pay for the morning doughnuts."

There was a light, metallic, scaly sound – sorry, but I don't know how else to describe it – as Mr. M. twined up a wooden leg and onto the table. Naturally he wanted to know what we were eating, and it didn't help when Ben described it as one of the five basic food groups. Fortunately he decided, after a couple of disdainful sniffs, that turtle-snakes did not care for pizza. He did, however, demand more coffee.

We stalled. Our first experience of Mr. M. plus caffeine had been eerily similar to us with magic stars: you didn't know what was going to happen, and it was likely to be more exciting than you bargained for. He demanded testily (his default state) whether we wanted him to solve our current problem or not.

Well, when he put it that way...

Fueled by another cup and a half of watery Center coffee, Mr. M.

raced around the break room while we finished off the pizza. And when I say "around," I don't mean east to north to west to south. I mean east to *up* to west to *down* and variations on that. After that last half-cup he was whizzing around us at such a rate that it was almost like being inside a ring of shining metal scales.

Ingrid quietly poured the rest of his coffee down the sink while cleaning up the other trash on the table.

"The problem is so simple that it is a waste of my unique abilities to solve it," Mr. M announced.

He was on the ceiling at the time. We twisted our necks to look up at him. Was he serious? His little turtle head didn't give a lot of clues. Box turtle faces have basically two expressions, Open Beak and Closed Beak. Mr. M., as you'll have gathered, favored Open Beak.

"The man Crowson is not at his residence," Mr. M. announced. "He appears to be in an open space with many trees and rushing water. Ah, there are also benches. Two scantily dressed people who are not running fast enough to escape any competent pursuit. A child..."

"Park!" Ben said. "Has to be a park. Open space, benches, joggers."

"You are familiar with the place?"

Ben slumped. "There are a lot of parks in Austin. You couldn't take us there?"

"Why? I thought it was the silver box you desired."

"The MacBook, yes."

"It does not look like a book. Is it perhaps the casing for one? And how does the scroll unwind?"

Explaining computers to a snakebot with a Babylonian mindset... oh well, Jimmy could take that on. Later. "It's not important now," I said before we could get mired between computer-nerdery and antique-book-nerdery. "We need to exchange the silver box we have for the silver box he has, without his knowing. Is that possible?"

"Not from here," Mr. M. said. "You must first bring the two boxes into compatible spaces."

There were a number of theorems that could be applied to the problem, but we didn't have time to experiment. "Can you take us to the park where he is so we can swap boxes?"

There was an irritable tap-tap-tap on the ceiling. Mr. M. was getting pretty good with that tail. "Of course not."

Ben took a hand. "Really? The greatest mage in ancient Babylon can't work a simple teleportation?"

Tap. Tap. Tap. "Of course I can take you to that park, but you will not be able to exchange the boxes. As I already told you, the man left his box at his residence."

He hadn't, actually, but just this once we all three managed to refrain from pointless bickering.

After all that angst, the transfer was relatively simple. We remembered Crowson's living room from -

"Oh, wow," Ben said. "It was just this morning, wasn't it? Feels like a week ago."

Stealing computers, evading men with guns, getting bawled out by Lensky had made for a rather full morning. And that's not even counting the part where we accidentally made the top half of a building disappear. Briefly.

Ben and Ingrid teleported together while I collected whatever change we could scrape together and went down to the vending machines for more liquid sugar. When we got back, Ingrid buried herself in her beloved machine to verify that nothing was lost or damaged, while Ben and I retreated to my offices.

"Any trouble?"

"None," Ben said. "It's a good thing we had an indoors location to jump to, though. There were about a million grackles raising hell outside."

"Grackles." Something was nagging at the back of my mind.

"What about them?"

"The man calls himself Raven Crowson. You think he's got some kind of deal with black birds?"

"Grackles aren't related to ravens. They're not even *Corvidae*." Biology majors know these kind of things.

"Yes, but do they know that? *I* didn't know it. And grackles have been giving us a lot of grief this week."

"Mmm. Crowson, Master of Ravens... and Grackles?"

It was all academic now, and rather anticlimactic. There was no desperate hurry to analyze Crowson's data now; he would have no reason to suspect we'd copied it and pulled a double-switch on him. We were all tired, and when Ingrid reminded us that we were committed to go to the Foundation party that night I decided to go home and enjoy some hours of solitude. Ben announced that he and Jimmy would take a preliminary look at the computer image until he went to pick up Annelise. "Just stay out of her dorm," Ingrid warned him.

Ben patted his jar full of light. "Conventional transport all the way. I'm going to drive home first and leave my little friends on the kitchen counter."

It was hot and I was too tired to enjoy the long walk to the apartment. Ingrid wasn't good for a ride; she wanted to go shopping for a new dress for the party. I collected Mr. M., put one hand in my pocket, visualized our ratty apartment and said to myself, "Brouwer!"

Apart from the bit where I lay on the living room floor counting dust bunnies under the sofa for fifteen minutes before staggering into the kitchen for something to restore my blood sugar levels, it worked like a charm.

As you might say.

CHAPTER 18

LINDA WASN'T AT HOME.

Neither were Pam or that guy Jerry. Had they all gone out somewhere while he was at Allandale House?

The house was unlocked, naturally, and there was a note on the kitchen table. *"Going out for lunch. Can you stay with Linda until we get back?"*

Linda wasn't with Pam and Jerry, and she wasn't at home. How long could it take a kid to walk three blocks? Lensky was out of the house and headed to the park before the small fraction of his brain that remained calm could compute the answer.

On the second block he saw Linda coming towards him. He almost didn't recognize her; she was walking briskly, head up, shoulders back. Practically bouncing!

"Looks like being alone in the park was more fun for you than showing me around," he greeted her.

"Oh – well, I wasn't exactly alone."

"Did a friend show up? Or what?" He was tensing in anticipation of the *or what.* Had Pam never taught Linda not to talk to strangers?

"Um, I was practicing. Talking. To the grackles." Her eyes shifted away from his face.

"You must have been pretty successful, if that entertained you all this time."

Linda rolled her eyes. "Uncle Brad, how about we start this conversation over? You say *Linda, I'm so, so sorry I had to leave like that.* Then I say *That's okay, I'm pretty good at entertaining myself.* And you say *Can I take you out to lunch to make up for it? Where would you like to go?*"

"How about we start over *after* the part where you tell me you remembered not to talk to strangers in the park?"

Linda shrugged. "What strangers? There wasn't anybody there except some joggers and the old guy who feeds the birds."

"Sounds like you know him pretty well."

His niece shrugged again. "He's okay. For, you know, an old guy. Now can we have *my* conversation?"

"How old exactly?"

"It's not polite to ask people their age," Linda said primly.

Vaguely dissatisfied, Lensky gave up for the moment. "All right. Where would you like to go for lunch?"

"Chuck. E. Cheese," Linda said promptly, and sputtered at the appalled look on his face. "I was just teasing you, Lens. That's for *little* kids."

"Softening me up, you mean, Lins? Where would you really like to go?"

"Can we go to Sonic? And they bring food out to your car window and we eat in the car?"

Lensky was so happy to be back to "Lens/Lins" and not going to Chuck E. Cheese that he would have agreed to far worse than Sonic.

I had way too much time to think before seven.

I had managed to avoid discussing exactly how I'd jumped to find Lensky. I had some hope that I'd never have to talk to him about it, but Ben and Ingrid would track me down eventually and I needed to decide what to tell them. Stress? The desperation of the moment?

Yeah, right. I might be able to slide that past Ingrid and Ben. It wasn't working on me, though.

After Ben's involuntary visits to Annelise, I'd realized that I too might be able to jump to a person rather than a place. If I knew the person. And there was some sense in which I knew this person far better than I should have, especially after just one week's acquaintance. Just as Ben knew Annelise, in some very important ways I knew Bradislav Lensky better than I knew even Ben Sutherland, my friend and colleague. Better than I knew Ingrid Thorn, my *roommate* and colleague. I couldn't explain how. I had made that jump on feelings, not reason. On the way his lips had felt. On the way *I* felt when he kissed me. On broad hands exploring my body with surprising gentleness. On a rock-hard body pressed to mine and generating extreme heat.

Yep. Even with talking turtles and snakebots and pornography and disappearing buildings and a pocketful of stars, I hadn't managed to lose that feeling.

But there were other things in the mix too. Talking in the shade of Scholz's, or while eating chips at El Patio; learning the obstacles he'd faced growing up. His surprising protectiveness towards me. The calm with which he'd handled his introduction to Mr. M. All that was the real problem: I *liked* the man.

And, yes, I still wanted to get back to that session on a broken couch and find out where we went from there. No, still lying to myself. I knew perfectly well what would happen if we got anywhere near a couch again, and I was *so* not going to go there. Not with somebody who belonged in a totally different world from mine, who was going to go back to Washington or thereabouts any day now, and who would almost certainly – once back in the normal world – look back on this week in Texas as a period of insanity and hallucinations. Who would, once he regained his sanity among normal people, never want to be anywhere near the Center again.

Not with somebody I liked but who had no desire to be in my life – not that I could blame him for that – sometimes I didn't much like being in my life.

I could predict the future of that path, and it hurt too much.

Far safer to keep him at a distance until he actually did leave.

Having made that decision, I dressed for the Foundation party.

~

His eyes widened when I came downstairs. "Wow. I... Just wow."

I think it was the sandals he liked: black, high heels, with skinny patent leather straps. The rest of me was pretty much business-as-usual: spiky black hair, spaghetti-strap black dress with a fitted top and a short, flared skirt. Oh, not *that* short. I'm not stupid enough to waste money on a dress that I can't wear to the Foundation's formal parties, especially since those are the only times I wear it. Contrary to Dr. Verrick's insinuations, the skirt is not so short that you can see all of Texas on my thigh.

You can't even see the Gulf Coast.

And despite Mr. M.'s complaints, I was *not* wearing him to the party. I did not want to have to explain him to the head of the Foundation or her VIP guests.

"You clean up pretty well yourself," I said. The close-fitting black T shirt and pants showed off his physique a lot better than the loose blazer he usually wore to cover his gun. "Where do you hide the gun in that outfit?"

"Ankle holster, if I were carrying, but I'm not. This isn't business, and Whitney Harris doesn't like guns in her house; I am actually civilized enough to cater to our hostess's preferences. Are those *the* sandals?"

"That I was wearing last time? Yep."

His eyes went up and down my legs, lingering on the patent leather straps.

"I can't imagine why Dr. Verrick – why any man with a pulse would object to your wearing those."

I wasn't going to touch that compliment with a ten-foot pole. I'd started feeling short of breath when he appraised my legs, and I'd already made my decision on that matter. "I think it was my *not* wearing one of them that upset him."

"Ah. Keep your shoes on and all will be well?"

"I only took them off because the heels were killing me. The champagne thing was definitely not my idea."

"Right. How drunk does a man have to be before he tries to pour champagne into a sandal?"

"Stick around tonight, and you'll probably find out."

I had been anticipating Tex-Mex or barbecue, but he surprised me again by having reservations for a place near Sixth Street. I'd never felt rich enough to go there, but it lived up to my image of a romantic restaurant with low lighting, flowers and candles on the tables, and a menu in French.

The prices were anything but romantic.

"You look a bit dubious. Don't you like this place?"

"I... It's awfully expensive. I'd be just as happy to go out for Tex-Mex again, you know."

Lensky laughed. "What – claim our reservations here, get seated, take one horrified look at the prices and rush out? Would we ever live that down?"

"Well, it's not like I'm likely to eat here again."

"That would be a pity," he said. He was looking at me, not at the menu. Well, I could understand wanting to avert his eyes from the prices. "I was thinking we could make it a tradition. You know, every time I come to Austin?"

He'd never been to Austin before and I doubted we could come up with enough terrorism and national security related problems to bring him or anybody else from his agency back here. Certainly not on a regular basis. Good of him to remind me why I'd decided to keep him at a distance.

I studied the menu – and thanked God for Aunt Alesia. They had descriptions of everything under the French names – they weren't delusional about Texans' foreign language abilities – but thanks to my aunt, I would be able to pronounce whatever I ordered.

"It's not exactly the usual student hangout."

"You're not exactly the usual student, Thalia."

"I'm not a student at all, not any more." Sometimes I felt sad about that. For nearly four years I had known exactly who I was and where I belonged: math major, UT Austin, Dr. Verrick's Honors Topology course. Being attached to a "research institute," that would never, ever be allowed to produce any publications occasionally seemed like a step backwards.

Lensky laughed. "With those stacks of textbooks on your desk, and weird line drawings pinned up on the walls, and notes on everything you've tried since you joined the Center? It doesn't matter whether or not you're registered in a degree program. You'll always be a student."

"I suppose you think that's impractical. Unrealistic. Immature..." My parents had given me a wide range of adjectives to use in this context.

"No," he said softly, "I think it's admirable." He put a hand over mine. I noticed again how warm and dry his hand was. It felt very good there. "We're not the same kind of people. I like finding out what the bad guys are trying to do so we can stop them. Straightforward, concrete results. I couldn't live in the world of abstractions you inhabit; I'd be like a fish out of water. But that doesn't mean I can't respect the work you do."

Our food arrived; in the process of arranging plates and finding cutlery his hand and mine got separated, and it seemed silly to reach across the table again, to try to repeat a casual contact. No matter how pleasant it had been.

"I'm afraid we haven't given you the best impression of our research this week." All we did, it seemed, was stumble from one crisis to the next, with no real understanding of what we were doing. And Lensky had been quite sufficiently acerbic about the process.

"On the contrary. I've been putting a great deal of pressure on you to find results. If you... all three of you... rushed into situations you couldn't control because of that pressure, the blame is mine. I just wish you would work *with* me instead of taking off behind my back and getting into trouble."

I took a few bites of salad. "Well. I don't think that will be a problem for much longer, do you?"

"Depends. Are you going to tell me you've suffered an attack of common sense?"

"No, but I think you'll be going back East soon. If Ben and Jimmy spent the afternoon picking apart Crowson's computer, they probably have enough information for you to wrap up this investigation." The trout meunière tasted like cardboard for some reason.

"And if they haven't got enough information?"

"Then I doubt there's very much more we can help with." I thought back over the week and hoped what I was about to say wouldn't be the death of our funding. "I don't think we did any more for you than one good computer hacker could have done. And they would have done it without any of the drama."

Lensky's lips twitched. "Ah, but it wouldn't have been nearly so much fun. My life would be immeasurably poorer had it not been enriched by experiencing involuntary teleportation and a talking turtle-headed snakebot. Not to mention The Case of the (Briefly) Invisible Building, and your account of Annelise's unforgettable 'explanations.' Very creative girl, that."

For some reason I felt cranky when he stopped there. "I'm glad to know we've provided you with some amusement. Is it time to go yet?" My big clunky plastic sports watch was fine for timing experiments - I mean proper, controlled experiments, not the wild-ass near-catastrophes we'd had this last week - but it detracted from the Little Black Dress look. So I wasn't wearing it.

"No, not nearly. We've got plenty of time for coffee and dessert." He pointed out an item on the dessert card.

"Death by Chocolate?" I was about to say that I was too young to die, but the description promised three kinds of chocolate. I hadn't more than picked at my healthy fish and salad, and it would be only prudent to have something in my stomach before visiting the Foundation's infamous open bar. "Bring it on," I said. Being prudent.

Some people might have considered the multiple layers of chocolate cake with chocolate custard filling and chocolate glazed icing to be more than slightly overdone. I looked on it as one of the seven wonders of the world and told Lensky so.

"I don't think I can eat all of it, though," I said regretfully. "I won't be burning off any calories teleporting or doing any other… transformations… tonight. Why don't you ask for an extra fork?"

He did just that, and loaded it with enough cake to give me pause. "I hope letting you have a fork isn't going to be a decision I regret all my life."

"It's hard to get through life with no regrets," Lensky said, demolishing another level of my dessert. "For instance…"

"Yes?"

He surprised me by putting his fork down and changing the subject. "Have I completely alienated you this week? If so, I'm sorry. Well, even if not, I'm still sorry. I know I've made some inappropriate comments. I'm really not like that… most of the time. The thing is that it's hard for me to look at you without thinking about sex, and the more I try *not* to think about sex the more those kinds of remarks come out."

When the man decided to quit fencing, he really let it rip, didn't he? I had a little trouble swallowing my comparatively modest bite of chocolate and chocolate with chocolate icing. "You haven't… alienated me. Although you *have* made some extremely inappropriate comments."

"But you like me anyway?" He sounded anxious.

"If I didn't, I wouldn't have let you buy me Truite Meunière and Mort au Chocolat."

"Oh? What would you have let me buy you? Coquilles Saint-Jacques and Iles Flottantes?"

His accent was atrocious.

"Nothing at all," I said, first taking advantage of his distraction to finish off the chocolate cake.

"In that case… "

"Not going to happen. I already decided that," I told him.

Damn the man, he still looked hopeful. "Then you were thinking about it?"

I nodded. "And what I was thinking was that the last thing I need is to get involved with someone who practically has his boarding pass for a flight back East."

"Long-distance relationships can work."

"Sometimes. When the parties have enough in common."

"We have a lot in common."

"What, exactly? Apart from the fact that we're both thinking about sex right now?"

His silence was answer enough. I filled in the blanks for him. "You're going to go back to your normal life among normal people, and after a little while you'll be embarrassed that you were ever crazy enough to hang out with someone who can do magic and who wears a talking turtle as a belt, and you won't really want me to come to Washington even if I can figure out how to jump that far, and I… don't want to have that conversation." I had to blink fast and swallow hard to get the last phrase out.

"What conversation would that be?"

"The one where you explain how you like me as a friend but you don't really want me to come to Washington."

"Actually, I live in Virginia."

"Tomato, tomahto," I said.

"And I didn't think your magic tricks involved predicting the future."

"This one doesn't require second sight."

"Dammit! Can't you give me credit for not being quite that shallow?"

"No. It'll hurt too much when I'm wrong. Isn't it time to go yet?"

"It certainly is," he said, pulling out a handful of bills and throwing them on the table. "*Past* time."

CHAPTER 19

DESPITE OUR UNCEREMONIOUS departure from Chez Nous, we were rather late getting to the party at Whitney Harris's house. This was all Lensky's fault and absolutely not my idea. He claimed that he got lost on the way to the house and that his GPS sent him up to the top of Mount Bonnell. Oh, all right, it was true that the GPS directions he was getting sent him there, but was that an error or had he given it the wrong address accidentally-on-purpose? I hadn't watched when he was entering it. Also, I told him the road we were on would dead-end there, and he didn't listen.

Mount Bonnell isn't much of a mountain, in fact hardly even a hill. But it falls off steeply to the west and gives a good view of the river. Lots of people go there at night. Purely to appreciate the view, naturally. And nobody disturbs the people sitting in parked cars below the stairway to the top of the hill. Wouldn't want to interfere with their aesthetic experience.

That Lensky not only knew where to park on the way to a party in a lake house, but knew to conceal the address he gave the GPS from me, demonstrated once again that his intelligence-gathering abilities, or his agency's, were superb. Mind you, I didn't object. We spent about an hour in his car while he tried to persuade me to change my mind about our relationship. I will say that he could be extremely persuasive. But I had promises to keep and a party to go to, and before we became unforgivably late I sat up, ran my fingers through my hair a couple of times, and reapplied lipstick.

"I really do have to go to this thing, you know. And I want to get there before Dr. Verrick leaves, so I can get credit for showing up."

"You *are* showing a great deal of up," Lensky murmured, tracing the outline of Texas with one finger. But he started the car, I pulled my skirt down, and this time he did give the GPS Whitney Harris's address.

The Moore Foundation parties were always at Whitney's house. The Foundation itself was housed in an unimpressive square building just off Balcones. Whitney Harris personally was housed in an extremely impressive modern house right on the lake, all glass walls and jutting shapes and spiraling iron stairs: a much better venue for a party.

Lensky whistled when we drew up in front.

"I thought you'd say that. Quite the showplace, isn't it?"

"How the hell does she get flood insurance?"

"Maybe she doesn't." *Men.* Show one of them a major work of modern architecture lit up like a fairy castle, and they talk about insurance. I'd always heard that the Harrises were richer than God; Whitney could probably replace this house out of the family's petty cash box.

He kept on muttering about things like insurance and mortgages and how much did the Foundation pay this woman, anyway? until we crossed an open deck and merged with the party that was spilling out of sliding glass doors and creating a serious noise pollution problem on the lake.

Just as we got there the music changed to something I knew all too well. "Oh-oh," I murmured.

"What's the matter?"

"Listen." Not easy, over the alcohol-fueled chatter, but the music was getting louder as we spoke. "Recognize that?"

"Isn't it the theme from *Star Wars*?"

I would have thought that too, if I hadn't been living with Ingrid for almost a year. "Nope. She's persuaded somebody to put on Wagner. That's *Ride of the Valkyries.*" Which Ingrid considered good music to wake up by... or to create havoc by.

The music seemed to be coming from under our feet. I edged through the crowd until I could look over an iron railing at a room half a flight of stairs below us. It was kind of like tracking a hurricane: what first looked like random movement gradually coalesced into a spiral shape moving through the crowd and spreading chaos behind it.

And the leading edge of the spiral was Ingrid, almost falling out of an extremely low-cut sparkling silver dress, the infamous horned helmet over her flowing gold hair, leading a conga line.

Lensky whistled again. "Who'd have guessed it?"

"It's certainly a creative adaptation to the loss of her sword. I didn't even know you *could* conga to Wagner."

Ingrid's voice rose above the music and laughter. "Another hero for Valhalla! And another! And another!" Laughing, the men she tapped chugged their drinks and joined the conga line. Ingrid saw us watching and headed her train of victims towards the stairs.

Two of them sat down on the stairs and gave up on the conga line, and the rest fell out of step but managed to hang on somehow. Ingrid was flushed with excitement. The guys not actually behind her in the conga line were flushed with the hope that with the next dance move she might actually fall out of that dress.

"And Dr. Verrick gives *me* grief about indecent exposure," I said to Lensky. "Hi, Ingrid. That's a nice dress you're almost wearing."

"A foretaste of the rewards awaiting heroes in Valhalla! Heijaha!"

To my recollection of Norse mythology, Valhalla was more about getting drunk and fighting than about fondling semi-clad Valkyries, but Ingrid always did have her own unique interpretation of these things.

"This could be bad," I told Lensky. "Not only is she wearing the magic horned hat, but also she's let her hair down."

"She certainly has," Lensky said, looking more appreciative of the view than *I* really appreciated in a man who'd just been trying to talk me into moving to the back seat of his car.

Our interchange caught Ingrid's attention and she tapped Lensky on the shoulder. "Come with me to Valhalla, hero!"

"Uh-uh," I said, getting between them. "Lay off, Chooser of the Slain. I don't choose that you should slay this one. Yet." I could always change my mind if he got obnoxious again.

"Let him choose! Will you have a hero's death and unending mead in Valhalla, or will you die a slave and be buried in the dirt?"

I nodded at Lensky. "Ah, if you pick the Valhalla option, pay up first, okay?"

"Pay?"

I indicated Ingrid's helmet. "You bet five bucks she wouldn't wear it."

"None of my bets are paying off," he grumbled, giving me a dirty look and five dollars.

The music was dying down and the conga line – excuse me, the Chosen Slain – were starting to grumble. "Restart!" Ingrid called, and the Ride of the Valkyries began again. "To the mead-hall!" She led her Chosen Slain back down the stairs and towards the bar. Always a popular direction, that.

I looked at Lensky. "How chivalrous are you feeling?"

"Want a dragon slain?"

"No, I want a drink, and the Valkyrie's Slain are blocking the bar."

"It might be better if you fetch the drinks. At least she's not going to try to take you to Valhalla."

A reasonable point, that. But before I could address it, a hand emerging from the crowd offered me a frozen Margarita. "No salt, no lime, am I right?" Bob Burkett smirked down at me.

"Bob, this is Bradislav Lensky, who's consulting with us at the Center. Brad, Bob Burkett, one of the trustees of the Moore Foundation."

Lensky narrowed his eyes. "Is this one of the men involved in the sandal incident?"

Bob looked down his nose at Lensky. "*Consulting.* Is that what you call it?"

Heaven knows what he meant to imply. But before any more less-than-friendly words were exchanged, the music changed again, this time from Wagner to something with a beat. "Lia, they're playing our song!" Bob said. "Dance with me!"

"Can't dance in these sandals."

"Yeah," Lensky put in, "she can barely stay vertical in them."

I glared at him. "Too bad you're so unlucky in your bets."

"*I* can fix *that*," Bob Burkett said, putting his hands around my waist and lifting. "We'll just dance like this, my Greek goddess, my sweet." He swung me round and we merged with the crowd of people shuffling and swaying in time to the music.

"My margarita!"

"Get you another," Burkett promised, somewhat breathlessly. "Just as soon as – the music – stops!"

Before he'd finished that promise, a guy with a short white beard tapped him on the shoulder. "My turn, Burkett!"

Bob passed me to him and struck out for the bar. I hoped he was sober enough to remember that I still wanted a margarita. No salt, no lime.

I didn't remember White Beard's name, but I thought he was on the U.T. Board of Regents. It didn't really matter, as within three turns he passed me off to the idiot who'd tried to drink champagne out of my sandal at the last party, and who was now trying to waltz to music that was seriously waltz-unfriendly. Andrew – Andy – somebody? At least being carried like this meant that I wasn't getting my feet stepped on.

Unfortunately, it also meant I had no way to resist when Andy Whoever decided that we should be dancing cheek to cheek. I just had to hang on and hope somebody else cut in fairly soon.

After a few turns I decided that Andy's motives were pure. He hadn't tried to feel me up. Most likely he just found it easier to balance my weight like this; it took serious wrist and arm muscles to hold even a small woman up and away from your body.

Lensky, now, could probably have done it all evening with no strain.

Just as I was thinking this, he floated into view with, oh joy, the margarita Bob had given me just before starting this mad dance. "You can put me down now," I told Andy.

"Ah, but why would I want to do that? Dance with me until dawn, my darling Lia!" He was slurring his words more than a bit, and I began to worry about being dropped. And probably trampled in the crowd.

Two large, strong hands took my waist from behind. "You heard the lady," Lensky said. He pulled, Andy lost his grip, and for a moment it looked as though we were about to make Moore Foundation history by all three hitting the floor when two of us weren't even drunk.

Lensky set me on my feet. During that slightly unbalanced moment he'd managed to turn so that he was between me and Andy. "I'm beginning to understand," he said grimly, "why Verrick warned you to mind your manners."

"Me? That's not fair! I am totally innocent. *I* haven't been picking people up and whirling them around."

"No, but you enjoyed it, didn't you?"

"Not nearly as much as I would have if anybody let me finish my drink." Lensky had stashed the margarita glass in the hands of a statue – well, I thought the flat black pieces were hands, anyway. They were the right height relative to the rest of the piece, which would make the red cube the head and the long white springs the legs and torso.

It wasn't a frozen margarita any more; more like a tequila slushie. A melting one. I took care of that and looked around for a refill. The bar, sadly, was still mobbed by Ingrid's admirers.

Lensky took the glass out of my hand. "You don't need any more." He gave the crowd a disapproving stare. "None of these idiots need another drink. They can't afford to drown any more brain cells in alcohol."

"Who died and made you God?"

He raised his hands. "Fine. Fine. Go drink yourself into a stupor if that's what you really want. With a little luck you'll destroy so many brain cells that you can't do math any more, and then you can be a normal person and get married and make some poor schlub's life miserable."

"Party pooper."

"Party animal."

"Tyrant."

"Where's Ben?"

You could get whiplash trying to follow Lensky's style of conversation. "I don't know, why?"

"Having seen the effect you and Ingrid have on this party, I am naturally curious as to what manner of havoc Ben is creating."

"Oh, well, he was going to bring Annelise. I expect he's trying to act normal."

Seldom have expectations been so thoroughly shot down.

Just in case, I listened for a few minutes. The party noise seemed to be at a constant level now. If Ben had been, oh, dancing the Mexican Hat Dance, there would have been another epicenter of noise and chaos around him. Wouldn't there?

But there was a disconcerting silence somewhere to our left.

"Where are you going?" Lensky demanded when I grabbed his hand and started slithering through the crowd on the left.

"Can't say."

"Then why are you in such a hurry to get there?"

I didn't have the energy to explain that I did actually know where I was going, in the sense that I was chasing down the location where there wasn't any noise. What I didn't know was how to describe it. Living room? Second State Drawing Room? Treaty Chamber? Whitney Harris's house was too modern for any description. Rooms furnished with modern sculpture and African tribal masks and chairs sculpted from unusual materials opened one into another, or occasionally into short hallways, with no particular pattern that I'd ever been able to identify. I made up names for some of the rooms just so I could keep them straight in my head.

The mysterious silence was beyond the Hall of Ugly Sculpture where we'd been standing, through the Chamber of Masks and catty-corner to the Sultan's Harem Pillow Collection. And, hallelujah, the room we were headed for was where one of the tables of party food had been set out and, for a miracle, nobody was screaming.

Um, not exactly hallelujah.

Not at all, in fact.

If the spectators weren't screaming, it could only have been because they were in shock. Annelise was standing in the middle of the room, with iced petits fours and lobster rolls and stuffed mushrooms and chocolate-dipped strawberries sort of dancing around her, and she looked absolutely terrified. Ben, standing by the food table, was muttering to himself and making little hand gestures, and I could just see tiny blue-white points of light at the tips of his fingers.

The idiot. Of all the times and places he could have chosen to experiment with his stars, this had to be the worst. Granted, he seemed to have excellent control, and I probably shouldn't choke him with his own petits fours until he told us how he'd achieved it. On the other hand, a quick glance around the room showed three Trustees of the Foundation, two Regents, half a dozen legislators, and assorted spouses and dates, all of whom were going to be in for years of therapy if I didn't clear this up quickly.

And I had come out without my stars. I didn't even have Mr. M. to help me.

"Thank you, thank you, ladies and gentlemen!" I shouted, moving towards Ben and catching flying hors d'oeuvres with my left hand. I extended my right hand towards Ben's hands with their aureole of white dots. Hoping. I didn't have more of a plan than that. But the stars had come to me first and it seemed just possible that they'd imprinted on me. *Come to mama*, I thought at them. I envisioned an open curve along the line of my open hand, with points of light flocking into it.

The stars moved and I held my breath. Once again they formed a spiraling shape pointed at my palm. There was a series of soft *splotch* noises behind me as the canapés I had failed to catch plopped gently to the floor. I lost my visualization but it was all right, the stars were still spiraling into the palm of my hand. There was a light prickling sensation again, and a momentary sense of being surrounded by something similar to my visualization but far larger and grander, a darkness shot through with the forces of the universe.

Then I closed my hand over the little cloud of stars and prepared to lie my head off.

CHAPTER 20

"THANK YOU," I said again, turning to face the room full of people, "for assisting with our first-ever.... um, our first..." *full-dress unmitigated disaster.* I choked on finding some better way to put that.

Annelise came to the rescue. She was still pale beneath her tan, and she'd clenched one hand over some canapé that had squirted oil over her hand and her dress, but she took over from me like a pro.

"Our first rehearsal of a new magic act," she said now. "We'll be appearing at the Slam Dunk Café next weekend, but as thanks to Ms. Harris for hosting this excellent party, the Superb Sutherland graciously agreed to provide a small demonstration tonight...." She kept blathering on while tossing desperate glances towards Ben. Finally he got the message.

"And let me thank my lovely assistant," Ben said, moving forward. He took Annelise's hand and raised it up. There was a spattering of applause; they both bowed low and then backed away. Annelise was well situated to slip out of the room; Ben wasn't so lucky, and serve him right if he was stuck here fielding questions from his impromptu audience for the rest of the night.

Or... not. He was as pale as Annelise now, and there were beads of sweat along his hairline. It was his own fault he was in this fix, of course, but it would be all of our necks if he let something slip that would generate the wrong kind of attention to the Center.

"Hold these," I whispered to Lensky, and placed my right hand over his, then closed his fingers over the tiny sparkling cloud.

With the stars safe, I moved over in front of Ben, hands up and outspread. "*Thank* you for your interest, ladies and gentlemen, but the Sublime Sutherland…"

"I thought he was the *Superb* Sutherland," one of the Regents grumbled.

"He's both," I said quickly. "Superb, Sublime, and… " Oh, help. The only su- word I could think of was "Superstitious."

"Superior," Lensky said under his breath.

"Sublime, Superb, and Superior. Your patience, please; you must know that a professional prestidigitator never reveals the secrets of his craft. You're all welcome to join us at the Slam Dunk Café, one week from tonight, for another demonstration of the Superb Sutherland's skills and another chance to guess how he performs these amazing feats." I grabbed Ben's hand and urged him to the door before the questioning could start again. Annelise was ahead of us, Lensky behind.

Halfway down the hall, a quiet voice said, "In here," and a door opened. We piled through and found ourselves on a redwood deck with a view of the city lights. I found a wall to lean on and slowly oozed down towards the bench behind me, deeply appreciative of the darkness and the cool, moist night air.

"I," I said without looking at anybody in particular, "need a *drink.*"

"After that, I think we all do," said the cool, quietly amused voice of the woman who'd ushered us out onto the deck. She pressed a button and said, "Santiago? A pitcher of frozen margaritas and four… no, five glasses, please. Yes, to the City Deck. And I believe some cleanup service is wanted in the Frank Erwin Room."

Of course it would be Whitney Harris herself who'd rescued us.

And of course she would have a button in every room to summon a superbly trained staff whose function was to smooth over life's little irregularities.

In the darkness she was nothing but a profile under a cloudy mass of dark hair full of twinkling lights... I gasped before I registered that these were LED lights and each one was significantly larger than our stars.

Lensky cleared his throat. "It must be difficult to train your staff to find their way around this place."

"I expect it would be," Ms. Harris said, "but I use a cleaning service. And I gave the caterers the same map the cleaners use. I *think* it shows most of the main rooms."

"You think?"

"I didn't build this place," she explained, "I bought it from a bankrupt real estate developer. I've never quite shed the feeling that I might go around two corners, open a door and discover a room I'd never seen before."

Her voice was light and tinkly, with a constant undertone of amusement that for some reason put my back up. She hadn't said anything to warrant it, but nevertheless I had a feeling that she was explaining the lives of elites like her to the deprived commoners.

The door to the hallway opened and a white-clad form bearing a tray appeared. Santiago, if that's who it was, set the tray carefully on a table formed by an angle in the deck railing and silently withdrew.

"Now," Whitney Harris said as she began pouring, "who would like to tell me what that was *really* about?"

Lensky cleared his throat again. "I'm afraid we can't do that, ma'am. It's classified."

"Indeed! You Center people don't mind frightening my guests, but you draw the line at explaining yourselves?" She didn't sound nearly as amused this time. "May I remind you that funding for the Center for Applied Topology comes through the Moore Foundation?"

"But is only passed through," Lensky countered. "The original funding comes from my agency."

"Which prefers to remain anonymous."

"Which *does* remain anonymous. I'm sure you signed the agreement, Ms. Harris."

Ben and Annelise were trying to bury themselves in their margaritas. I tapped Ben's shoulder and gestured for him to pass one to me.

"Do you need that?" Lensky asked, temporarily abandoning his fencing with Whitney Harris to return to bossing me around. Or trying to.

"Anybody who can say 'prestidigitator' without even practicing is not *nearly* drunk enough for this party," I told him, and let the icy drink slip down my throat. The tequila actually burned; whoever had mixed these was far more generous with the alcohol than were the owners of El Patio, where I consumed most of my margaritas. I made a mental note not to finish the drink too quickly.

Ben was embarking on a confused and rambling 'explanation' of his impromptu magic show. Apparently Lensky didn't object so long as the name of his super-secretive agency was not mentioned. Well, it wouldn't be, would it? None of us actually knew it, though we had our theories.

I sipped my frozen drink more carefully, to avoid either brain freeze from the slush or brain death from inhaling tequila too fast, looked at the stars – the real ones, I mean - and let my pulse rate slow down. This evening had been over the top in far too many ways.

I remembered that Lensky was holding something for me. "You can give them back now," I murmured under cover of Ben's 'explanation.'

"Give what back?"

"What I asked you to hold for me."

"Thalia, you gave me a handful of *nothing.* Are you sure you should be drinking that?"

"Yes," I said, prudently transferring the glass to the hand farthest away from Lensky. I opened my free hand, palm up. "Just give me back the... nothing, okay?"

I guess he really did not see the little sparkling cloud that appeared when he opened his hand. Neither, to judge from their lack of reaction, did Whitney or Annelise. Ben, however, was startled enough to lose the thread of his story for a moment.

"Those are *mine.*" He grabbed my wrist and almost made me spill my drink.

"You have just as many without them," I reminded him. "Haven't you made enough trouble for one night?"

"What *are* you arguing about?" Whitney asked. She sounded as if she were really saying, "What are the children fighting over now, and can't they be quiet?"

"Uh, Thalia accused me of hoarding the margarita pitcher," Ben improvised.

"But he's going to give me a refill now," I said, raising my glass. With a sour look, Ben dumped half of his own drink into it. Never let a good lie go to waste, that's my motto. I sipped my spoils while Ben went back to rambling about grackles, computers, the Axiom of Choice and the external hard drive onto which Jimmy DiGrazio had copied an image of Crowson's laptop.

"It took Jimmy all afternoon to get a look without triggering its self-destruct security option," he was saying now, "but tomorrow we can analyze the data, and then Boris here can decide whether to stay on here or go back to Washington."

This was news to me; I'd imagined them dissecting the data from the hard drive today. Oh, well. It didn't make much difference; in a day or two we'd have finished our part. Lensky would still be heading back within a few days.

"Indeed!" Whitney said. "I had no idea that topology had so many interesting applications." She sounded less than cheerful about it, but maybe that was because of her next words. "I'm afraid I should be getting back to my other guests. But do stay as long as you like. Shall I have Santiago bring another pitcher?"

"No, thank you," Lensky said, much too quickly. "We really must be going now."

Annelise, evidently the only one of us who'd been well brought up, supplied the appropriate social noises about Whitney's lovely house and the lovely party and how fortunate we were to have been invited, while Ben skulked behind Lensky and avoided my eyes. Once outside, he grabbed Annelise's hand and said, "See you later, my car is over there."

I got in his way. "First tell me what you thought you were doing in there."

"I wanted to impress Annelise," Ben muttered sulkily.

"You certainly did that," Annelise told him. She sounded as icy as a frozen margarita. "And not in a good way. In case you were wondering."

Ben spread his hands. "You *knew* I could... do things, Annelise. It was in your job description!"

"Yes. Silly me, I thought this was a *date*, not part of my job!"

"But you rescued us anyway, for which I can't thank you enough," I interrupted the lovers' quarrel. Ben could apologize to Annelise on his own time; what I really wanted to know was how he'd been able to calibrate the stars' power so precisely. Judging from last night's experiments, I would have expected the entire table of canapés to fly through the air.

Ben smirked. "I selected a finite subset," he said. "Started with one star, worked up to a dozen."

"Now that," I said, "was really clever. Not what you used it for, but the idea of working with a finite subset instead of the whole cloud. I suppose the one-through-twelve experiments are what you were doing this afternoon, when I naively thought you and Jimmy were going to analyze his image of the laptop?"

"Like I told Whitney, we had to get around the self-destruct code... well, Jimmy did; I wouldn't know anything about that. In fact, now that we've got the laptop duplicated to an external hard drive, analyzing the data is pretty much pure computer geekery. He didn't need my help."

"And of course, once you figured out how to use a subset of the stars, you *had* to demonstrate. In public. With the Dance of the Seventy-Seven Canapés."

"Seventy-two, actually." Ben smirked again. "One star for every six pieces."

That *was* impressive precision. I really needed to stop wasting my time with the spook and get back to serious research, figure out exactly what the stars augmented and how, develop algorithms...

"Algorithms" sounded better than "spells," though I was no longer sure it was a more appropriate description. I sighed. "Take me home, Bradislav. Ben needs to start groveling to Annelise, and I need to get my head clear."

"You're *thinking* again, aren't you?" Lensky said as we picked our way along the edge of the road to his car.

"There's a lot to think about."

He sighed. Much more dramatically than I had done. "I knew it. I can practically see your brain fizzing and shooting off sparks."

"You object to me using my brain?"

He opened the passenger-side door for me. "Experience suggests that this level of thinking is incompatible with a stop at Mount Bonnell on the way back."

I fastened the seat belt and waited for him to walk around the car. "I do respect a man who can accept defeat gracefully." He was right, of course. When he'd led me up the garden - Mount Bonnell - path, I'd been vulnerable to hormones overpowering my good sense. Now I was back to sanity.

"Normally," he said mournfully as he started the car, "plying a girl with drink makes her more receptive to my advances, not less."

"Maybe you should try doing that next time you're in Austin." Which would be, like, *never*. "You spent most of this evening trying to get between me and my drinks, not plying me with them."

"Normally," he said again, "a girl who's passing you a handful of nothing – and then asking for it back - is already drunk enough for all practical purposes."

A handful of nothing to him, a pocketful of stars to me. The gap between us couldn't have been clearer.

"I'm not. Normal. I did try to tell you." It hadn't taken him long to make the leap from "I'm fascinated," to "This is too weird," had it? Even Rick had hung in there for a few days before deciding to dump me. Clearly the spook was more efficient about cutting his losses.

He took me straight home with not one detour.

Efficiency.

CHAPTER 21

THE PECKING at her window woke Linda. It was a grackle! A large one – maybe one of those the Bird Whisperer had been talking to yesterday? She pushed up her window. "Gaaak?"

"Gaak, gaak, gaakle," the bird answered.

"I'm sorry," she said – quietly, so as not to wake Pam and Jerry. "I don't understand grackle yet." Maybe it was telling her to come to the park for another lesson?

One of the bird's legs looked rather lumpy – no – was that a note tied to its leg? "I have to take the screen off," she apologized. The grackle flapped noisily up to perch on the gutter, just as if it had understood her.

Linda had meant to loosen the screen and drag it inside, but the first step required a hard push outwards and the second step never happened. She held her breath as the window screen spiraled downward and came to rest in a bed of lantana. Fortunately, Mom's bedroom downstairs was at the front of the duplex; the rustling of lantana around the back probably wouldn't wake her.

The big grackle flapped again and landed on her windowsill. It was an imposing bird, maybe twice the size of an ordinary grackle and gleaming blue-black and blue-purple in the sunlight. Tentatively,

Linda extended her hand towards what she was now very sure was a message for her. It seemed rude to just grab the bird's leg and pull on it.

"May I?"

"Gaak, gaak, gaakle," the bird said, just like before. Then it hopped to the inside of the windowsill and let out an impatient *"Gaak!"* Even a person who didn't – yet – speak grackle could understand that. It was saying, "Get a move on already!"

Very slowly and carefully, Linda reached for the end of black string dangling down the grackle's leg. She unwound it, passing her fingers between the grackle's legs, until the piece of paper it held plopped onto the windowsill. A breeze stirred it; Linda grabbed; the grackle fluttered off the sill with another series of harsh cries.

Downstairs, Pam stirred, muttered, "Damn grackles," and pulled the pillow over her head.

"Apprentice bird whisperer," the note read, *"this is the time for your second lesson. Come at once to the place you know of, and tell no one."*

Linda drew a deep, gratified breath. She had been accepted as an apprentice! She scrambled into her jeans and t-shirt, picked up her sneakers and tiptoed downstairs. In the kitchen she paused for a moment, then wrote in caps on the whiteboard, "GONE TO LATONYA'S LOVE YOU MOM." Hadn't she been clever to invent LaTonya as a cover for playing by herself in the park! Now that invention would be truly useful. The injunction to tell no one was probably a test of her dedication.

The thought did just flicker through Linda's mind that even without that warning, she might not have wanted to tell Pam that she was going out, first thing on a Sunday morning, to meet a man who'd promised to teach her bird language. You never knew when a mother might do something stupid like insisting on meeting this man for herself, and Linda felt sure that would have been dreadfully insulting to the Bird Whisperer.

She eased the back door open and, for possibly the first time since they'd moved to Austin, held the screen door so that it wouldn't slam back against the door frame and irritate Pam. Once it had been very gently closed, she sat on the steps and tied her sneakers before quietly walking around the house, then running down the sidewalk.

~

Sunday morning at Allandale House was a bit livelier than usual.

Lensky was in Jimmy's office, presumably unlocking the secrets of Raven Crowson's laptop.

I was there to work on using the stars in the way Ben had thought of, starting with a small finite subset and gradually adding to it until I had just the degree of augmentation necessary for what I wanted to do. It wasn't completely straightforward because the stars didn't seem to be with the program. They were sociable little guys; select one and half a dozen others would cluster with him. I was working on a selection condition that would get me a finite subset – for starters I would have taken any finite subset.

Ben, of course, had already worked out something like this to get his little collection together, and now I understood how that could have taken him the whole afternoon. And yes, of course I could have simply asked him for his process. But it was the kind of problem I preferred to solve for myself, because once I'd worked through a solution I would never forget it.

Besides, Ben was busy. Yes, he'd come into the office too, but I suspect it was only so he could use the phone; he'd had it tied up most of the time that he'd been there, talking to Annelise. I thought he was making progress; he'd certainly groveled quite spectacularly. It remained to be seen whether she was stupid enough to let him back into her life.

Ingrid and I were actually sharing the break room and comparing notes, as she too was working on the problem of extracting a finite subset of stars. Last night I'd had to wait until she took off her horned hat before she got sane enough to appreciate what Ben had pulled off. Well, I'm not sure "sane" was the right word; she'd wanted to start working on the problem immediately, but she fell asleep with her fingers covered in stars. Nobody had been getting between *her* and the bar.

This morning, for once, she hadn't been singing in the shower. More like tiptoeing carefully under the shower and complaining that the noise of water droplets hitting her forehead deafened her. I smirked, but quietly; if I hadn't been handicapped by Lensky's interference I would probably have been feeling the same way now.

We agreed that experimentation would be better done at Allandale House, where Dr. Verrick had responsibility for damage to the building, than in our shabby apartment building where the landlord was already looking at us sideways. So she drove us over to campus; one good thing about Sunday morning, there was plenty of parking space.

We were in the break room, rather than skulking in our individual offices, because Lensky had brought in another sack of pastries and neither of us trusted the other alone with them. Selecting subsets of stars wasn't as draining as all those teleportation experiments had been, but it was only prudent to make sure we had enough fuel to do the job right.

Upper Crust's marzipan pockets and cheese Danishes are some *fine* fuel. It was close to heresy to couple them with break room coffee, but we had no alternative.

No, not drinking coffee was *not* an option. It wasn't even noon yet.

Walking to the Drag for some decent coffee, on the other hand, was beginning to look more and more attractive. Ingrid had already suggested I should go. I'd suggested that she could go. It appeared that nobody was going anywhere while there was still a marzipan pocket on the tray.

Ingrid's approach was more sophisticated than mine, involving ultrafilters on a compact Hausdorff space; I was more comfortable with simple point set theory. It remained to be seen which, if either, approach would work best. At present we were both still shaking clusters of stars off our fingers.

Outside the break room, Ben slammed the phone back on its cradle. Perhaps that was why he refused to get a cell phone; you can't really hang up on someone satisfactorily with one.

Immediately after he did that, the phone began ringing again. "Oh, for the love of Riemann!" Ben exclaimed. We heard him galloping down the stairs.

"This girl has really gotten under his skin," Ingrid commented. She twisted her wrists and fingers and skimmed off a huge clump of stars. Possibly her Hausdorff space hadn't been compact.

"I just hope he hasn't put her off working here. Do you realize we actually had a receptionist who wouldn't get a nervous breakdown around us? I was looking forward to making Dr. Verrick keep his promise to hire her." I lost my focus on rigorous selection and got stars all over my own fingers.

"Isn't anybody going to answer that phone? It's driving me crazy."

"Well, *I* don't want to listen to Annelise complaining about Ben, do you?"

The insistent ringing stopped just long enough for us to draw breath, then started again. I made a preemptive strike on the last marzipan pocket and took it with me to the desk at the head of the stairs. "Center for Applied Topology, how may I direct your call?"

"It's about time," said an angry voice. A male voice. A vaguely familiar male voice. "I've been trying to get through all morning. Put me through to Brad Lensky."

We don't have a switchboard. We don't even have an answering machine. I set the phone down and walked over to Jimmy's office. "Lensky! For you."

As he came out, I remembered where I'd heard that voice before. It had been only yesterday, and the owner had been saying, "Give it back now, and nobody gets hurt."

While holding a gun to Annelise's head.

We really couldn't blame her, I thought, if she had decided to shake the dust of this place off her shoes and never return.

While thinking that, I turned sideways and walked through the wall to the Research Division. There was an extension to the office phone in there, so that in the absence of a receptionist – in other words, the usual situation – anyone working in there could answer the phone without shimmying back and forth from one side of the wall to the other.

I eased the receiver off carefully and put it to my ear.

"No, *I'm* telling *you* how it's going to work," Crowson snarled. "You're going to leave that external hard drive on a bench at Mayfield Park. The one on the south side of the main lily pond. You have fifteen minutes to deposit it there. I'll collect it when I'm ready, take it away and verify that it's the right one. Then I'll let the little girl go and tell you where to pick her up."

There was a click and the buzzing noise of the dial tone, and through the wall I could hear Lensky swearing. Probably in Polish, as there seemed to be a lot of consonants involved.

"Jimmy, do you have another external hard drive here?"

By the time I got back to the public side, Jimmy DiGrazio was giving Lensky a hard drive. Of course, he didn't know what the stakes were.

I did.

"Lensky! You're not going to give him a blank drive!"

He stared at me, wild-eyed. "What choice do I have?"

"Jimmy, don't give it to him. Crowson wants the real drive, the one with his data on it, in exchange for Linda. His niece," I amplified. "She's eleven years old. Lensky, you can't have thought this through. If Crowson finds out you've cheated him, what happens to Linda?"

"Oh, I've thought," Lensky said grimly. That little vein at his left temple was jumping again. "What do *you* think happens to Linda if I hand over our only bargaining chip and let him walk away with it? Do you think we'd ever see her again? I'm going to capture him when he comes to collect the hard drive and then offer to trade *him* for Linda. Whatever parts of him are left when he sees the wisdom of agreeing."

"Make a copy?" Jimmy suggested.

"We don't have time. I have to be there in fifteen minutes." He glanced at his watch. "*Thirteen* minutes, now." He headed for the stairs; I followed him, with Jimmy and Ingrid on my heels.

"Okay, not a bad idea. We'll come too."

"I don't need that kind of help."

"You have no idea what kind of help you might need."

"Leave me alone! Haven't you done enough damage already?" He was out of the building and running for his car, while I fought back angry tears. It was Ben, not I, who'd been blabbering about the hard drive last night. But right now he probably despised all of us equally.

"Where's he going?" Ingrid asked.

"Mayfield Park."

"Well, he can't stop us going there too. It's a public place. Anybody know it well enough to teleport there? No? Come on; I'll drive."

Jimmy had his phone out as we piled into Ingrid's car.

"Who are you calling? The cops?"

"I thought we could use Annelise and Ben too."

"Ben doesn't have a cell phone."

Jimmy smirked. "No, but Annelise does."

"They won't be – "

Well, actually, they were together; he was right about that.

Love. I guess I just don't understand it.

In any event, the two of them would probably get to Mayfield Park only minutes behind us. Well, several minutes. Possibly more. Ingrid was displaying a remarkably cavalier attitude towards red lights, stop signs, one-way streets and other polite suggestions of the traffic cops.

"Ingrid! We won't get there in time if we get a ticket."

"We won't," she said without taking her eyes off the road. "They can't see us. I'm using Camouflage."

Un-, as far as I knew, -calibrated. She was wearing great galloping clusters of stars all over her arms and hands.

So to others' view, we weren't there and neither was a rolling half-block of street and parked cars. That seemed like a great way to get hit by a truck. Fortunately, on Sunday morning the streets around the university weren't crowded. I heard some screaming now and then, and saw a few people pointing, but the closest we came to a collision was an intimate encounter with a stop sign that did no good to Ingrid's side view mirror and paint job.

She couldn't have driven better, or more recklessly, if she'd still been wearing her horned helmet. I decided there was no point in worrying about sudden death; it would happen or it wouldn't. Instead, I concentrated on feeding Mr. M. scraps of the marzipan pocket that had still been in my hand when we left the building. There hadn't been time to give him coffee; I just hoped that sugar would have an equally energizing effect.

CHAPTER 22

THE ROOM WAS dark and smelled bad. Well, it was really the people in it who smelled bad. They'd been in the back of that truck for days, then one night they were hurried out of the truck and up those strange stairs made of metal twisted like taffy into fancy designs, and into this room with no lights, inside or outside. There was a bathroom, but by now it smelled just as bad as everything else. She had made the circuit of the room when they were first herded in here, reaching up the walls as high as she could, so she knew that the room probably did have windows. They were just boarded up with plywood. Maybe people outside would see the plywood – on the *inside* of the windows – and realize that something was wrong here.

More likely the plywood was covered up, to the people who might look in, by pretend curtains. And most likely nobody would care anyway. In her brief life she had already learned that most people didn't care, didn't want to know, got angry if you asked them to quit looking the other way. There was no good reason to suppose that anything would be different in this new place.

There was one comfort about being stinky and dirty: nothing was going to happen to them right away. When They wanted to do whatever they did, the first step was always to wash one of them and hand out clean clothes. Then the clean person went away and did not come back. They said "gone to a good home," but she didn't believe that for a minute. Anybody who had really gone to a good place, wouldn't they make the good people come back and let the rest of them out of this room?

She went back to her project, twisting a coin between one corner of a sheet of plywood and the wall it was nailed to. She did that until her fingers hurt, then rested and started again. Only, today her fingers hurt all the time, so she had a different rule: twist the coin fifty times, put it back in her pocket and rub her hands for a count of a hundred, then start twisting again. The coin was moving farther than it used to, this one corner of plywood was coming loose. She thought. That might make it easier to get the second corner loose.

Of course she had no way to reach the top corners, so this was probably pointless. But you never knew. Maybe if the bottom two corners were loose from the wall, it would be possible to twist the whole sheet of plywood, or jiggle it loose, or something. Maybe, if she got that far, she could get one of the others to stop crying and help her.

There was a noise at the door and her hand jerked, but she didn't drop the coin. She slid it into the pocket of her shorts and tried to look as if she was just leaning against the wall, as filthy and dispirited as the rest of them.

It wasn't hard.

The door opened just a crack, just enough to let one of Them shove a slender girl inside. The new girl stumbled, went down to her knees and jumped back up again, shouting in Inglés. "You can't do this! My uncle is going to kill you!"

The new girl was wrong, of course. Lupe had already learned that They could do anything they liked. But it was probably going to be worse for this one, because she had fair hair, which They liked, and because she already smelled good and had nice clothes.

Lupe could understand the Inglés a little, enough to follow orders, but she had never spoken the language. Now she approached the fair-haired girl and tried to warn her in Spanish. "You are clean... I am sorry. That means they will take you next."

~

It was a nice Sunday morning and Mayfield Park was so popular, there was no place to park. Lensky's rental car had snagged the last space.

I was out of the car as soon as Ingrid slowed down in the parking lot. Dodging around strolling families, I got to the central lily pond just in time to see Lensky walking away from the bench on which he'd placed the empty hard drive. How had the man expected to trap Crowson with no backup? Lucky for him we'd disobeyed his instructions to stay put.

This called for Ingrid's specialty: telekinesis. I defined a non-metric space overlapping the Euclidean space of the real world, narrowed my eyes and nudged the hard drive a little way along the bench. There was a sudden tornado of grackles, cackling and flapping in a black spiral from sky to ground, and when they dispersed the Master of Ravens was there. I couldn't see where Lensky had gone. As Crowson reached for the hard drive I tugged on it mentally and it floated off the bench, away from him, over the central mass of plants and flowers in the middle of the shallow pond, where it stalled out. I could feel it getting harder to move, as though it had suddenly become a great deal heavier.... Or as though an opposing force was trying to bring it back to where Lensky had left it. This wasn't good enough; the relevant word for the pond was *shallow*. Crowson could easily wade out to grab the hard drive.

I stuck one hand in my pocket and applied the force of more stars to my transformation.

A flock of grackles swooped down on the hard drive and I felt the pull of the opposing force getting stronger, enough to balance out my best effort even with the augmentation of the stars.

Well, Crowson wasn't the only one who could wade into the pool... but why bother, when I could get there faster with a single word? *"Brouwer,"* I said, and I was standing in several inches of water among plants and flowers and – oh, hell. That thick, shiny black ribbon wasn't a vine; it was the midsection of the largest cottonmouth water moccasin I'd ever seen, and it wasn't happy about being stepped on.

Water moccasins are bad-tempered and can strike with unbelievable speed. A normal person wouldn't have been able to splash out of range in time to escape being bitten. That thought just flashed through my mind as I grabbed the hard drive and said *"Brouwer"* again.

The instantaneous jump got me safely out of the pond. Unfortunately, I'd been looking across the pond at Crowson when I spoke, so that was where I teleported to. He grabbed me and pulled me back against him. I hung onto the hard drive. The water moccasin sliced through the water, heading for us.

And Mr. M. shimmied out of my belt and threw himself on the venomous snake with a shrill cry of rage.

"Hojotoho Lia!" Ingrid's voice cut through the clamor of an increasingly upset crowd of onlookers. She was on the far side of the pond, where I'd been standing a moment earlier. The grackles swooped down between us, aiming their cawing fury at her.

Not a good move. Ingrid was still mad at them over the incident of the Grackle Poop in the Oleanders. I could just see the bright points of stars flying from her fingertips and attacking the grackles, turning bird after bird into a clump of black feathers that hung in the air for a moment before floating gently down to the water's surface.

A harsh cry from the sidelines indicated that the Mayfield Park peacocks had joined the fight, though on whose side was anybody's guess.

Crowson distracted me from my aesthetic appreciation of Ingrid's grackle slaughter and Mr. M.'s epic battle with the cottonmouth. A hard round thing being poked into your side by a man who was last seen waving a gun will have that effect. He dragged me backwards away from the pool, step by step, and I didn't dare fight him. "Everybody back off if you want her to live!" he shouted over the cacophony of peacocks, grackles, and screaming onlookers.

I couldn't see who he was shouting at. I hoped it was Lensky. I hoped Lensky had a better plan than trading my life for Linda's, but I couldn't think what it might be. Nor could I think of an algorithm that would put me and the hard drive a nice safe distance from Crowson and his gun. If I teleported myself back across the pond while he was hanging onto me, he and the gun would come with me. He might be too surprised to shoot.

Or he might be surprised into shooting.

I didn't really want to take that bet.

At this point Mr. M. and the cottonmouth took center stage again. The water snake had already tried twisting around to bite his attacker, and I hoped chomping down on Mr. M.'s steel scales had hurt its mouth. There were dents and scratches on the prosthetic body, but the cottonmouth evidently hadn't been able to turn sharply enough to get its fangs into Mr. M.'s head and short neck, the only parts that might have been vulnerable to its venomous bite. Then it had dived under the water, but apparently that hadn't incommoded Mr. M. either. Now it reared up out of the pond and came right at us. Probably it was just trying to escape the mini-monster gnawing on its spine and squealing a war cry, but I was terrified. *You* try looking into the eyes of a seriously pissed off giant cottonmouth!

Crowson must have felt the same way, because the pressure of the gun against my side abruptly lifted. There was an extremely loud noise, the cottonmouth's softball-sized head exploded, and something knocked into us and threw both Crowson and me to the ground. The hard drive spilled out of my arms and I dived after it.

Crowson didn't come after me when I scooped the drive up again, but my knees were shaking too much for me to do anything sensible like getting up and running. I swiveled around, still clutching the drive, and saw Lensky on top of Crowson. He seemed to be banging his head on the ground. Seemed like a good idea to me.

"Where – is – Linda?" he demanded.

Crowson bared his teeth. "Kill me, and you'll never find her!"

Someone screamed – again; the screaming had briefly died down, but now a siren was adding to the noise and confusion. "There they are!" a man yelled.

"On the ground, on the ground, *on the ground!*" someone else shouted. "Hands on your head!"

The cops were pointing their guns… at Lensky.

"Officers!" Lensky kept talking, without releasing Crowson. "Case Officer Bradislav Lensky, Special Actions Division. Reach into my pocket and you'll find my badge. This man is a terrorist. Don't let him get away!"

"No, he isn't! I heard everything. They were fighting over a girl!" A gray-haired woman shoved her way to the front. She pointed at me. "Is your name Linda?"

"Lia," I said. "And he's telling the truth."

All that bit of discussion availed was to distract everybody enough for Crowson to punch Lensky and flee down the steep hill at the end of the park. Lensky drew his own weapon and fired twice without result.

"*Linda,*" he said desperately.

"Lia! Are you OK?"

That was Ben's voice. Good. If he was here, Annelise was probably with him, and maybe she could weave one of her 'explanations,' and make the cops help us. Or at least go away.

And… we might not have time for that. She'd just have to do it without Lensky and me. Explaining Mr. M. would be the tricky part; I hoped he would have the sense to play dead. Dropping the hard drive, I inched closer to Lensky until I could put both hands around his ankle. "*Brouwer,*" I said for the third time that morning.

We hit the floor in Allandale house, hard: I had been kneeling, and my grab at Lensky had gotten him off balance. I made a mental note that teleporting was much less uncomfortable if everybody was standing up, stable, and prepared for the experience.

As if that was going to happen on a regular basis around here.

"Linda," Lensky said again.

He could certainly focus well. That might be a help in the experiment I was going to try.

"We can be with her in a minute," I said with somewhat more confidence than I felt.

"What – How?"

"Remember when I turned up in the park to get your help? I'd never been there before. I wasn't jumping to a place; I was jumping to a person. I knew you well enough to use you as my focal point." I hadn't intended to let him find that out, but my feelings didn't matter now.

"You don't know Linda that well."

"But you do. You love her. I don't know, but if you concentrate on Linda while I visualize the theorem, maybe the two of us together can jump to where she is."

Now that I'd put it into words, it sounded terribly weak. I wasn't at all sure how this was going to work out. We might not be able to leave Allandale House at all if I didn't have our destination in mind. We might wind up in some unreal variant of spacetime where we couldn't exist; get squeezed down to points, or spread out to cover a plane.

Or we might find ourselves with Linda.

Before the Master of Ravens could get to her. If Ingrid had destroyed enough of his grackle helpers, he might have to stay in this physical world while he went to where Linda was, and that might give us a chance to get to her first.

There were way too many "if" and "might" words floating around there. I pushed them out of my brain and wrapped myself around Lensky, who was standing up now.

"What do I do?"

"Just think about Linda and stay really focused on her," I said. That was how I'd found Lensky in the park. Could we split the tasks this way? *"Brouwer,"* I said, deliberately visualizing two glowing surfaces completely separated in space. If this worked, Lensky's vision of Linda would become the meeting point.

Darkness, glowing curved surfaces meeting at one point, nothing to breathe, a jolting transition, more darkness. I sucked in a breath.

We were definitely in some kind of physical reality; I couldn't see anything, but I could smell the air. It was thick with the scent of unwashed bodies. Dizzy from the two rapid jumps with a passenger, I tried to get my balance so I could stop hanging on to Lensky. For all I could tell he might need his hands. Or his weapon. Because now I could tell that those unwashed bodies were all around us.

As my eyes gradually adjusted to the darkness, I realized that we were surrounded by people who were mostly under four feet tall, and several of whom were crying softly. Not terrorists.

Little girls.

"Uncle Brad! I knew you'd come."

That blotch of light hair must belong to Linda.

"Linda. What's happened?"

She didn't know. All she knew was that the man she called the Grackle Whisperer wasn't a nice old guy at all; he'd grabbed her and put a hand over her mouth and there'd been feathers all around them and then they were in a nice place but he opened the door and shoved her in here and this room wasn't nice at all and she wanted to go home.

"Good idea," Lensky said.

But what were we going to do about all these other children? I didn't want to jump us out of here into safety for the three of us and leave this roomful of tearful little girls to whatever nasty fate had been planned for them, and I certainly didn't have the strength at this point to teleport them all to Allandale House. I wasn't sure, I told Lensky, that I could even move him and Linda.

"If it comes to that, take Linda, leave me," he said calmly. "I can take care of myself. For the moment, let's see if we can't get out of here before Crowson turns up."

"We need Ben," I said as Lensky rattled the door. "He does locks."

"So," Lensky said, "does *this*. Everybody stand back and cover your ears."

Linda and I did as he said. The other children in the dim room milled around wailing as if they hadn't even heard what he said. Linda jumped up and down and waved her arms. "*Aqui! Hacer como mi!*" I

195

thought the Spanish might not be quite right, but it worked; the other girls joined Linda in the corner and put hands over their ears like her.

There was a deafening noise followed by a series of quiet pings as the components of the lock gave up their positions. Lensky swung the door open. "Linda, can you tell them to come with us?"

"I don't think I need to." The girls had mobbed the door as soon as it was open. Two of them were holding onto my shorts, several more were holding bits of Lensky, and one very small girl had climbed up onto his shoulders.

Thus encumbered, we made our way down the hall to a spiral wrought-iron staircase... of a style that I'd seen before, very recently. "Lensky. Is this Whitney Harris's house?"

"Looks like it."

Indeed. Whitney Harris herself was standing at the bottom of the staircase with a gun in her hand. "Stop right there!" she commanded. "What are you people doing in my house?"

She didn't sound quite so calm and amused now.

CHAPTER 23

LENSKY PAUSED. He must have been calculating the odds. The way Whitney's hands were shaking, it was quite likely that she'd miss him. But he was the center of a cluster of little girls. If Whitney fired, somebody was sure to get hurt. True, she appeared to be working up a defense of "I knew nothing about it," and being willing to shoot a child would not be compatible with that defense. But we couldn't count on her recognizing that in the heat of the moment.

I had been behind Lensky on the stairs; now I took a quiet step back, detached the girls who'd been clinging to me and transferred their sweaty little hands to Linda's belt. One more step back, and under my breath... "*Brouwer.*"

Even shaky as I was, that small of a jump was easy enough; from the top of the stairs to just behind Whitney Harris. And I already knew what to do next. I whacked her gun hand with both of mine before she even knew I was there, and the gun fell to the floor and skittered away from her. A second later Lensky was restraining her.

And the children were crying and screaming.

I picked up Whitney's gun, just in case Crowson showed up now. Then I called 911.

There are times when you actually do want the police.

~

"Well, I guess that explains why she didn't have a resident staff," I said, hours later, when we'd all told our – suitably censored – stories multiple times and had worked out what had really been going on. Part of the reason this had taken hours was that the Austin police, no dummies, knew that our stories were thin in places, flatly impossible in others, and failed to account for many of the observed phenomena. They could write off onlooker stories about fireworks and talking snakebots and hard drives floating through the air. The dead water moccasin was easy enough; somebody had shot it, and considering the public relations disaster a giant water moccasin in the park could have created, they weren't going to look too hard for the guilty party. But there were all those exploded grackles littering the park, and there was Lensky's car at the park miles from Whitney Harris's house and no explanation for how he and I had gotten to the house, let alone into the locked-off top story.

However sure they were that we were leaving things out, they had no actual theory of *what* we were leaving out. And the expensive-looking lawyer who'd turned up to support Lensky persuaded them to abandon their initial plan of, "There's something we don't understand and we're going to keep all these people right here until they explain it to us."

They settled for keeping Whitney Harris and the hard drive image of Crowson's laptop, and warning the social workers who came for the children to keep them available for further questioning. Ben and Ingrid and I had been told not to leave town without permission.

Lensky had not.

After taking Mr. M. home and changing into a clean dress (Ingrid) and a clean T-shirt and denim skirt (guess who) we'd joined the others at El Patio. That evening we were using up the entire front seating section. The owners preferred to have large parties sit at the long table running through the middle of the back room, but we needed to be able to see each other and talk across each other; it wasn't an occasion for getting stuck at a long table where you could only talk to your nearest neighbors.

"I still can't believe she had the nerve to throw a Foundation party while she had half a dozen trafficked children locked in an upstairs room." Ben was trying to monopolize a basket of tortilla chips, but Annelise, whose blood sugar hadn't even taken any hits during this hectic day, was matching him chip for chip. Maybe there was a future for those two after all.

"Why not? The Harrises have more money than God. She's probably never been held accountable for anything before." Ingrid had gone for the nachos: immediate fuel, slightly higher quality than chips and salsa.

"I don't think they have enough money to bury this." I'd outraged El Patio tradition by eating three pralines as an appetizer, not as dessert. I'd done more jumping than anybody else, and the vending machines in the police station had been limited to peanut butter crackers and Mountain Dew. I still had low blood sugar and the guacamole cheese enchiladas weren't out yet.

"God, I hope not," Jimmy said. He'd seen more of the porn pictures than any of us except Ben.

"If that happens, can you come back, 'Boris'?" Ingrid asked.

"I'll probably have to return to testify," Lensky said, side-stepping the issue of whether he'd be able to give us any other help.

Raven Crowson had disappeared, as had any fingerprints that might have been left in his house and office. Police investigators were following up on all the contacts revealed in his laptop; given that the head of the Moore Foundation had been in this dirty business up to her neck, nobody on his contacts list was going to be presumed innocent.

There were loose ends dangling all over the place, enough to trip us up a dozen times over, but the general outline was reasonably clear. The emails that had started Lensky's investigation had been coded, all right, but they referred to sex trafficking of children from Latin America, not to movement of terrorists. The 'birthday party' referenced in the emails would not have involved bombs, just a group of vile people getting their pleasure from terrified children. Including Whitney Harris, who apparently really did think that the commoners were not real people. If we'd had time to think we would have realized she had to be involved; who else could have told Crowson about our copy of his laptop?

And this ended Lensky's official involvement. His agency was not supposed to operate domestically, except in cases involving counter-terrorism and the crossing of borders. He had been told not to wait for the closing of the police case; he was supposed to return to the office immediately, to avoid even the appearance of involvement with a domestic matter.

He already had a ticket for the first flight to Washington tomorrow morning. After he left this extremely public meal, I probably wouldn't see him again. That should be a good thing; I hate long drawn out good-byes.

I was still reminding myself what a good thing this was when he disappeared, between one beer and the next, quietly and efficiently.

I changed my mind half a dozen times before the Uber driver let me off in front of Lensky's motel room. He probably wasn't even here. He would be out with Pam and Linda, celebrating the successful conclusion of his case. Even if it hadn't been anything like we'd all expected.

So, fine. I would just knock and go away when no one answered, and it would really be better that way, and given that, why even bother knocking? What did I think I was accomplishing here?

I guess I needed to know that I wasn't a coward. I wouldn't run away before I established that he wasn't here.

I was going to knock, I swear to God. But he swung the door open before I was ready.

"You!"

He grabbed my wrist and pulled me into the room and slammed the door behind me, all in one motion. Then he backed off and sat down in the room's only chair. "What are you here for? And make it fast, because I have limited tolerance for sitting in a hotel room with you and..." He rubbed the back of his neck. "Limited. Tolerance." What an unreasonable man. Who just yanked whom inside, anyway?

"If it's inconvenient, I can go. Away. I was about to do that, actually."

"The door's not locked."

Oh, God. This really was going to be the most hideously humiliating experience of my entire life, wasn't it? On a scale of one to ten, with *ten* being the night Rick let me know we were through by stranding me at the party and taking Cyndi Simmons home with him, this was shaping up to be a solid eleven.

"I've been thinking." My mouth was dry. "About... regrets."

Lensky ran one hand through his hair and sighed. Deeply. "Oh? If this is going to be another excursion into your philosophy of avoiding emotional pain at all costs, spare me! You've made your feelings perfectly clear."

"Have I? Because they're not so clear to me." I moistened my lips. "Because what I was thinking is that I can spend the rest of my life regretting something I did... or regretting something I didn't do. And on the whole... I'd rather regret *doing* something than regret *not* doing it. If it doesn't put you out, of course, and..." My courage was leaking out. God, why was I such a fool? The man had said the door wasn't locked. Obviously he was just waiting politely for me to use it. "Never mind, it's not your problem, sorry to have bothered you, I'll just be going now..."

He was out of his chair and holding me by the shoulders before I'd even half turned for the door. "*Thalia.*" He bent his head and kissed me. Hard, hungry. "If you don't mean it, you'd *better* go now. Because my tolerance for this is officially used up. *Now.*" He didn't explain how I was supposed to go anywhere when he had me backed up against that door and was grinding himself into me until we were seconds away from having our first serious sexual encounter with both of us fully dressed.

Which seemed rather a waste.

He picked me up by the hips and lifted me to a more accessible height for his purposes. I didn't have any objection. In the next few minutes he disposed of the clothing barriers – I never did find those panties – and demonstrated that yes, he could hold me up indefinitely even while distracted by doing other things.

I may have screamed just once or twice.

Then he was just holding me and kissing me and there were actually glints of moisture in his eyes. "Where'd that rational, reserved little mathematician go?"

"Oh, *her*? Turns out she had her priorities scrambled, so I sent her home."

"And brought the wild party animal over here." He was doing his energetic best to kiss my neck all the way down to my nipples, and my T-shirt was going to go the way of my panties if I didn't do something.

"I realize this is a boringly conventional suggestion," I told him, "but if you'd put me down on the bed I could take this off."

We got to the bed, but as soon as his hands were free he got one up under my shirt and filled it with me. The noise he made seemed to indicate that he found my assets adequate. "Do you always not wear a bra, or has this week been specially for me?"

"Oh my God, you tore my bra off and I didn't even notice!" The look of shock on his face was the funniest thing I'd ever seen. I started giggling uncontrollably and barely managed to choke out, "J-just kidding, I don't usually wear a bra, I don't really need one."

"An admirable philosophy," he said, pausing in his fondling just long enough to haul the T-shirt over my head so that he could get down to properly appreciating my breasts. "*I* certainly don't need you to be wearing one." He didn't seem to have a problem with the fact that I wasn't exactly built like Ingrid - something the late, unlamented Rick had managed to mention at least once every time he got my shirt off, and why the hell had I ever wasted even five minutes on that loser?

He was seriously overdressed compared to me. I started to do something about that, but he grabbed my hands. "There's something we have to settle first," he said.

"Settle away," I said lightly, "I'm all for it." If "settling" was a necessary precursor to ripping off his clothes, I could be very cooperative.

"I love you," he said.

I wasn't quite ready to use the L-word yet, but I made encouraging noises. If he wanted to go on in this vein, I could wait a few minutes before we got to the ripping-off-clothes part.

Unfortunately, he wasn't headed in quite the direction I was anticipating.

"Thalia, you came *this* close to getting shot today. Twice! You need to understand that it's not like the movies. If you take a bullet that doesn't kill you, you do not tell the medic "It's just a flesh wound," look brave for a few minutes while he bandages you, then leap up and rejoin the action. A bullet is a tremendous insult to the body. Any time you take one, you could be looking at weeks of painful physical therapy, loss of muscle tissue, and a strong chance of permanent damage."

"And you're telling me this from personal experience?"

"Actually, yes."

"You don't seem permanently damaged to me."

"That's because I'm an obsessive maniac when it comes to rehab and physical therapy."

"Can I see your scars?"

"*Later.* Thalia, can't you focus on one thing for more than a minute?"

Of course I could. Right now I was focused on the promised showing of scars, and wondering where they were and how much he'd have to take off to display them. But I wanted to make him happy - and get this whatever-we-were-settling out of the way. So I nodded. "Right, Lensky. That's me. Laser-like focus."

"I love you and I can't stand to think of you getting hurt. And apart from everything else, if I have to worry about your being injured because you're in the middle of a firefight, it screws *me* over. My attention's split and my priorities are fucked up, because all of a sudden my top priority is protecting *you*. Now do you understand?"

"Right. Got it." And at that point I really thought I did. "Stay away from bad guys with guns if you're anywhere in the vicinity. Only get involved if you're not around."

He made a noise that reminded me of a garbage disposal eating a fork. I didn't know the human larynx was even capable of such sounds. Maybe those long Polish words that looked like a train wreck of consonants were just a warm-up for speaking Jammed Garbage Disposal.

"Thalia, the point is that you're to keep out of these situations *regardless* of where you think I am." He said a couple of things in Polish that I didn't ask him to translate.

"You're leaving town," I pointed out. "Whatever I do or don't do won't be your problem after tonight." And given that schedule, I could think of better ways than bickering to spend this night. So I didn't even mention that the 'situations' might not have turned out so well if I had stayed out of them the way he claimed to want.

"Thalia, you're *always* going to be my problem."

That wasn't logical, but evidently he was as tired of bickering as I was, because his mouth covered mine and he pushed me down on the bed and - do spooks get special training in Stealth Clothing Removal? Because I discovered that his pants were out of the way already, and I hadn't even begun to rip.

By the time I came up for air, I couldn't even remember what I'd meant to say next. I was pretty much reduced to panting and gasping. Lensky had more control: without losing focus on what we were doing right now, he started talking about what he wanted to do to, with and for me next. Which only raised my gasp-to-speech ratio even higher.

When he got around to the first part of those future plans, some time later, he implemented it with admirable thoroughness and attention to detail. I would have mentioned that in his performance review if I'd been up to talking. By the time he was finished, the only thing that kept me from becoming a boneless puddle was my desire to reciprocate.

That - during the reciprocating, I mean - was when I first got a good look at one of his scars. It was a long, ugly, raised and crinkled line that ran from his pelvic bone diagonally down to his inner thigh.

"How did you get *that?*"

"Ricocheting bullet."

"Came awfully close to the family jewels, didn't it?"

"Can't you concentrate on what you were doing? Before you stopped for this friendly little chat?"

I gave him some of my finest undiluted concentration then.

"Jesus," he said afterwards, "I felt like my brain was going to explode out of the top of my skull. You're a dangerous woman."

"You're no slouch yourself," I said, "apart from your brutal control-freak side."

"Which gets you hot, admit it," he growled into my ear.

"Me? Oh, no, this is just how I react to men in general, any man..."

You'd have thought that by this time it would have been safe to tease the man.

Not Lensky.

CHAPTER 24

FOUR WEEKS after the Foundation Fiesta and the Battle of Mayfield Park, life at the Center was getting back to... well, I hesitate to use the word "normal" in connection with this group. With Lensky and his demands for results gone, we were free to do the serious research of analyzing our new abilities and integrating them with existing topological theory.

Yes, I felt about as excited as that sentence sounds. But this was, after all, what we were here for. If I just kept working on it, the excitement would probably return.

It wasn't all theory. Ben and I felt that as dedicated researchers, we were obliged to investigate the exhilaration/low blood sugar effects of teleporting long distances. So far we had extended our workable range to the outskirts of Round Rock, but that was dependent on a series of kluges. First we put a box of doughnuts in the break room. (Chocolate covered for preference.) Then, having threatened the rest of the Center with violence should they touch our vital research materials, we persuaded Jimmy or Annelise or someone else to drive us out of town to a point at least a mile from our previous longest jump. We jumped back from there, scarfed enough doughnuts to keep from fainting, and wrote up trip notes.

After the first couple of longish jumps we learned that it was best to wait until the exhilaration wore off before completing the trip report. Dr. Verrick was scathing about reports consisting mainly of "Whee!" and "Better than Six Flags!"

We were still a long way from being able to teleport as far as the East Coast. Not that I had any intention of doing that anyway.

I didn't even know what Lensky's place back East looked like.

Ingrid showed no interest in joining us on these excursions. Her excuse was that she had to catch up on the course work that she'd neglected at the end of the semester, and then she needed to prepare for the written and oral qualifying exams that would get her into the doctoral program. I thought something else was eating her; she spent a lot of time staring into space, and she wasn't sleeping all that well. I knew because I wasn't sleeping either. I wasn't willing to discuss what was keeping me awake, so I didn't ask her about her insomnia. We were doing a pretty good job of ignoring each other, these days.

Our expanded, non-research staff didn't quite fill up the third floor of Allandale House, but we were using enough offices to get the trustees off our backs and to remove the threat of sharing with the Office of Diversity Compliance.

Annelise had graduated and was installed as our full-time receptionist and Ben's part-time girlfriend. He managed to tick her off on a regular basis, to the extent that they were only "together" about a third of the time. The rest of the time she treated him with an icy civility that perceptibly lowered the temperature on the public side.

Jimmy DiGrazio's consulting job had become a permanency: Dr. Verrick's excuse was that the Lensky investigation had been a harbinger of a future in which we would have to deal with computers, and we needed someone on the staff who spoke their language. Jimmy was the obvious choice, being possibly the only computer expert in Austin who would work for the pittance Dr. Verrick paid just to be close to magic and Ingrid. He seemed perfectly happy to be snubbed daily by Ingrid. I think his master plan was to be standing close to her the next time she put on that horned helmet.

Meadow Melendez was also on the expanded staff, though I

didn't know how long we'd be able to keep her. On graduation she'd received numerous offers from engineering firms that used words like *bonus* and *stock option*. For now, though, she talked about specializing in neuro-mechanical programming. She spent long hours with Mr. M., designing new capabilities for his prosthetic body. So far she'd equipped him with wi-fi and GPS. He was agitating for torpedos, or at least a machine gun mount, but Meadow told him she couldn't add projectile weapons because he wasn't heavy enough to handle the recoil. It might even have been true.

When not tinkering with robot snake bodies, she spent her time reading the in-house (uncensored) report on the late investigation and going, "Holy shit!" at intervals.

Nobody had yet moved into the office Lensky had been using.

On this particular fine June morning, Ben was arguing with Annelise instead of preparing for the next test of our teleportation range. I could have gone on my own, but we had agreed to have two people on every test, in the hope that if one got in trouble the other could save the day with prompt and decisive action. That was possibly the only time the words "prompt and decisive" had been used in connection with the Center. And in this context, "hope" was short for "forlorn hope." Or possibly "delusion."

Anyway, I didn't feel wildly excited about seeing another chunk of Round Rock. So I sat in the break room, surreptitiously nibbling on a chocolate-covered Berliner that should have been reserved for post-jump blood sugar treatment, and listened to Annelise turn down Ben's request for a date with one of her trademark fantasies.

"Annelise," he said, sounding exasperated, "that story may work on other guys, but I *know* you are not committed to a speaking part in a Matt Damon movie being filmed on location at the Driskill. Why don't you just say you don't want to go out with me?"

"All right. I don't want to go out with you," Annelise said promptly. Tiny icicles dripped off each word. "Not to hear Money Chicha tonight, not to Jitterbug Vipers this weekend, not to any live music venue ever again in this life."

I wondered what Ben could have done to put her so totally off live music.

"I *promise* not to jam with a remotely controlled saxophone ever again."

Oh.

"It wasn't just that you did it in public and frightened the band," Annelise said, "you were *flat*."

Personally, I thought Ben should give up on this argument and come do another jump test with me. But what did I know about maintaining relationships? Less than nothing.

Someone was coming up the stairs two at a time. Annelise and Ben stopped arguing to gawk and I moved to get a better view of our visitor from the break room door.

It was a broad, blond-haired man in a rumpled tan sport coat and a blue shirt that lit up his blue eyes. They lit up even more when he spotted me lurking in the break room, and he made a beeline in my direction.

"You have chocolate on your face," was his deeply romantic greeting. Or no, I guess the prolonged kiss that followed that comment was the romantic part of the greeting. Though I could have done without the background accompaniment of claps, whistles, and "Get a room!"

"So do you, now," I answered when I caught my breath. I wanted to spit on a paper towel and rub the chocolate smear off his cheek, but that was too much of a girlfriend sort of thing to do before I knew what was going on. "Why are you dropping in this time?" Another investigation for his agency would be fine news. A long-running investigation. But more likely he was just in town to visit Linda – and, as an afterthought, me.

Ben dropped his hopeless attempt to win Annelise round and butted into our conversation. "What does the agency want now, 'Boris'?"

"Nothing in particular," Lensky said.

I knew it. Just a flying visit.

For all I knew, he could have a girlfriend in every city that boasted a direct flight from Washington, and I was just his Austin stopover.

Sure, he'd used the L-word the last night we were together. But I hadn't heard any words at all from the man in the subsequent weeks.

He was grinning. "Following my report," he said, "the agency has decided that this Center is a potentially valuable asset which must be preserved if at all possible. Not only will funding continue, but I've been assigned here permanently because the report also made it clear that you maniacs need somebody sane to protect you. I'm also ordered to discourage the FBI representatives who've been sniffing around since you broke the sex trafficking ring."

"How did you know about them?" Annelise asked.

He looked surprised. "You really have been approached by the FBI? I just put that in my report in the interests of, ah, creative verisimilitude."

"You did know the FBI took over once we knew it was sex trafficking, not terrorists? Several agents wanted to know how we did, um, what we did," I told him, "except they didn't *really* want to know, if you take my meaning. Annelise has been defending our privacy with fantastic tales that take time to check out."

"Excellent," Lensky pronounced. "The agency will never recall me now. This Center is far too valuable to let the Fibbies get it." He glanced around the open space. "Ah, good, you haven't given away my office. I'll just…"

"Drive us to Round Rock," Ben said. "You can settle in later."

I didn't really need another long jump; I was already exhilarated, out of breath, and craving sugar. I hoped the traffic between here and Round Rock was terrible.

It was. And Lensky made Ben drive while we sat in the back seat and caught up.

THE END

KEEP READING for a preview of the next book in the Stars series, *An Opening in the Air.*

AN OPENING IN THE AIR

PREVIEW

THE JOB applicant Dr. Verrick had brought over edged into my office, kicked the trash can, dropped a sheaf of papers and went down on his hands and knees to scoop them up. "I'll take those," Dr. Verrick said when he stood again. "Miss Kostis, Mr. Edwards." He collected the forms Mr. Edwards was clutching and disappeared. He probably considered that a lavish and informative introduction.

"Call me Colton," the young man said with a tentative smile. "Colton Edwards." He pulled a chair out of the corner, banged it into his own shins, and sat without, thank goodness, further mayhem.

Asking if he was naturally clumsy or just nervous would probably scare him even more, so I repressed the question. Though I did wonder. Given his appearance, I was voting for natural clumsiness. He didn't look like a college graduate; more like a farm boy from a West Texas high school, one who had shot up eight inches and two shoe sizes the previous year and hadn't yet learned to manage his extra height. Shaggy blond hair fell over a wide forehead and framed an open, friendly face. The rest of him seemed to be trying to figure out what to do with his outsize hands and gigantic boots.

Before I could even introduce myself, the interview was interrupted by a crash of furniture and a string of curses in the office next door. "Would you excuse me for just a moment?" I abandoned the job applicant and zipped around the corner to the next office. What had happened to Ben? Unlike this Mr. Edwards, he was not given to falling over the furniture.

His office was built on much the same lines as mine: a tall narrow room partitioned off by flimsy temporary walls that looked shabby against the exquisite woodwork of the oak floor. That's the kind of décor that happens when you turn the top story of a Victorian house into office space.

He had knocked over a stack of three chairs in the corner of his office, his hair looked even more like a light brown bird's nest than usual, and there was a quilt trailing from his desk to the floor. Ohio Star pattern.

I'm used to adding up clues, though in the research division of the Center for Applied Topology the addition was likely to involve numbers like the square root of minus one rather than anything as simple as two plus two. "Ben. Were you walking around with a quilt over your head? And why?"

"I'm trying to use Riemann surfaces to make light. Operating on the molecular level."

"I still don't get the function of the quilt in this theorem."

"I thought maybe I had made light, only it was too dim to see in here." He gestured at the sunlight pouring in through his office windows. "So I was trying to create a dark working space."

For a topologist at the Center, this was as close to making sense as it got. "Well, next time just sit in the supply closet, okay?" I was dying to know how he thought a Riemann surface would enable him to make light out of nothing, but the theoretical discussion would have to wait until I didn't have a nervous job applicant in my office.

When I got back, the young man facing me across the desk looked even more nervous. I couldn't blame him. Before Ben's little problem, Mr. Edwards had walked through a wall in a way that twisted space around on itself – and that was only the start of the tour. That, and signing the stack of non-disclosure forms and agreements that Dr. Verrick had carried off. Since the spook from the nameless three-letter agency had come to stay, there were a lot of new rules and procedures aimed at preserving the secrets of the Center for Applied Topology. If this guy had even glanced at the fine print on the forms he'd just signed, he would know that he had acceded to terms of service even worse than Microsoft's. Whether or not he got hired, discussing what he was about to see here with anybody outside the Center would guarantee that he spent the next twenty years in jail, and not a nice American one, either.

That was the kind of arm-twisting Lensky's agency did for us. Before they'd taken a hands-on interest in the Center, our secrecy-preserving measures had been more ad hoc: Dr. Verrick warned research fellows not to pursue their research in public, yelled at us when we did so, and hired an exceptionally gifted fabulist to persuade anybody asking inconvenient questions that they hadn't actually seen what they thought they saw. Annelise was, in my opinion, a much better security system than a bunch of signed forms, but that's not how Washington does things.

"So, Mr. Edwards, why do you want to work for the Center for Applied Technology?" The question wasn't a mere formality. Only a certain type of crazy person would want to do academic research for a miserly stipend, out of an office in a creaky Victorian building, with no prospect ever of publishing any results.

"I don't know that I do," Colton Edwards answered, and I blinked.

"Well then, what brought you here?"

"Dr. Verrick. I took a topology class from him last year, and he... well... some odd things happened, and he suggested I come and talk to you people. Strongly suggested," he amplified, and I understood a little better. Dr. Verrick's strong suggestions could have turned the Titanic around. His force of will had been what created the Center in the first place: our office space here on the University of Texas campus, our funding, our shaky position as a part of the University's research efforts. A strong suggestion from Dr. Verrick could, in fact, do almost anything except make the Center's research fellows behave like normal human beings, and he hadn't yet given up on that.

"But the suggestion wasn't strong enough for you to act on it immediately?" Spring semester would have ended last May. It was mid-October now.

He twitched slightly. "Summers, I usually go home and straighten out the books on the family farm. They were counting on me to do the same thing this year. Actually, they were counting on me to stay, now that I've got my degree." I took a moment to skim his transcripts, which were heavy on things like Calculus Concepts for Business Majors and Statistical Inference in Management, but remarkably light in terms of actual mathematics. "What inspired you to take first-year honors topology in your final year?" Most students' final semesters were heavy with the boring required courses they'd put off in the hope that they might die before actually having to take them. Annelise, our receptionist, had spent her last semester as an undergraduate doing little but satisfying the Diversity and Anti-Bigotry requirements.

He offered me a crooked smile that showed where one tooth had been chipped and never repaired. "It looked interesting?"

"But your entire background was in business-oriented math?"

"Which is boring," he said. "I wanted to have a little fun before going back to be the accountant on the family farm." He took a deep breath. "Introductory Topology turned out to be… a little more fun than I'd bargained for."

"What did you move?" We'd all started out with a little unintentional telekinesis on small, light objects; I was willing to bet Colton's experience had been similar.

"Ah, the chalk?"

"A stick of chalk?"

"Um, no, the chalk on the board." He wriggled his shoulders unhappily, "See, Mr. Nesmith was putting up a proof, but he'd got one line backwards, and I was thinking really hard about the way the third line should have gone instead of what he'd actually written and trying to get him to look at me so I could, you know, signal him or something, and instead… Well, you probably won't believe this, but…"

"The writing on the board changed."

His eyes blazed with hope. "Yes! You get it. You really do get it!"

"Oh yes, Mr. Edwards. All of us got here through similar experiences." Some more traumatic than others. Colton had gotten off easy.

A colored bubble floated through my open office door. A glowing colored bubble. Bubblegum pink, if you're interested. It was followed by friends in a rainbow of different colors. Each bubble in turn hovered over my desk, shrank down to a pinpoint and disappeared. I wondered if Ben had planned the color show, or if this was just a temporary stop on the way to full-spectrum lights.

"Ben, keep the closet door closed!" I called out, then gave Mr. Edwards an apologetic smile. "At least we don't have to give you the what-we-do-here tour. Mr. Sutherland is taking care of that all on his own."

Colton grinned back. Without the grin he'd just looked like a clumsy farm boy, all big boots and too-long legs and big hands. With it – well, he still looked likely to fall over furniture and small animals, but his face lit up in a very appealing way. I wondered – briefly – whether he was likely to give Ben competition in the unending courtship of our lovely, lying receptionist. Well, not my problem.

"So are you looking for a short post-grad stint before going back to become the family business manager? Or for something more permanent?"

"More permanent would be really good."

"There's more money in accounting," I warned him.

"There's more *boredom* in accounting. Also, I spent way too much of this summer trying to explain to my big brother why it would be a really bad idea to keep two sets of books. Now somebody who's not related to him will have to tackle that issue. I mean – if you – if I can – "

A panicky yell from the supply closet interrupted his incoherent words. I raced around the corner and yanked the closet door open. Colton was right on my heels.

There was a faint smell of something burning, but it didn't seem strong enough to justify panic. "What did you set on fire?"

Ben gestured towards the floor. "I think it's in the middle of a supporting beam. We can't just let it smolder indefinitely. And if we open up the floor to dump water on it, the fire will blaze up. What are we going to do?"

I was tempted to say, "What do you mean we?" but the fact was that he had created a problem for all of us. Our tenure of the third floor of a Victorian mansion on campus was based on the requirement in Chester Allandale's will that the university preserve and use his home in return for the rest of his extremely generous bequest. Setting a supporting beam on fire was exactly the sort of thing the trustees would not understand as part of "preserve and use."

"Can you invert the process and, I don't know, create water inside the beam?"

Ben shook his head. "I'm afraid to try. I don't even know how the fire started. I was only trying for light."

When in emergency... I nipped back to my office and grabbed the three-foot silver snake coiled up like a paperweight on my desk. "Mr. M.! Help!"

The turtle head at the business end of the snake opened one eye part way. "I'm hibernating."

"It's only October, and it's still hot in Austin! And we need your help."

The coil of silvery scales shook, expanded, became a long metallic snake body behind an organic turtle head. Mr. M. slithered out of my arms to the floor, undulated around the corner towards the closet, lifted his head and sniffed. "Apply the Lights to the problem."

"Are you sure? Seems to me we need less light, not more."

"You disturbed my sleep to demand advice. I have given it. Do as you wish." The turtle beak closed with a snap. So did both the turtle eyes.

"Ben?"

He was already opening the glass jar from his desk. A cloud filled with sparkling points of light streamed from the jar into his hand. Behind me, Colton sucked in his breath. This was possibly not the ideal way to introduce him to the infinite set called the Lights of the Medes. Or to Mr. M. himself, for that matter.

Ben knelt and placed his open hand, palm down, on the closet floor, and closed his eyes. I could feel the miniature stars moving from his hand down into the wood. There was also a feeling of... not-enough? There were infinitely many stars. Not enough topologists, then? I stuck a hand in my pocket, then knelt and laid my palm beside Ben's. Now I could feel the movement of my own stars. They swirled joyously around the grain of the wood and returned to my hand, slightly warmer. The sense of smoldering heat slowly dissipated and Ben looked at me. "I think it's all right."

"I think so too." I would save my blistering recommendation that he repeat the Elementary Physics semester on heat, sound and light until later. It would be nice if Colton could maintain the illusion that we were all one big happy family until he'd been formally written into the program.

I scooped up Mr. M. and returned to my own nice, dry, not-on-fire office, followed by Colton. "Where were we?"

With a visible effort, Colton averted his eyes from the sight of Mr. M. coiling himself back into a tight spiral on top of my papers. "I thought that was a paperweight."

"No, he's more of a... colleague." It would probably be best to save the detailed story, which involved Nebuchadnezzar, a magic-damping ring, a beheading, and the involvement of a robotics engineer, until Colton had had time to assimilate what he'd already seen. Even the White Queen had limited herself to six impossible things before breakfast.

"You'd have your own office, though," I promised Colton. "The only reason Mr. M. has to share with me is that he's not very good with doorknobs."

"Then – am I hired?"

"Oh, yes," I said. By the time Dr. Verrick brought an applicant over to the closed side, he was as good as hired; this interview was just a chance for the topologists to object. Nothing objectionable about young Edwards, as far as I could see. "You're definitely crazy enough to fit in here. I don't have any more questions. What about you?" When he started on about pay and benefits, I'd shunt him back out to Annelise.

"Just one," he said, surprising me. "What's a Riemann surface?"

I started to answer him, but the building fire alarms drowned me out. They drowned out just about everything except Meadow Melendez, from the public side, shouting, "Ben, what the [fornicating] [expletive] did you do now?"

The automatic sprinklers went on. Mr. M. uncoiled, slithered to the floor and headed for the stairs in the public section. I scooped up most of the papers on my desk and followed, towing Colton by the hand. Leaving the private section was easier than getting into it, but the kid could be excused for being too rattled to realize that.

By the time we'd crossed to the other side of the wall, Mr. M. was a silver flash on the heels of Meadow and Annelise, and Ben and Ingrid had joined us on the public side. Jimmy DiGrazio grabbed Ingrid's arm and barked, "Downstairs!" as if he thought she was too dumb to move without orders. That wasn't going to improve their relationship.

I really, really hoped the stairs weren't on fire, because the trustees had felt that fire escapes would be a blot on the visual integrity of the building.

www.ingramcontent.com/pod-product-compliance
Lightning Source LLC
Chambersburg PA
CBHW061143170626
46809CB00003B/973